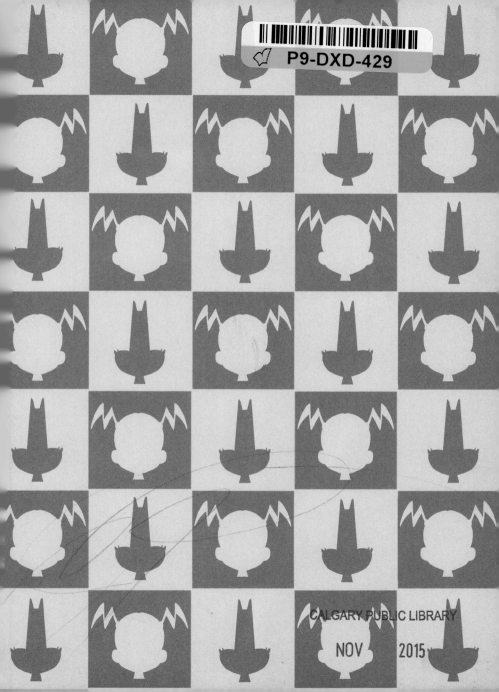

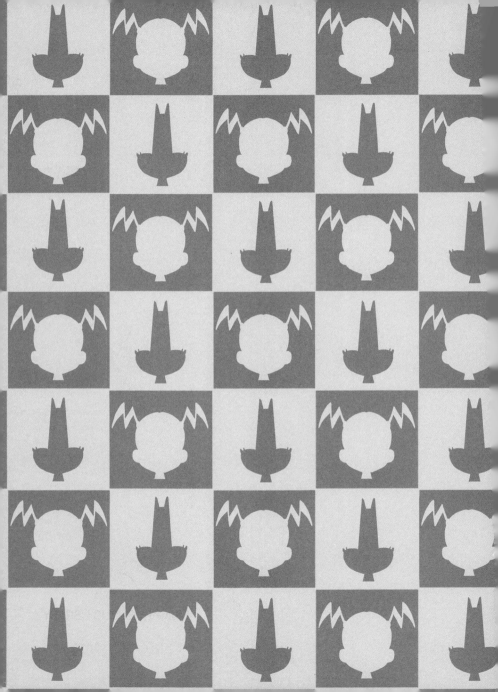

The Misadventures of SALEM HYDE

5

Frozen Fiasco

Frank Cammuso

AMULET BOOKS
NEW YORK

Hardcover ISBN: 978-1-4197-1651-5
Paperback ISBN: 978-1-4197-1652-2

Text and illustrations copyright © 2015 Frank Cammuso
Book design by Frank Cammuso and Alyssa Nassner

Printed and bound in China
10 9 8 7 6 5 4 3 2 1

Amulet Books are available at special discounts when purchased in quantity for premiums and promotions as well as fundraising or educational use. Special editions can also be created to specification. For details, contact specialsales@abramsbooks.com or the address below.

ABRAMS
THE ART OF BOOKS SINCE 1949

115 West 18th Street
New York, NY 10011
www.abramsbooks.com

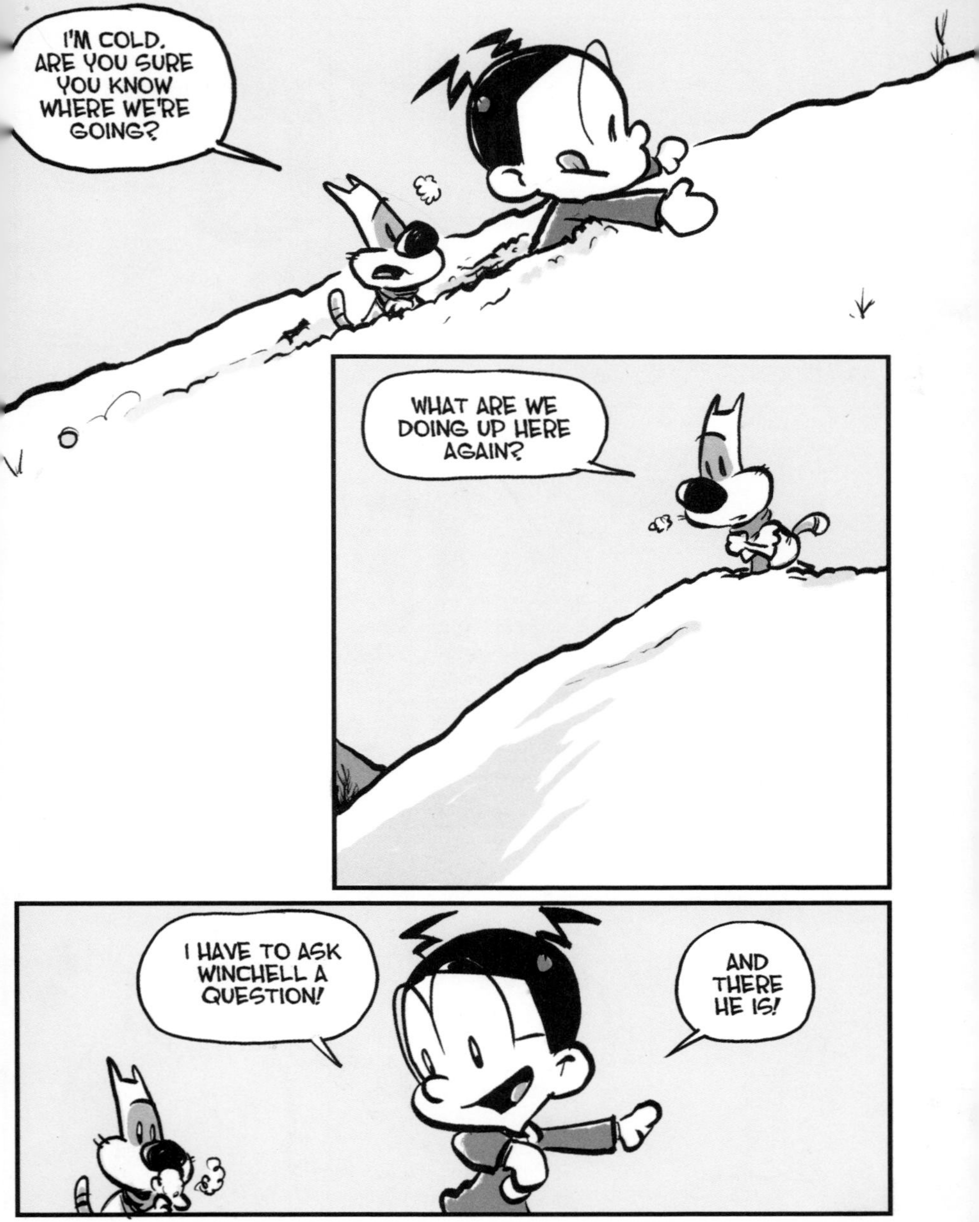

I'M COLD. ARE YOU SURE YOU KNOW WHERE WE'RE GOING?
WHAT ARE WE DOING UP HERE AGAIN?
I HAVE TO ASK WINCHELL A QUESTION!
AND THERE HE IS!

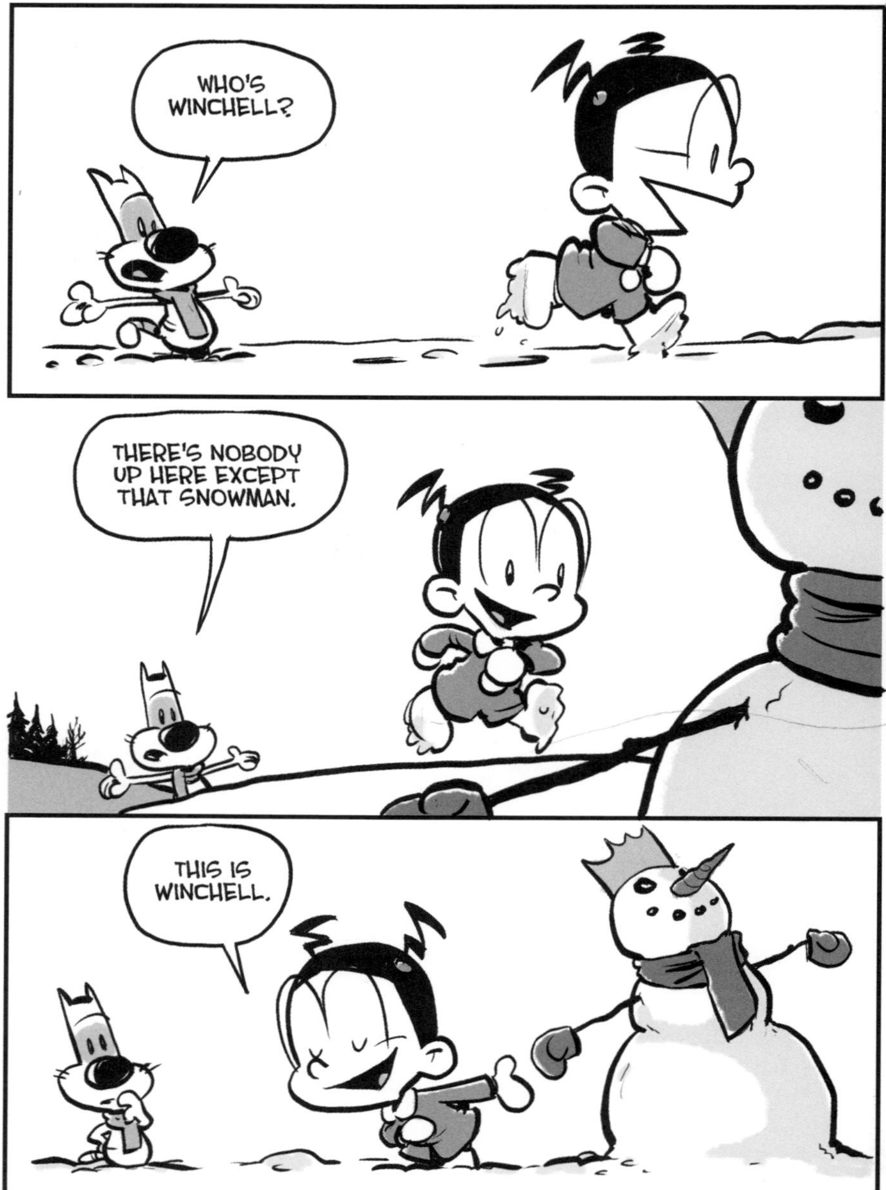
WHO'S WINCHELL?
THERE'S NOBODY UP HERE EXCEPT THAT SNOWMAN.
THIS IS WINCHELL.

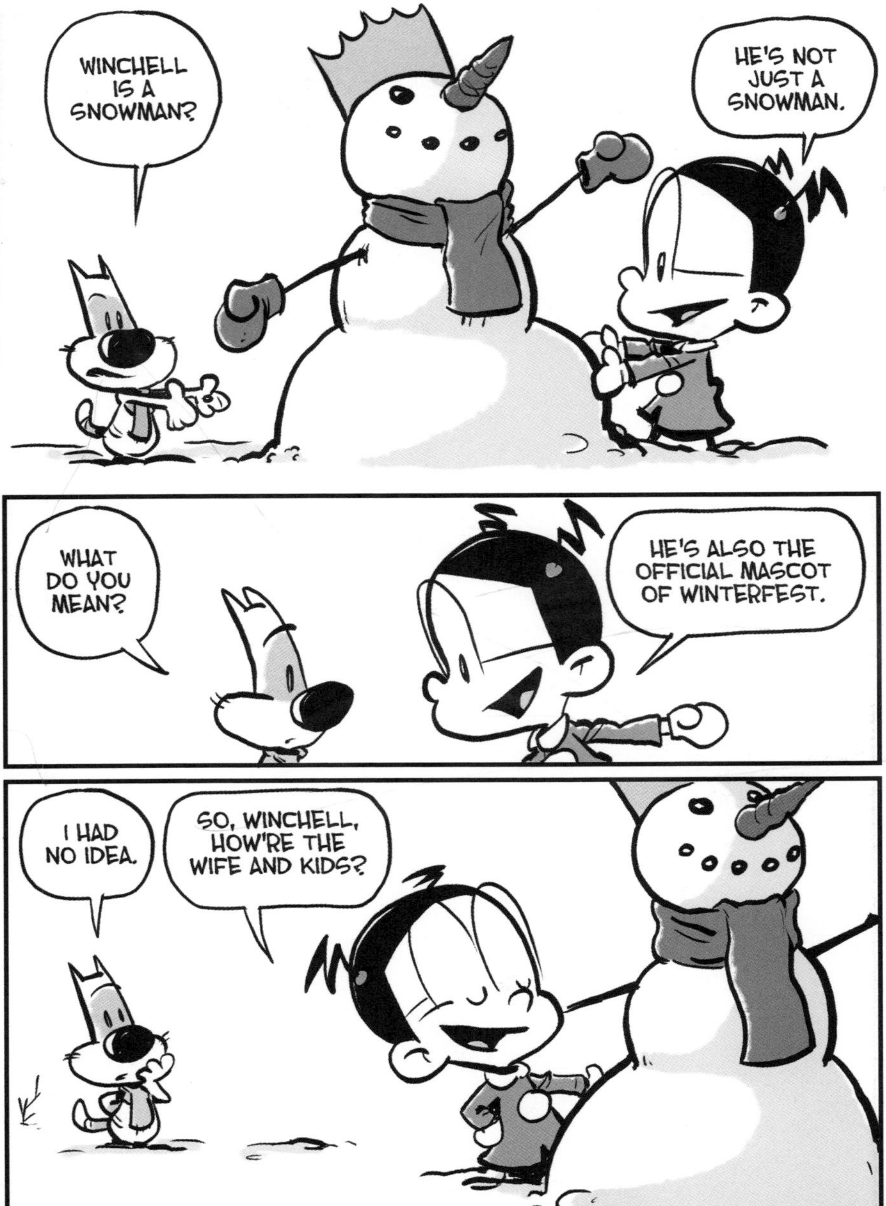
WINCHELL IS A SNOWMAN?
HE'S NOT JUST A SNOWMAN.
WHAT DO YOU MEAN?
HE'S ALSO THE OFFICIAL MASCOT OF WINTERFEST.
I HAD NO IDEA.
SO, WINCHELL, HOW'RE THE WIFE AND KIDS?

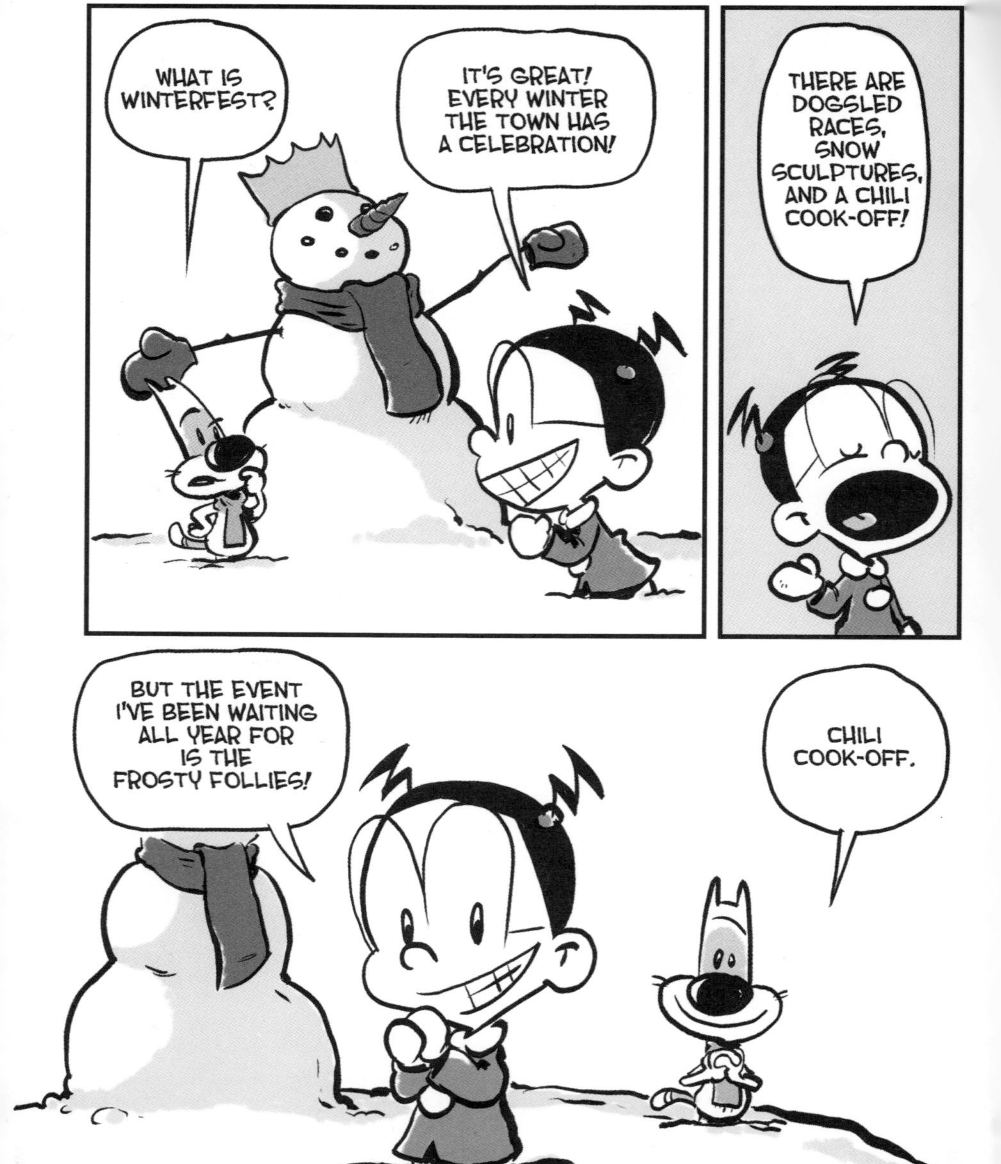
WHAT IS WINTERFEST?
IT'S GREAT! EVERY WINTER THE TOWN HAS A CELEBRATION!
THERE ARE DOGSLED RACES, SNOW SCULPTURES, AND A CHILI COOK-OFF!
BUT THE EVENT I'VE BEEN WAITING ALL YEAR FOR IS THE FROSTY FOLLIES!
CHILI COOK-OFF.

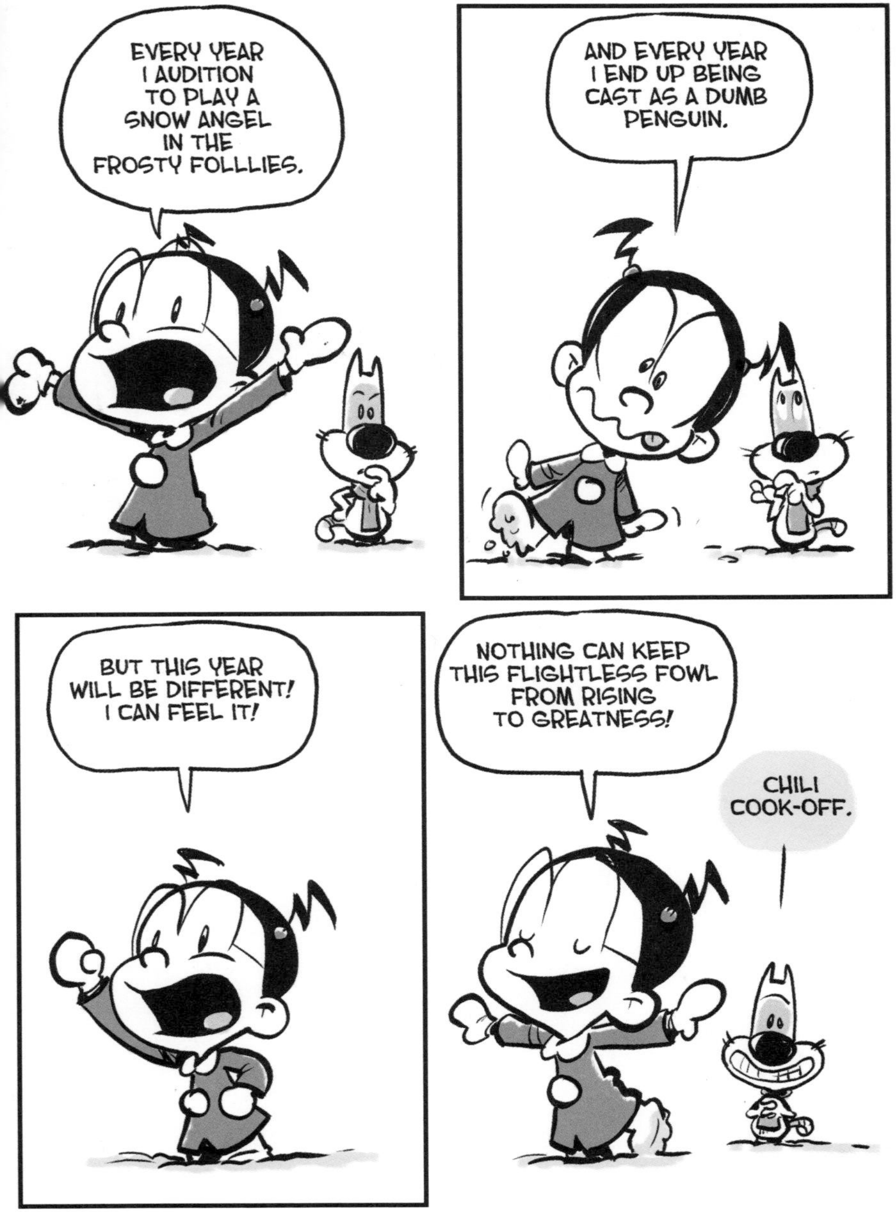
EVERY YEAR I AUDITION TO PLAY A SNOW ANGEL IN THE FROSTY FOLLLIES.
AND EVERY YEAR I END UP BEING CAST AS A DUMB PENGUIN.
BUT THIS YEAR WILL BE DIFFERENT! I CAN FEEL IT!
NOTHING CAN KEEP THIS FLIGHTLESS FOWL FROM RISING TO GREATNESS!
CHILI COOK-OFF.

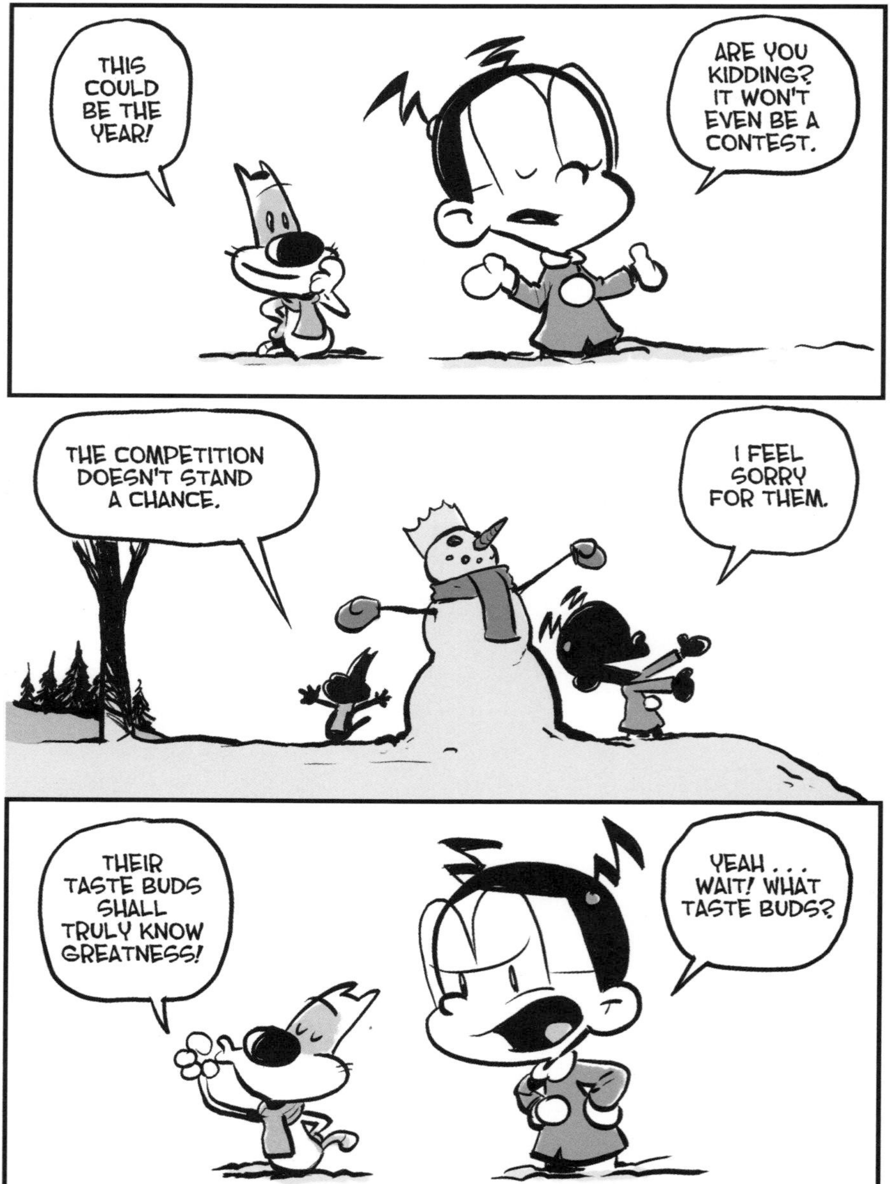
THIS COULD BE THE YEAR!
ARE YOU KIDDING? IT WON'T EVEN BE A CONTEST.
THE COMPETITION DOESN'T STAND A CHANCE.
I FEEL SORRY FOR THEM.
THEIR TASTE BUDS SHALL TRULY KNOW GREATNESS!
YEAH . . . WAIT! WHAT TASTE BUDS?

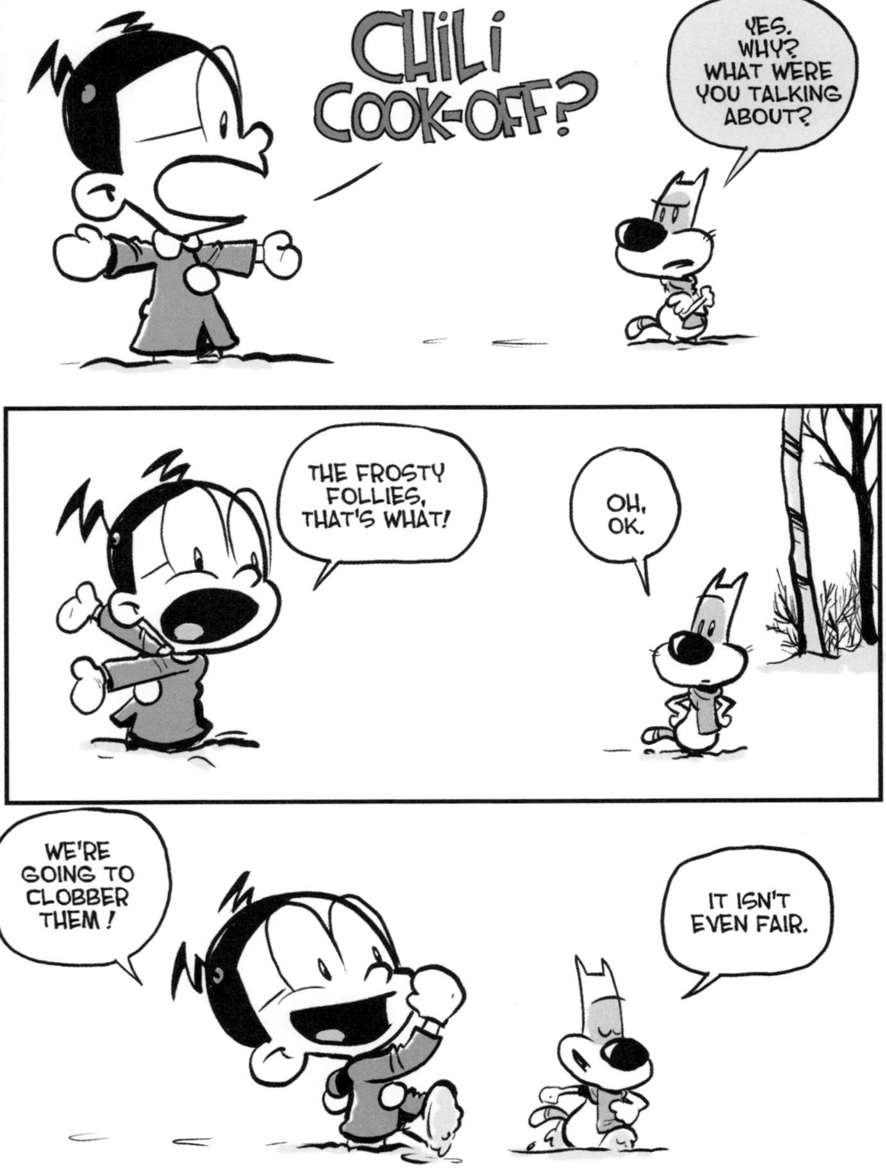
CHILI COOK-OFF?
YES. WHY? WHAT WERE YOU TALKING ABOUT?
THE FROSTY FOLLIES, THAT'S WHAT!
OH, OK.
WE'RE GOING TO CLOBBER THEM!
IT ISN'T EVEN FAIR.

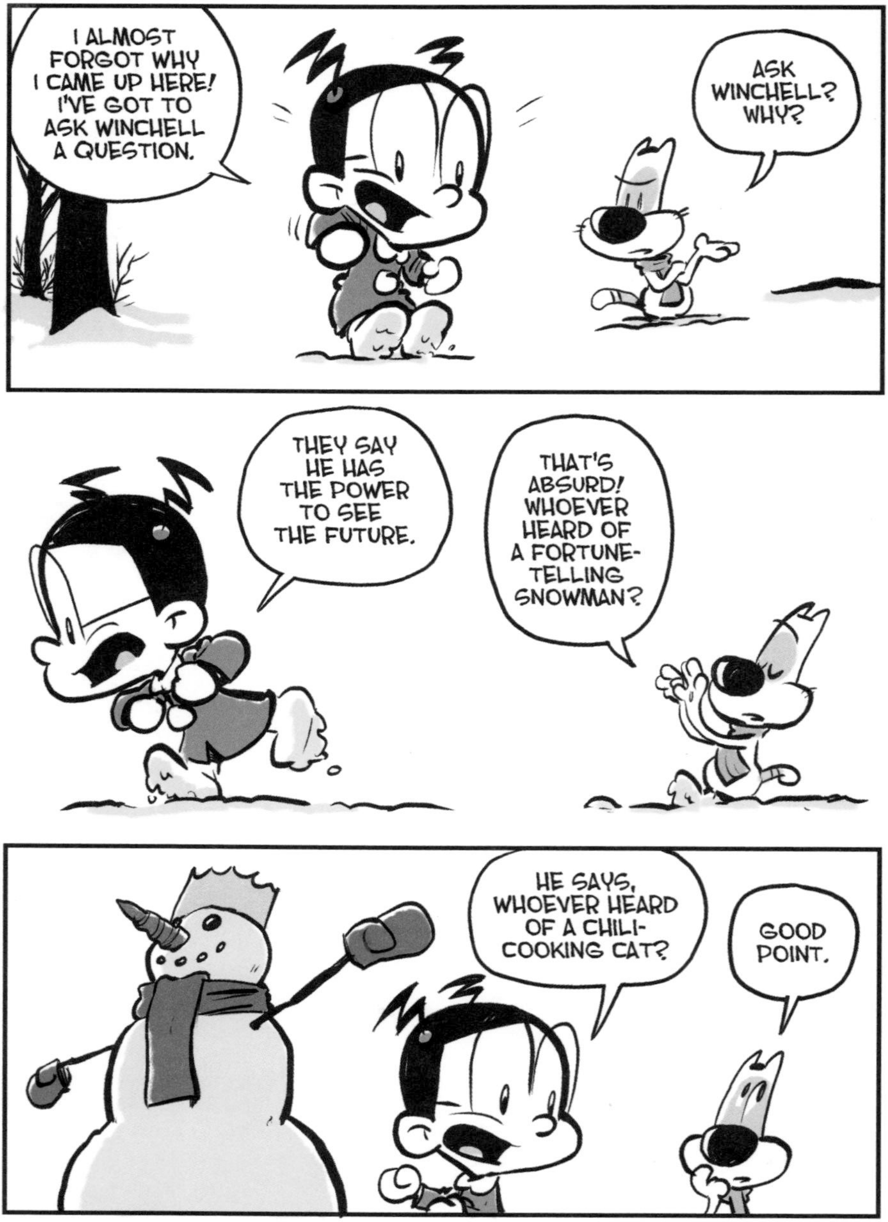
I ALMOST FORGOT WHY I CAME UP HERE! I'VE GOT TO ASK WINCHELL A QUESTION.
ASK WINCHELL? WHY?
THEY SAY HE HAS THE POWER TO SEE THE FUTURE.
THAT'S ABSURD! WHOEVER HEARD OF A FORTUNE-TELLING SNOWMAN?
HE SAYS, WHOEVER HEARD OF A CHILI-COOKING CAT?
GOOD POINT.

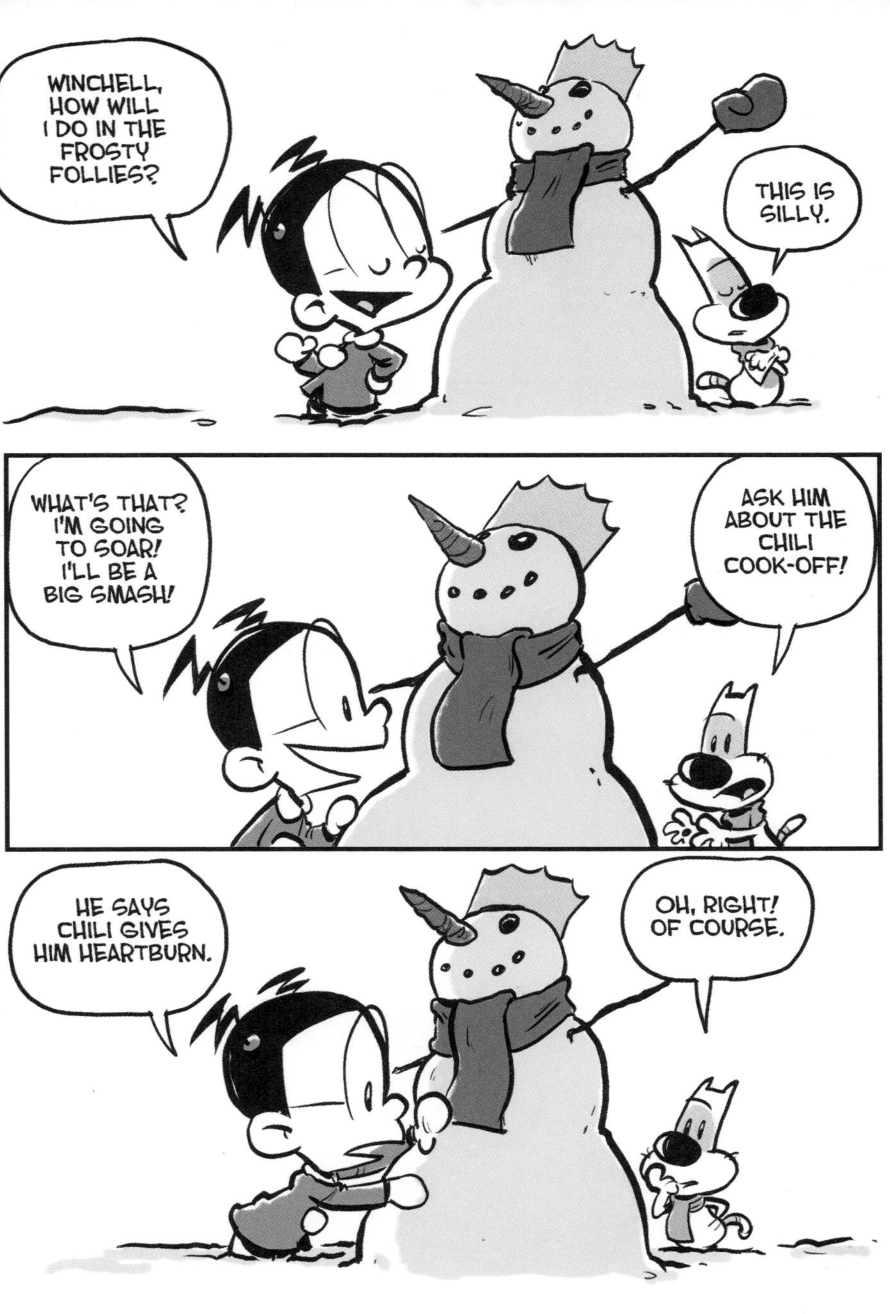
WINCHELL, HOW WILL I DO IN THE FROSTY FOLLIES?
THIS IS SILLY.
WHAT'S THAT? I'M GOING TO SOAR! I'LL BE A BIG SMASH!
ASK HIM ABOUT THE CHILI COOK-OFF!
HE SAYS CHILI GIVES HIM HEARTBURN.
OH, RIGHT! OF COURSE.

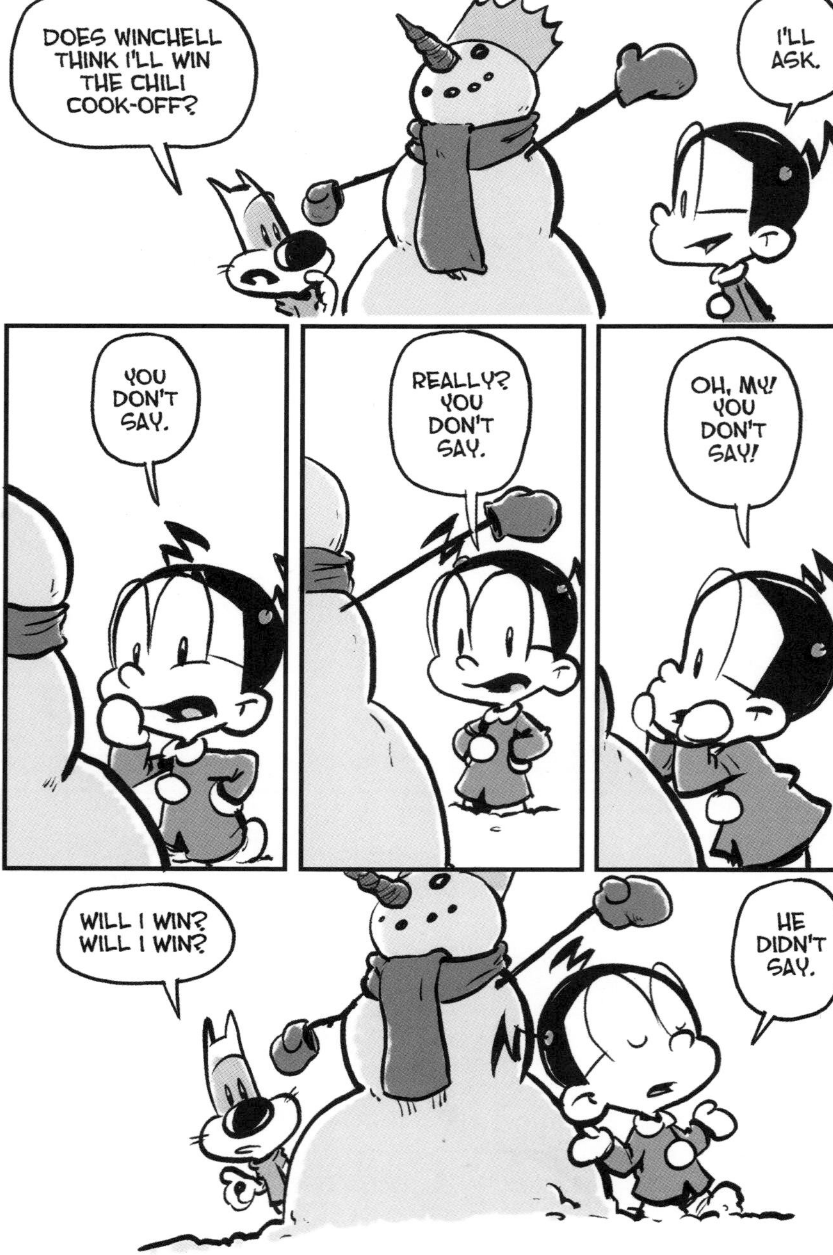
DOES WINCHELL THINK I'LL WIN THE CHILI COOK-OFF?
I'LL ASK.
YOU DON'T SAY.
REALLY? YOU DON'T SAY.
OH, MY! YOU DON'T SAY!
WILL I WIN? WILL I WIN?
HE DIDN'T SAY.

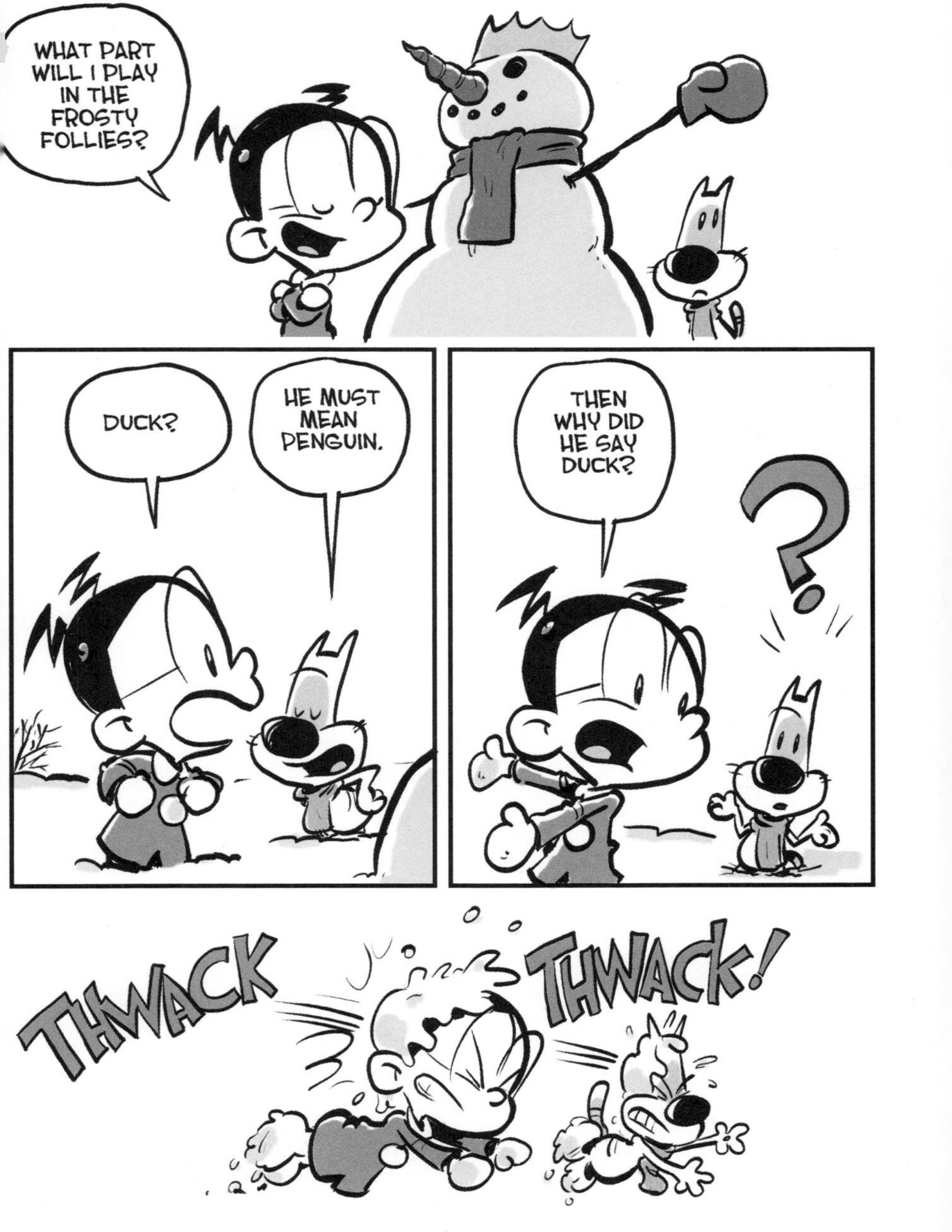
WHAT PART WILL I PLAY IN THE FROSTY FOLLIES?
DUCK?
HE MUST MEAN PENGUIN.
THEN WHY DID HE SAY DUCK?
?
THWACK
THWACK!

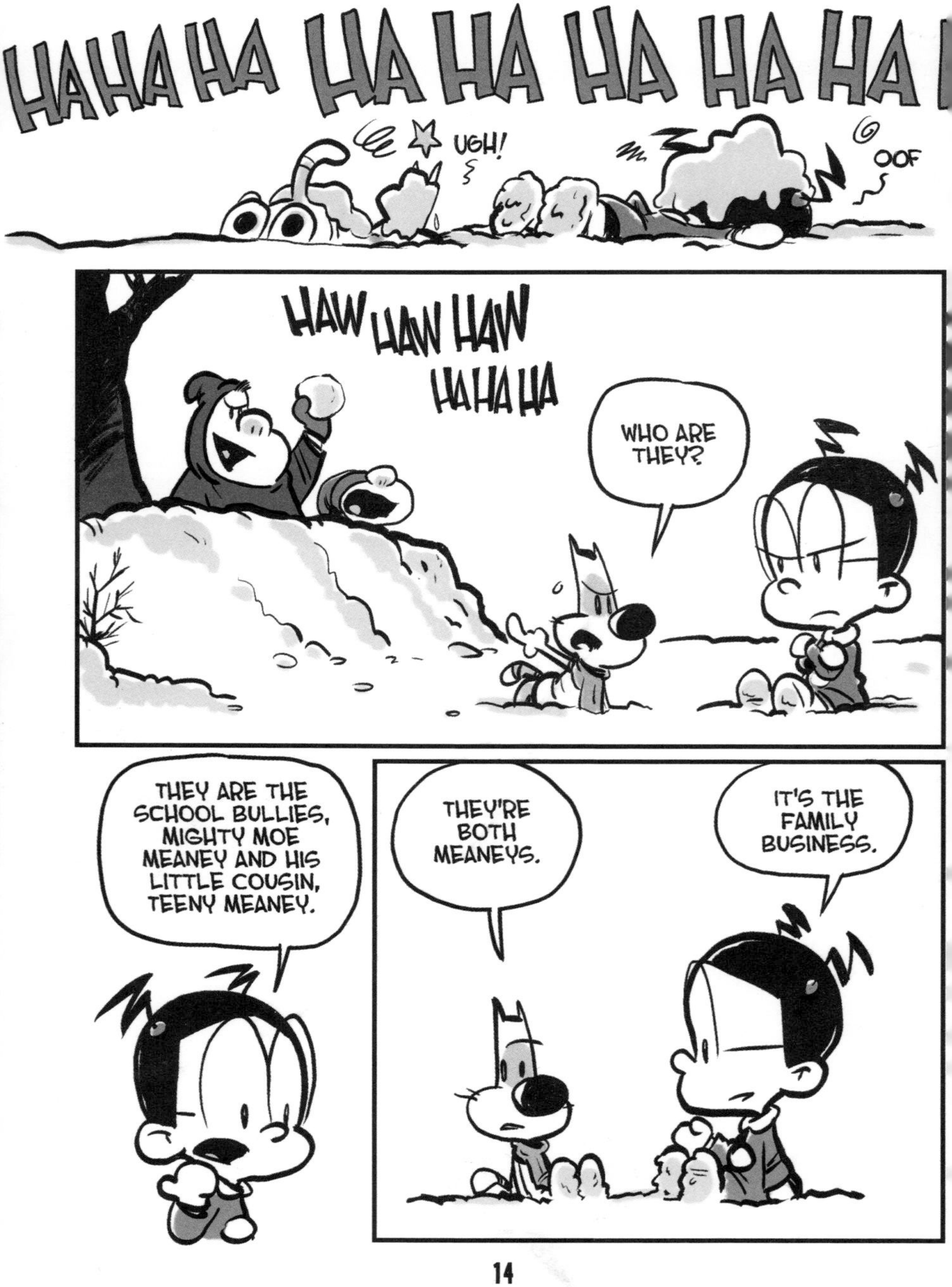
HAHAHA HA HA HA HA HA HA HA
UGH!
OOF
HAW HAW HAW
HAHAHA
WHO ARE THEY?
THEY ARE THE SCHOOL BULLIES, MIGHTY MOE MEANEY AND HIS LITTLE COUSIN, TEENY MEANEY.
THEY'RE BOTH MEANEYS.
IT'S THE FAMILY BUSINESS.

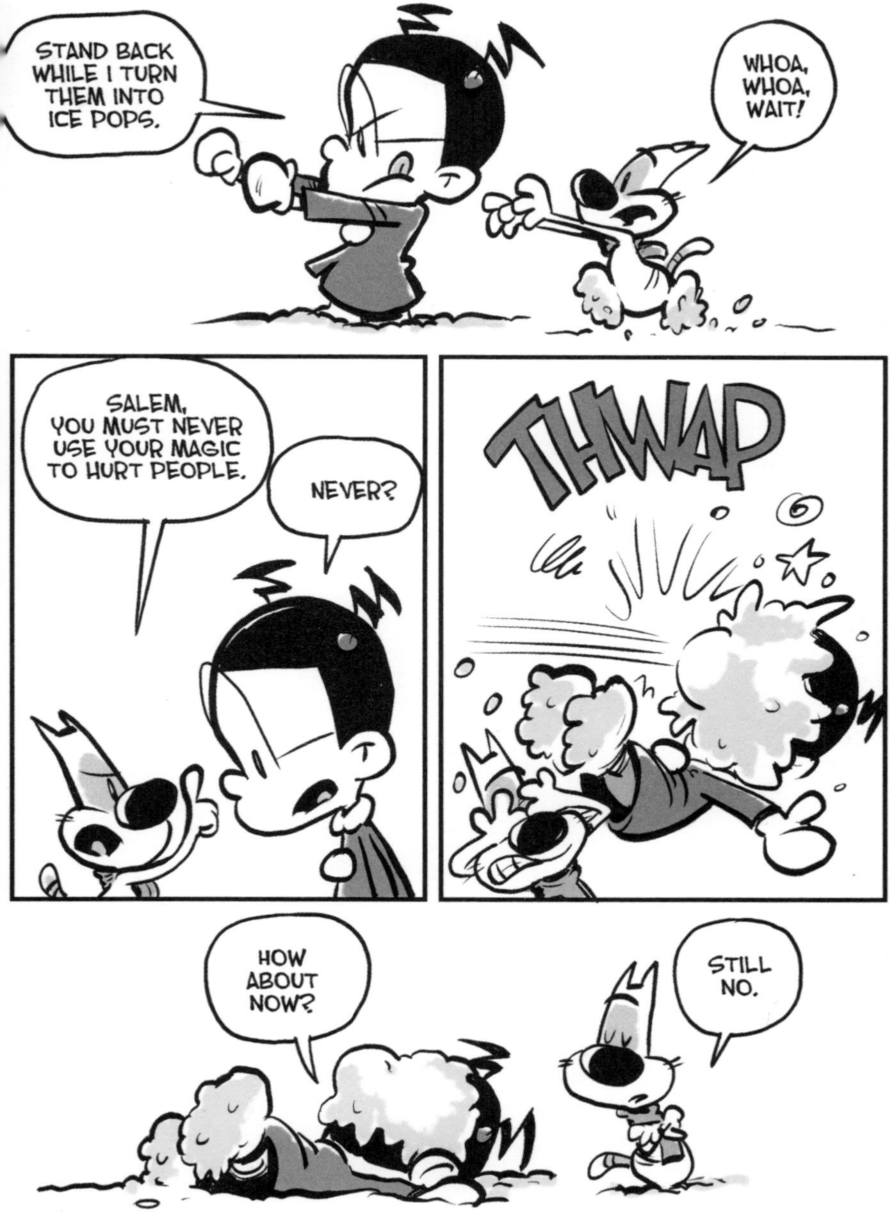
STAND BACK WHILE I TURN THEM INTO ICE POPS.
WHOA, WHOA, WAIT!
SALEM, YOU MUST NEVER USE YOUR MAGIC TO HURT PEOPLE.
NEVER?
THWAP
HOW ABOUT NOW?
STILL NO.

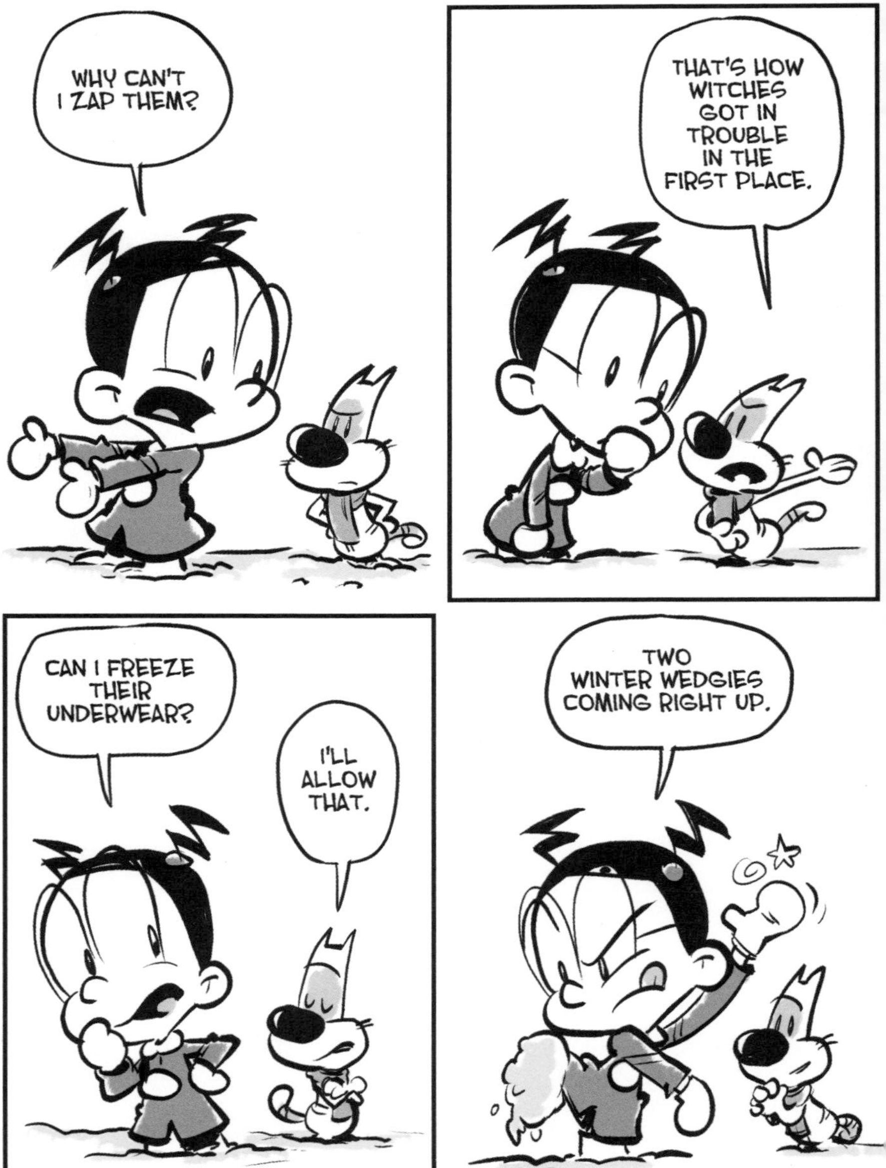
WHY CAN'T I ZAP THEM?
THAT'S HOW WITCHES GOT IN TROUBLE IN THE FIRST PLACE.
CAN I FREEZE THEIR UNDERWEAR?
I'LL ALLOW THAT.
TWO WINTER WEDGIES COMING RIGHT UP.

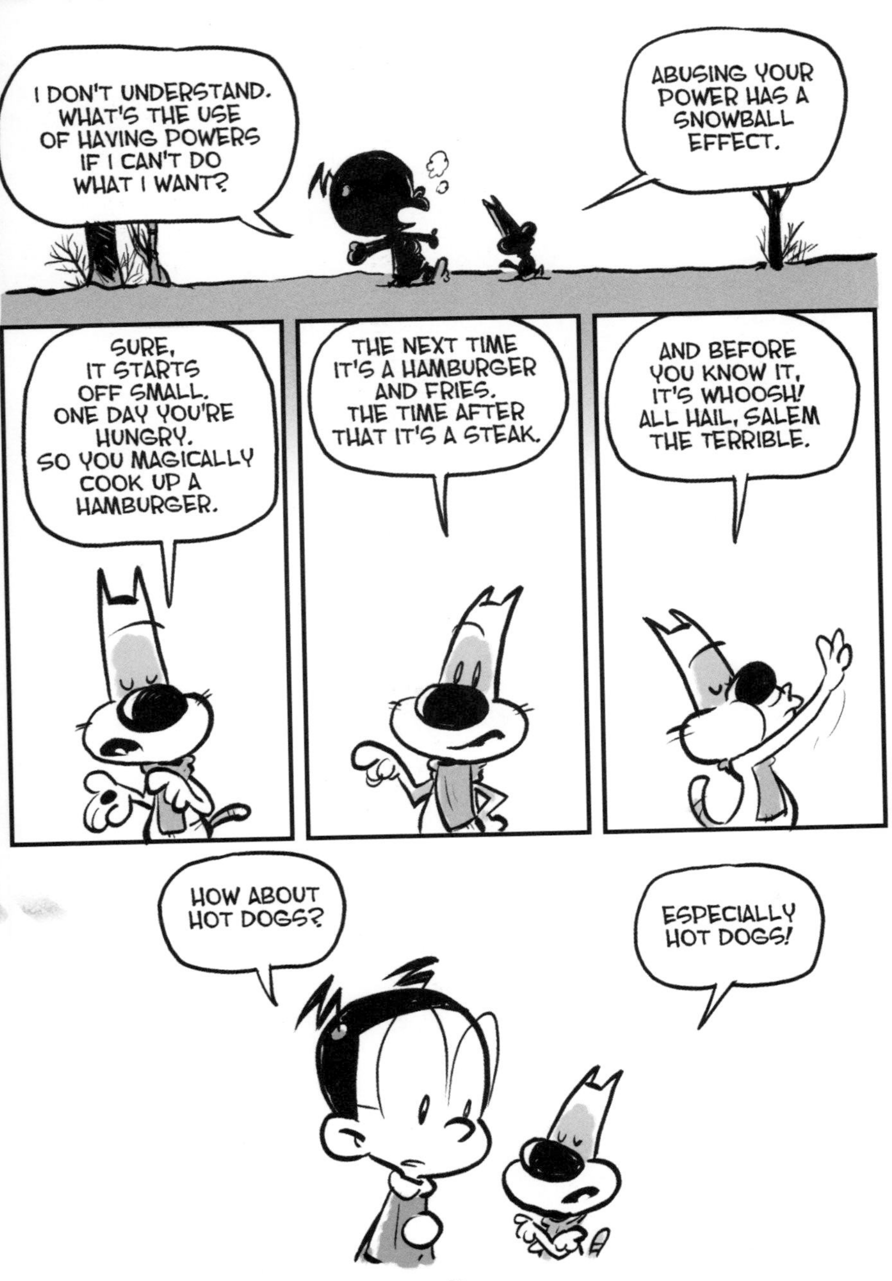
I DON'T UNDERSTAND. WHAT'S THE USE OF HAVING POWERS IF I CAN'T DO WHAT I WANT?
ABUSING YOUR POWER HAS A SNOWBALL EFFECT.
SURE, IT STARTS OFF SMALL. ONE DAY YOU'RE HUNGRY. SO YOU MAGICALLY COOK UP A HAMBURGER.
THE NEXT TIME IT'S A HAMBURGER AND FRIES. THE TIME AFTER THAT IT'S A STEAK.
AND BEFORE YOU KNOW IT, IT'S WHOOSH! ALL HAIL, SALEM THE TERRIBLE.
HOW ABOUT HOT DOGS?
ESPECIALLY HOT DOGS!

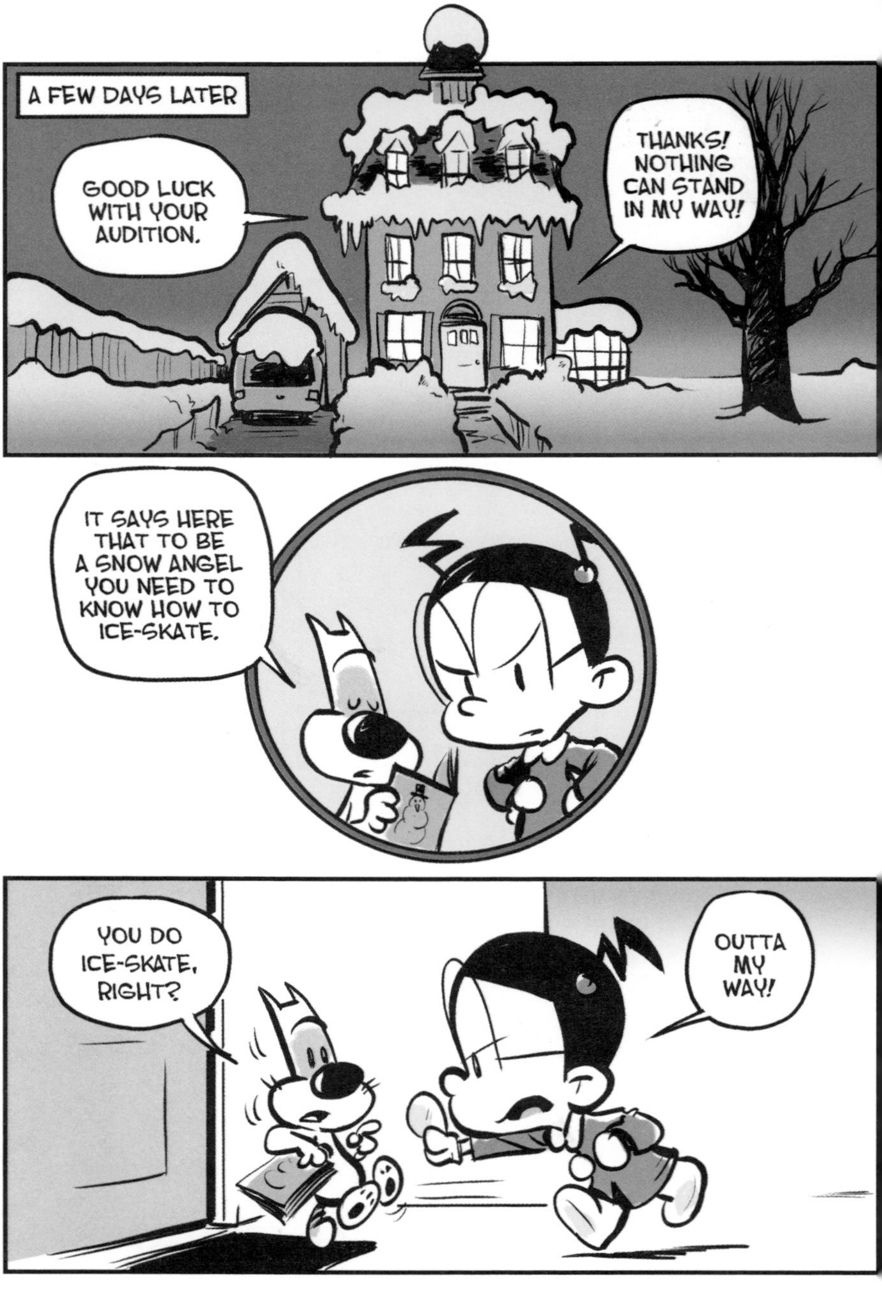
A FEW DAYS LATER
GOOD LUCK WITH YOUR AUDITION.
THANKS! NOTHING CAN STAND IN MY WAY!
IT SAYS HERE THAT TO BE A SNOW ANGEL YOU NEED TO KNOW HOW TO ICE-SKATE.
YOU DO ICE-SKATE, RIGHT?
OUTTA MY WAY!

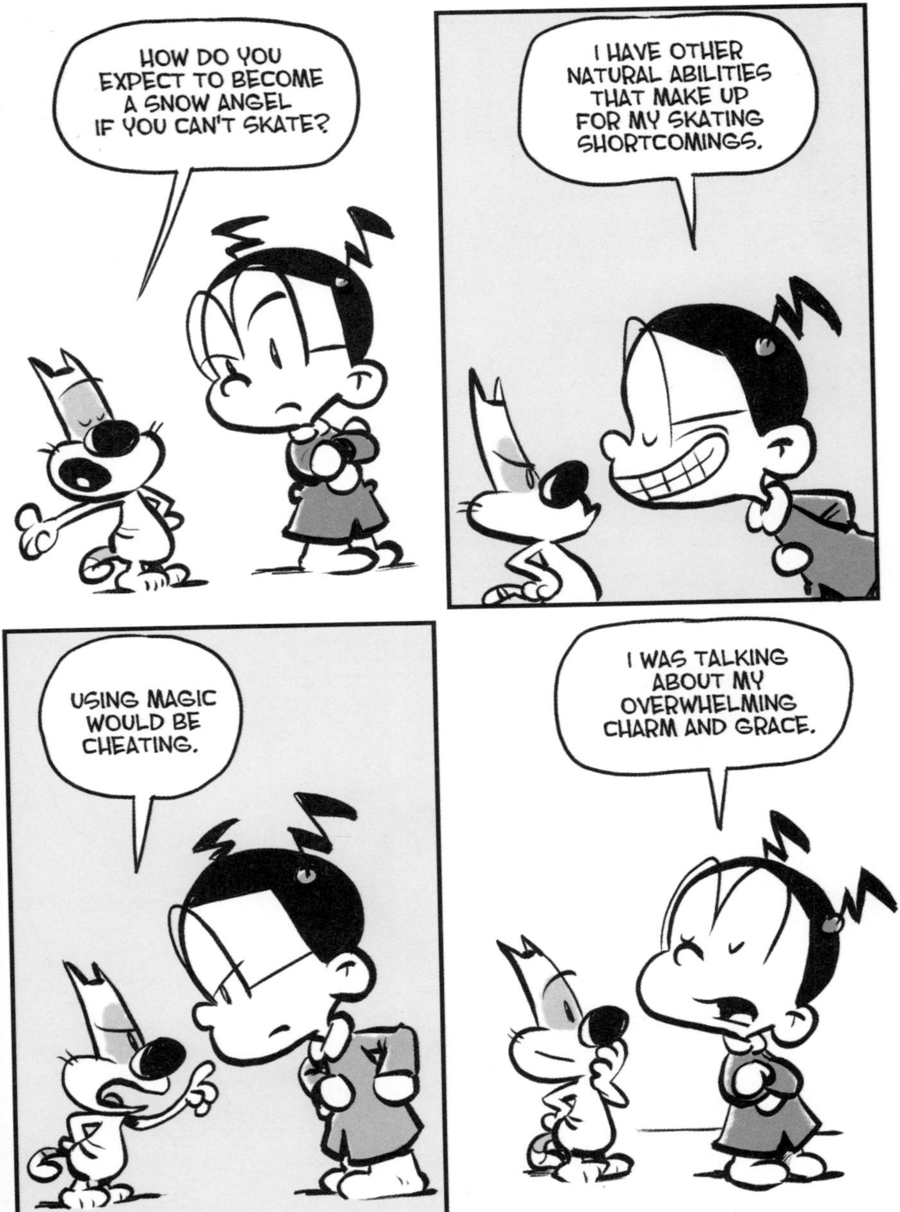
HOW DO YOU EXPECT TO BECOME A SNOW ANGEL IF YOU CAN'T SKATE?
I HAVE OTHER NATURAL ABILITIES THAT MAKE UP FOR MY SKATING SHORTCOMINGS.
USING MAGIC WOULD BE CHEATING.
I WAS TALKING ABOUT MY OVERWHELMING CHARM AND GRACE.

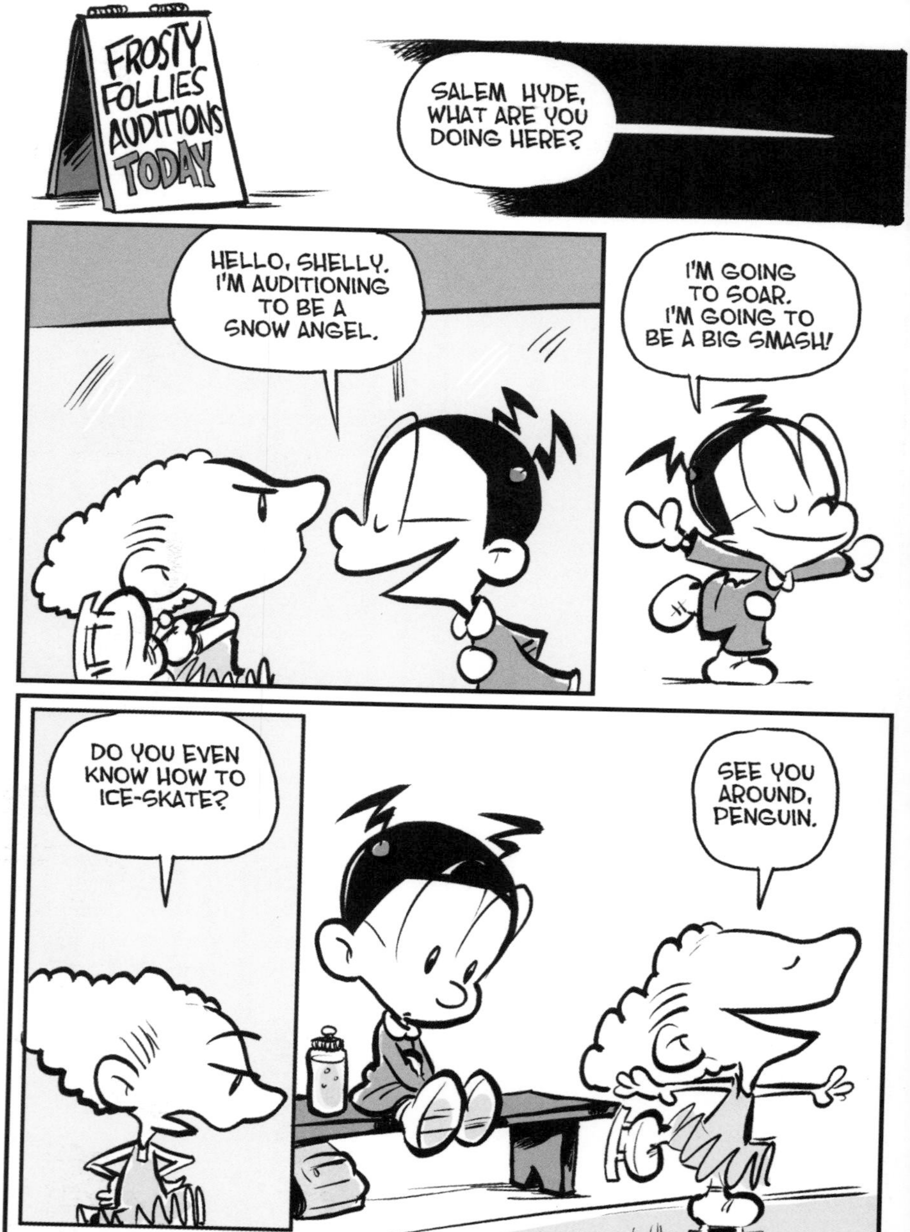
FROSTY FOLLIES AUDITIONS TODAY
SALEM HYDE, WHAT ARE YOU DOING HERE?
HELLO, SHELLY. I'M AUDITIONING TO BE A SNOW ANGEL.
I'M GOING TO SOAR. I'M GOING TO BE A BIG SMASH!
DO YOU EVEN KNOW HOW TO ICE-SKATE?
SEE YOU AROUND, PENGUIN.

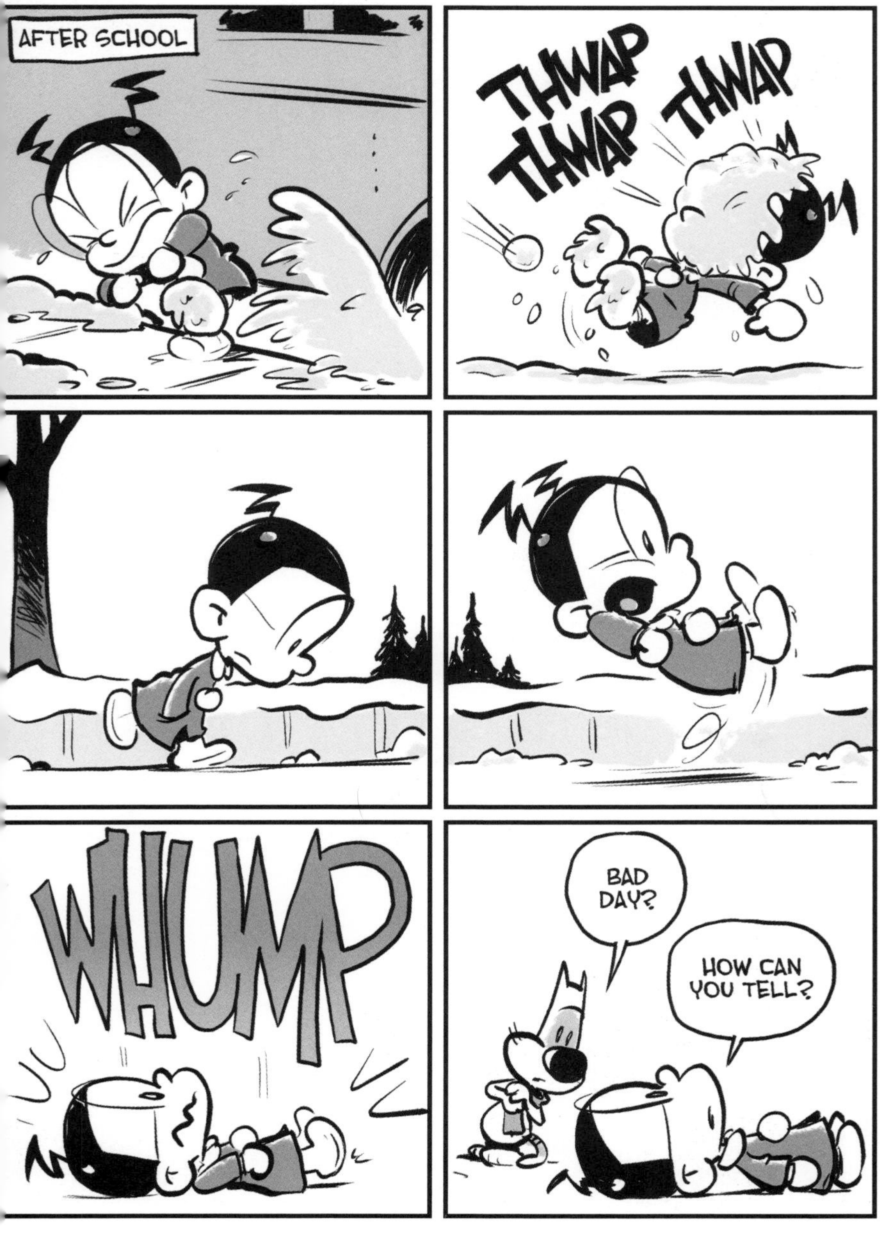
AFTER SCHOOL
THWAP
THWAP
THWAP
WHUMP
BAD DAY?
HOW CAN YOU TELL?

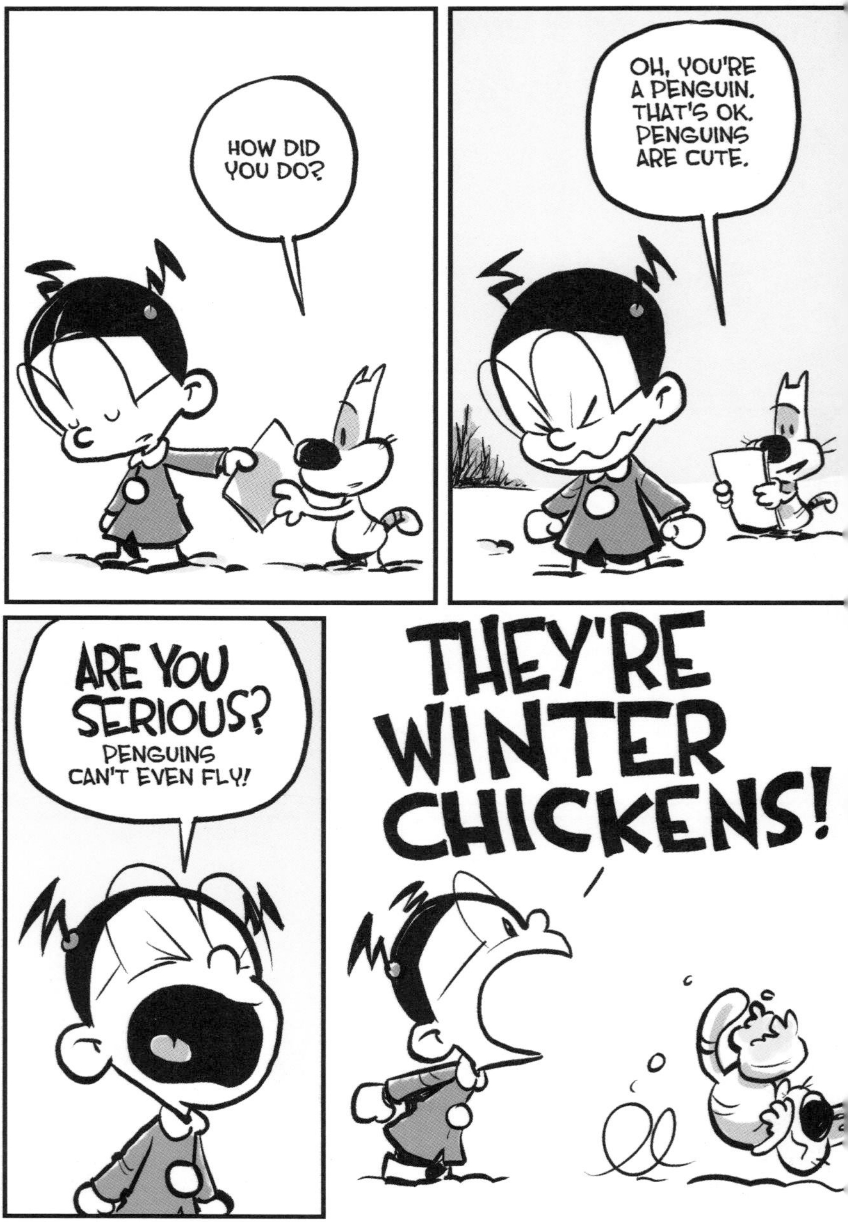
HOW DID YOU DO?
OH, YOU'RE A PENGUIN. THAT'S OK. PENGUINS ARE CUTE.
ARE YOU SERIOUS? PENGUINS CAN'T EVEN FLY!
THEY'RE WINTER CHICKENS!

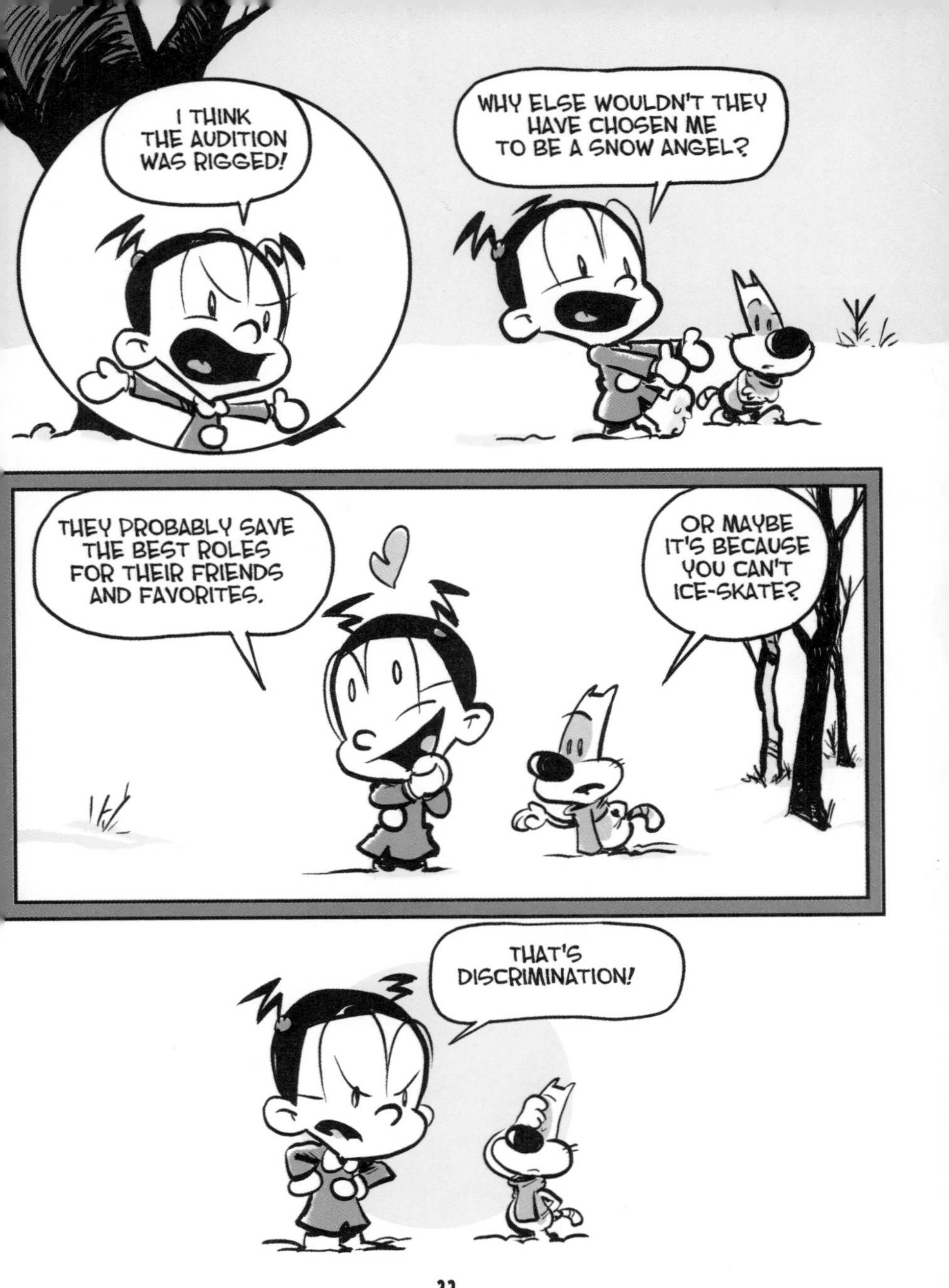
I THINK THE AUDITION WAS RIGGED!
WHY ELSE WOULDN'T THEY HAVE CHOSEN ME TO BE A SNOW ANGEL?
THEY PROBABLY SAVE THE BEST ROLES FOR THEIR FRIENDS AND FAVORITES.
OR MAYBE IT'S BECAUSE YOU CAN'T ICE-SKATE?
THAT'S DISCRIMINATION!

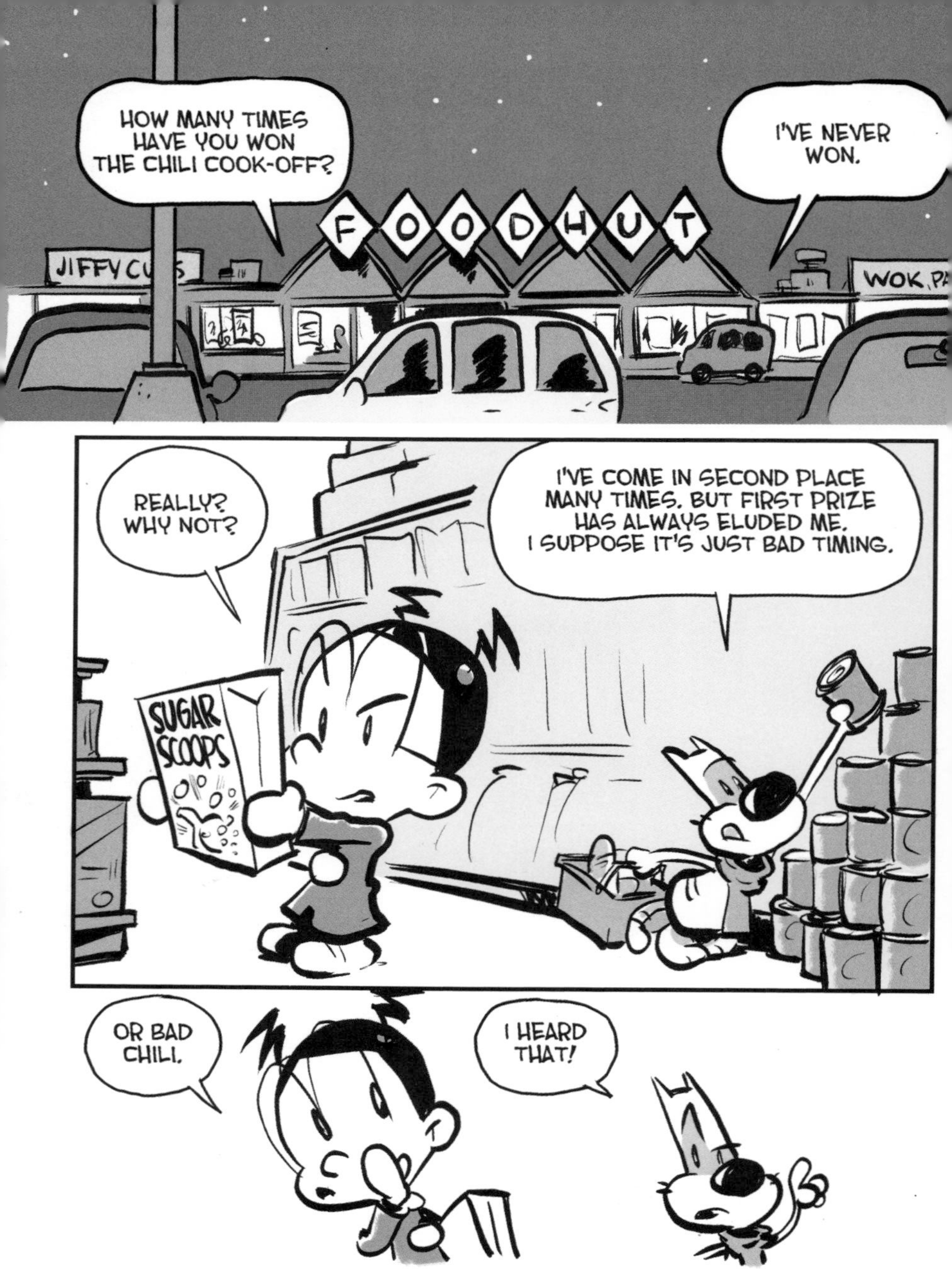
HOW MANY TIMES HAVE YOU WON THE CHILI COOK-OFF?
I'VE NEVER WON.
FOODHUT
JIFFY CU
WOK PA
REALLY? WHY NOT?
I'VE COME IN SECOND PLACE MANY TIMES. BUT FIRST PRIZE HAS ALWAYS ELUDED ME. I SUPPOSE IT'S JUST BAD TIMING.
SUGAR SCOOPS
OR BAD CHILI.
I HEARD THAT!

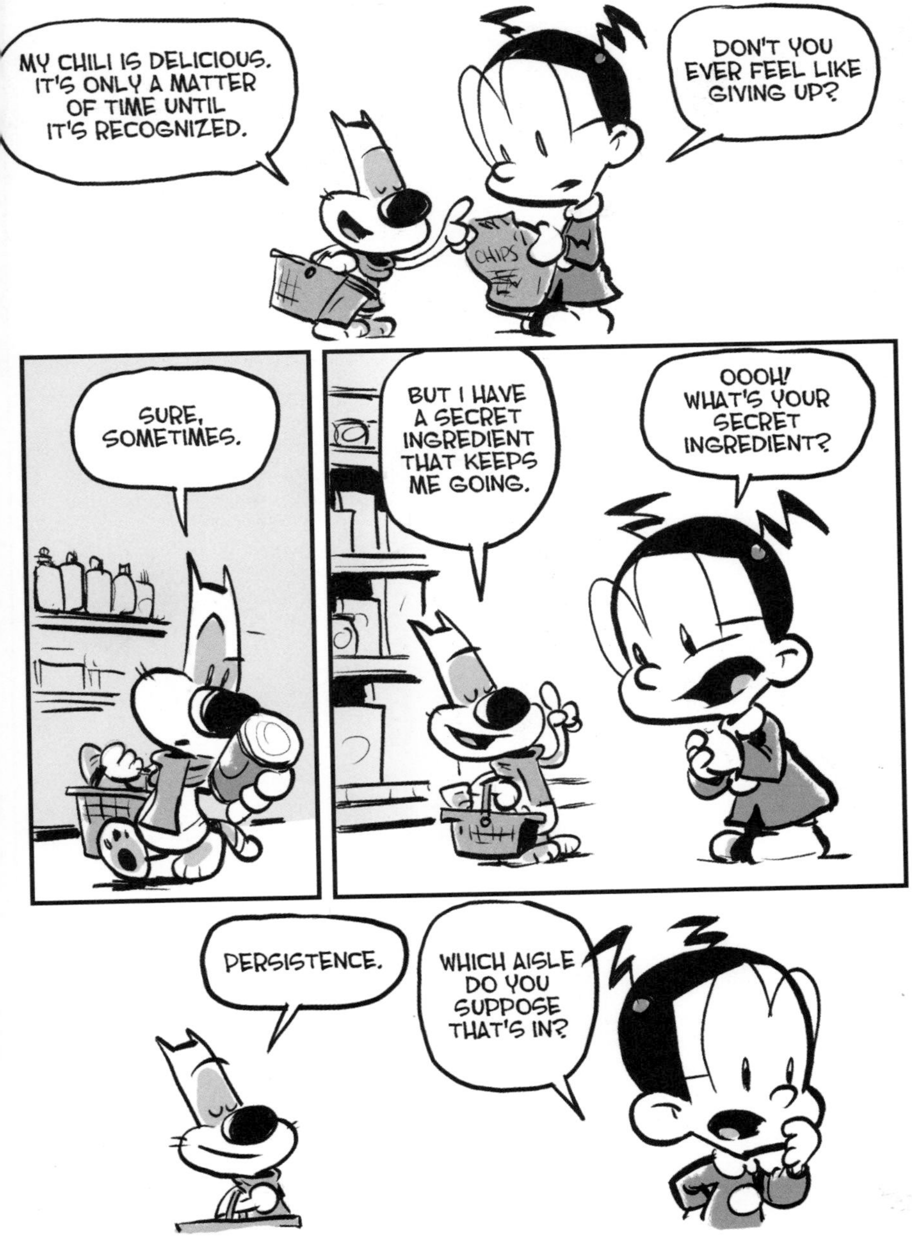
MY CHILI IS DELICIOUS. IT'S ONLY A MATTER OF TIME UNTIL IT'S RECOGNIZED.
DON'T YOU EVER FEEL LIKE GIVING UP?
CHIPS
SURE, SOMETIMES.
BUT I HAVE A SECRET INGREDIENT THAT KEEPS ME GOING.
OOOH! WHAT'S YOUR SECRET INGREDIENT?
PERSISTENCE.
WHICH AISLE DO YOU SUPPOSE THAT'S IN?

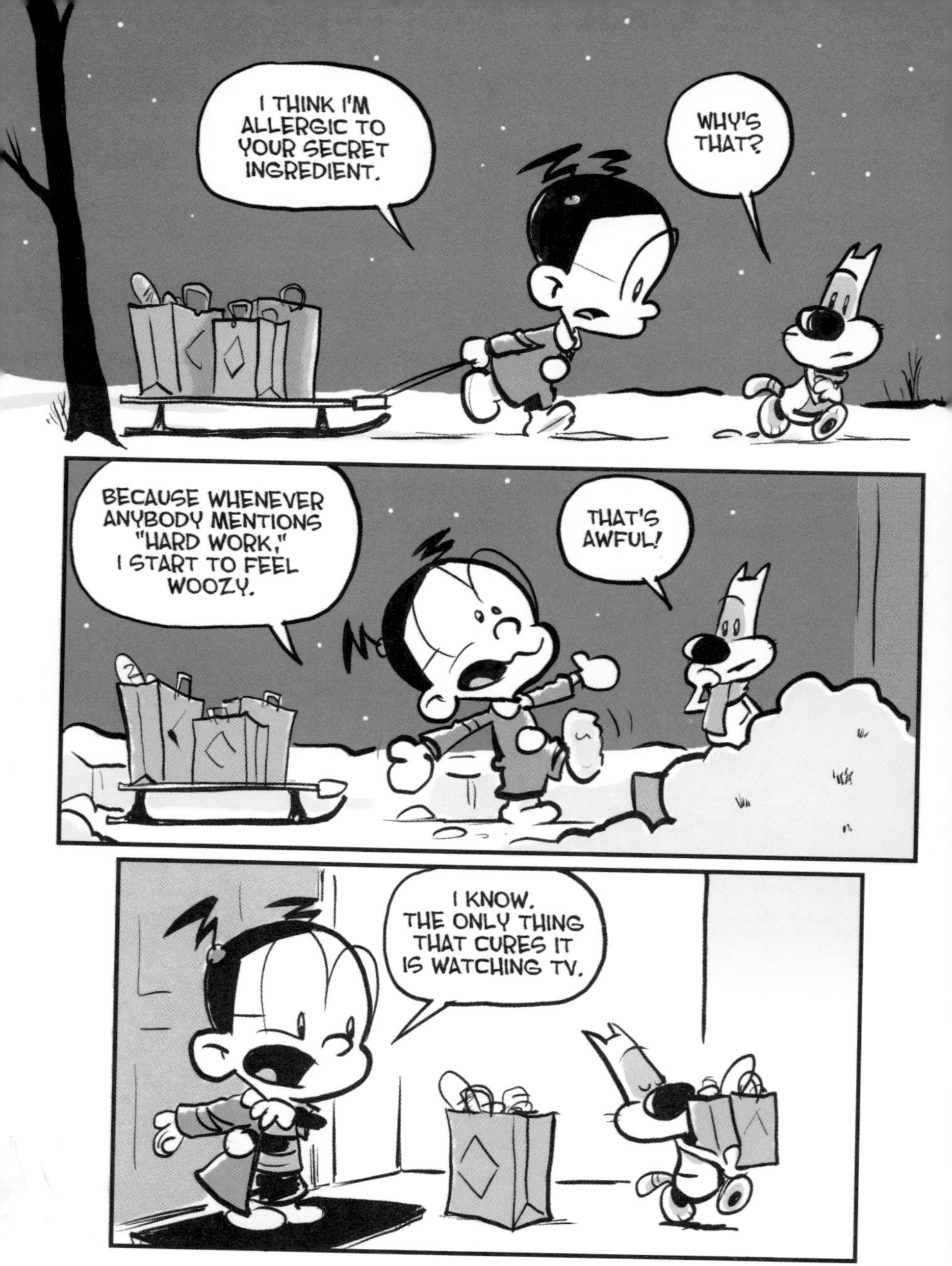
I THINK I'M ALLERGIC TO YOUR SECRET INGREDIENT.
WHY'S THAT?
BECAUSE WHENEVER ANYBODY MENTIONS "HARD WORK," I START TO FEEL WOOZY.
THAT'S AWFUL!
I KNOW. THE ONLY THING THAT CURES IT IS WATCHING TV.

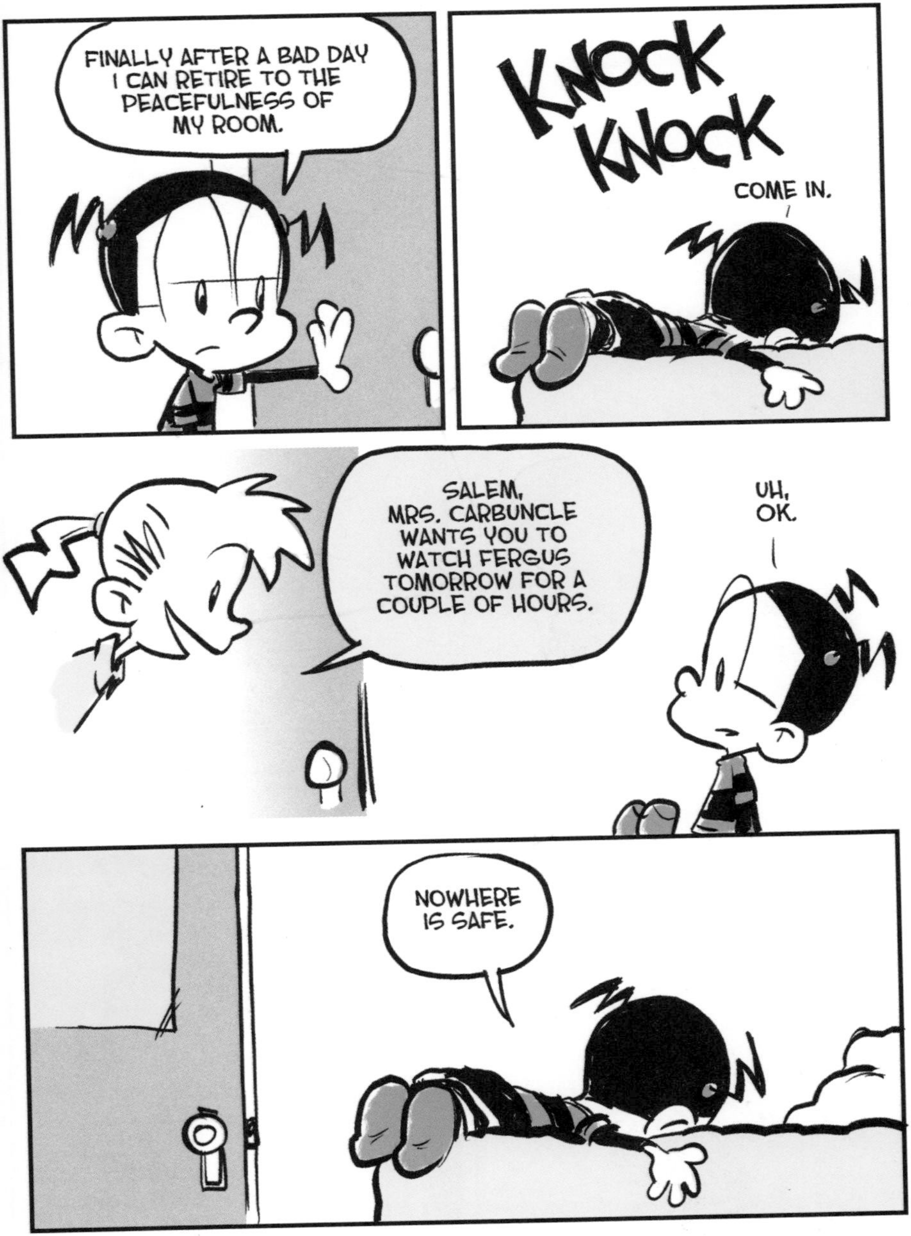
FINALLY AFTER A BAD DAY I CAN RETIRE TO THE PEACEFULNESS OF MY ROOM.
KNOCK KNOCK
COME IN.
SALEM, MRS. CARBUNCLE WANTS YOU TO WATCH FERGUS TOMORROW FOR A COUPLE OF HOURS.
UH, OK.
NOWHERE IS SAFE.

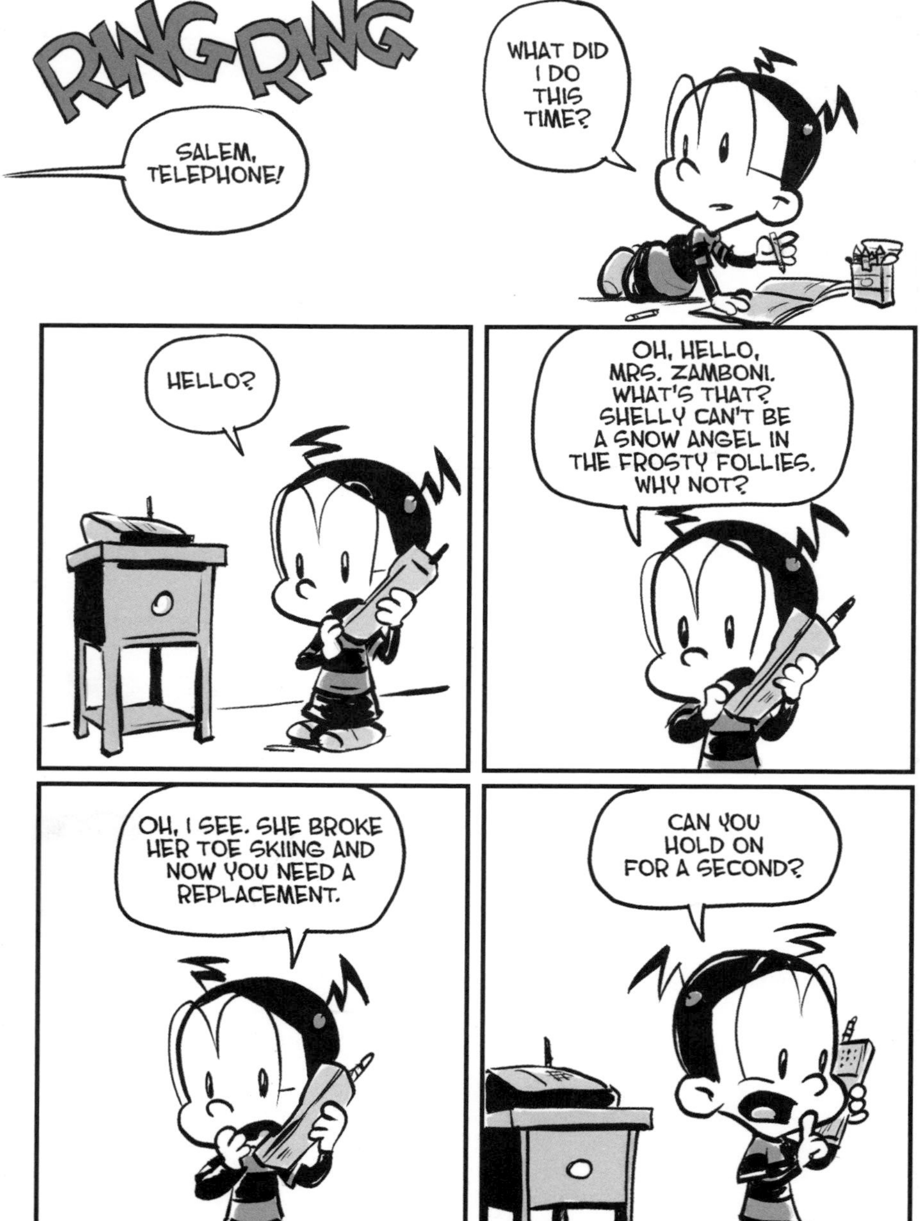
RING RING
SALEM, TELEPHONE!
WHAT DID I DO THIS TIME?
HELLO?
OH, HELLO, MRS. ZAMBONI. WHAT'S THAT? SHELLY CAN'T BE A SNOW ANGEL IN THE FROSTY FOLLIES. WHY NOT?
OH, I SEE. SHE BROKE HER TOE SKIING AND NOW YOU NEED A REPLACEMENT.
CAN YOU HOLD ON FOR A SECOND?

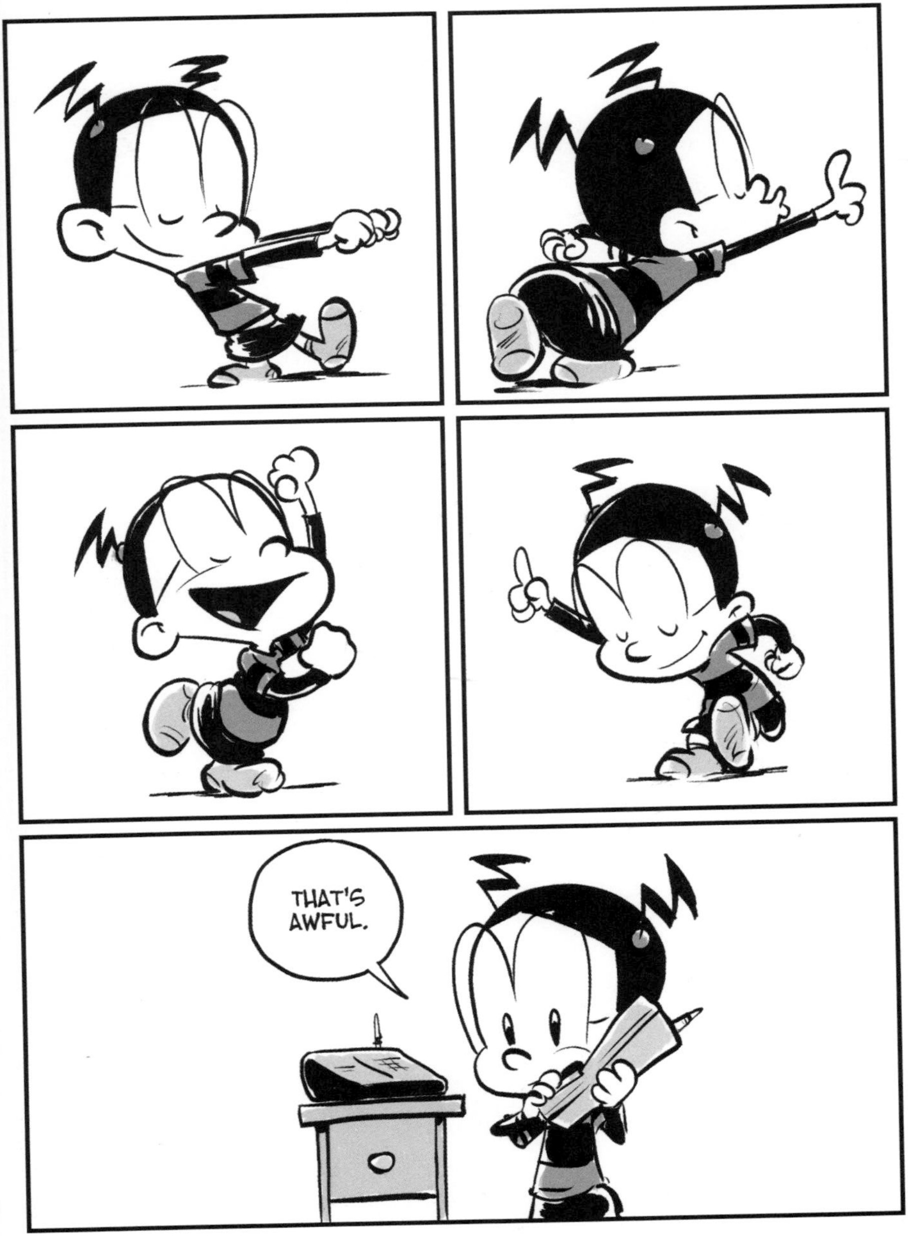
THAT'S AWFUL.

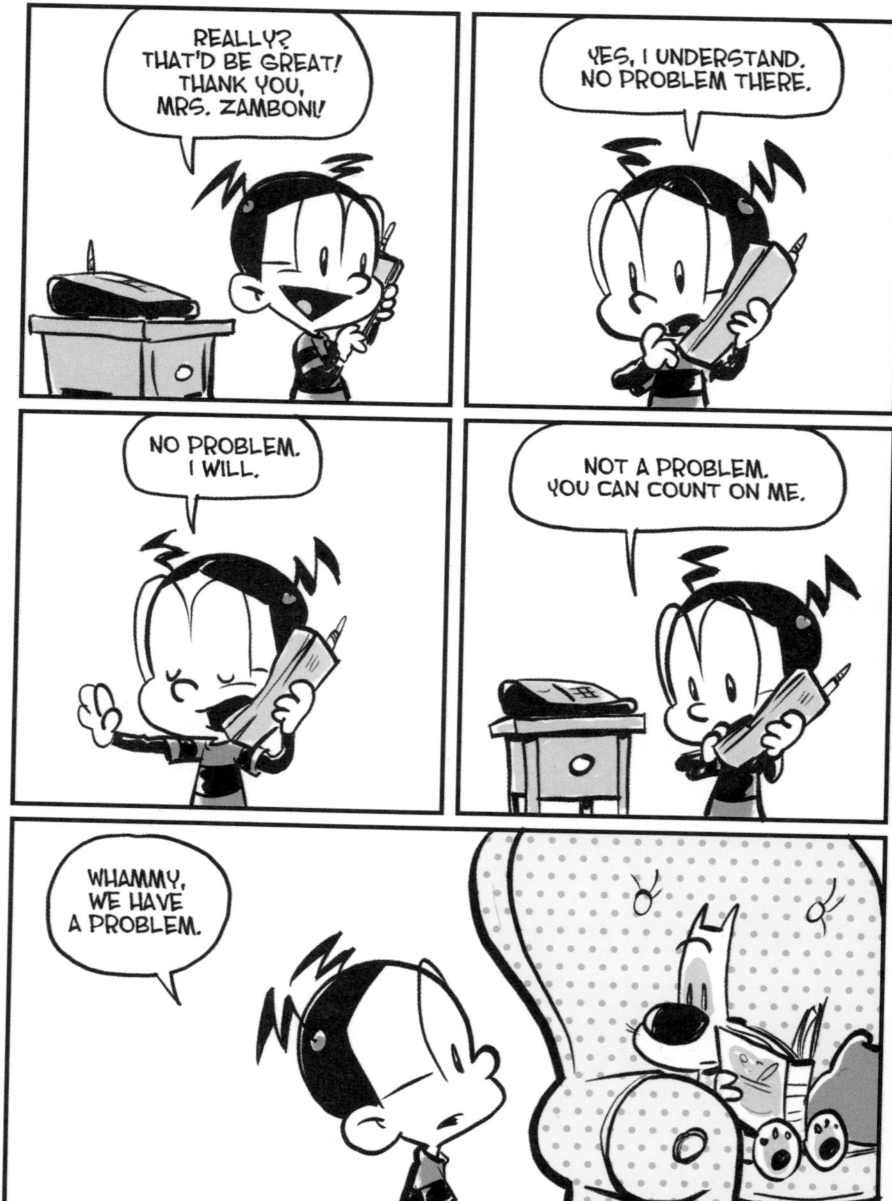
REALLY? THAT'D BE GREAT! THANK YOU, MRS. ZAMBONI!
YES, I UNDERSTAND. NO PROBLEM THERE.
NO PROBLEM. I WILL.
NOT A PROBLEM. YOU CAN COUNT ON ME.
WHAMMY, WE HAVE A PROBLEM.

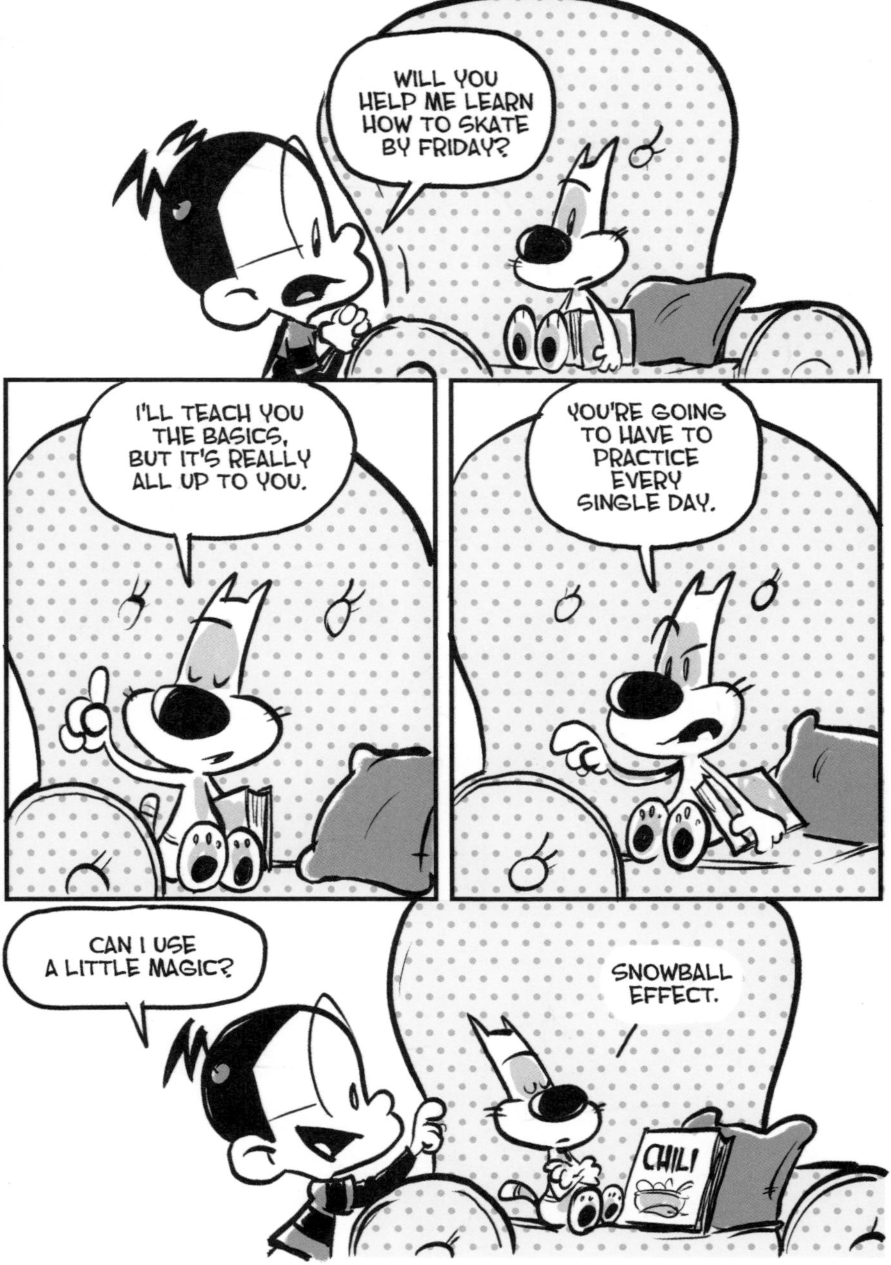

WILL YOU HELP ME LEARN HOW TO SKATE BY FRIDAY?
I'LL TEACH YOU THE BASICS, BUT IT'S REALLY ALL UP TO YOU.
YOU'RE GOING TO HAVE TO PRACTICE EVERY SINGLE DAY.
CAN I USE A LITTLE MAGIC?
SNOWBALL EFFECT.
CHILI

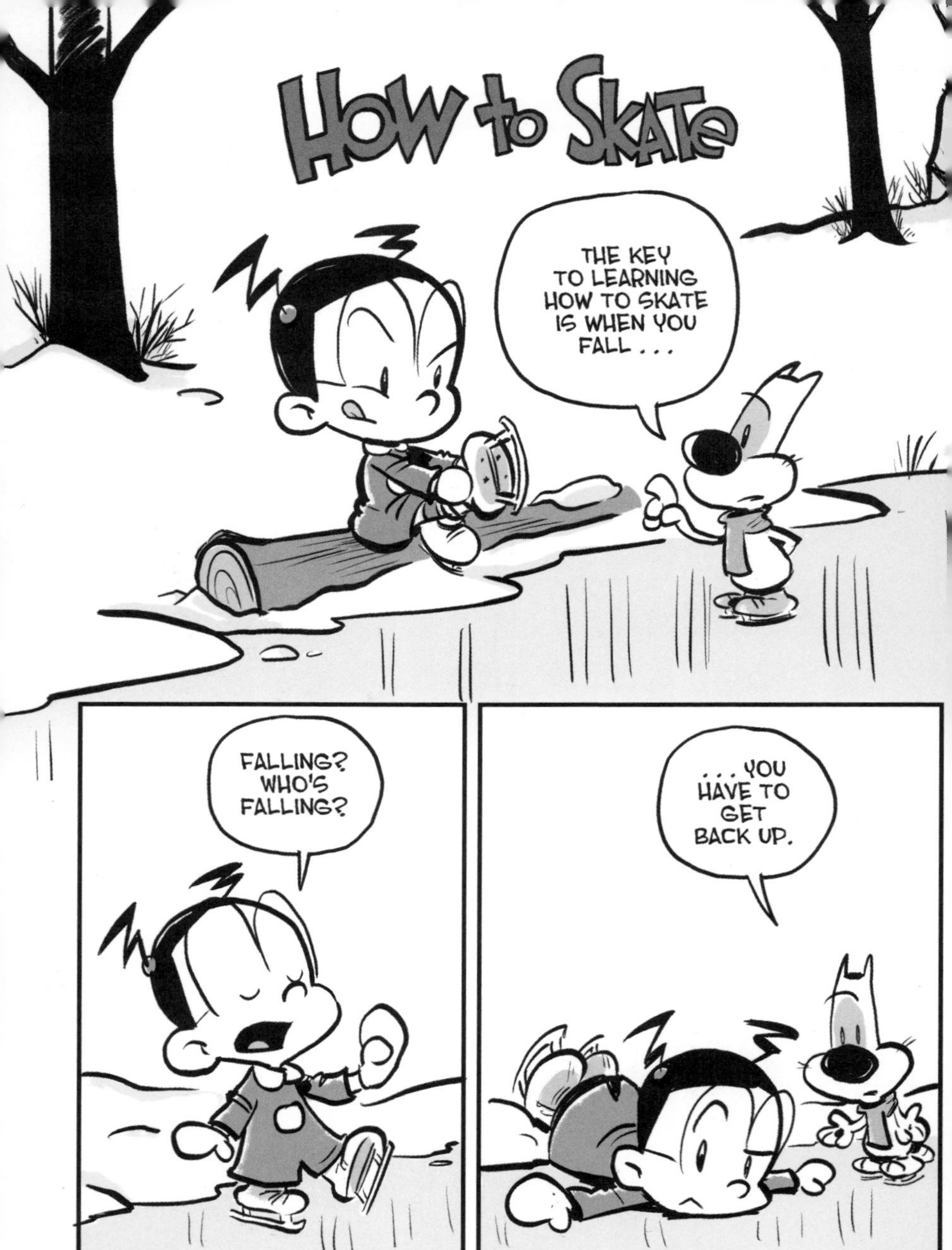
How to Skate
THE KEY TO LEARNING HOW TO SKATE IS WHEN YOU FALL . . .
FALLING? WHO'S FALLING?
. . . YOU HAVE TO GET BACK UP.

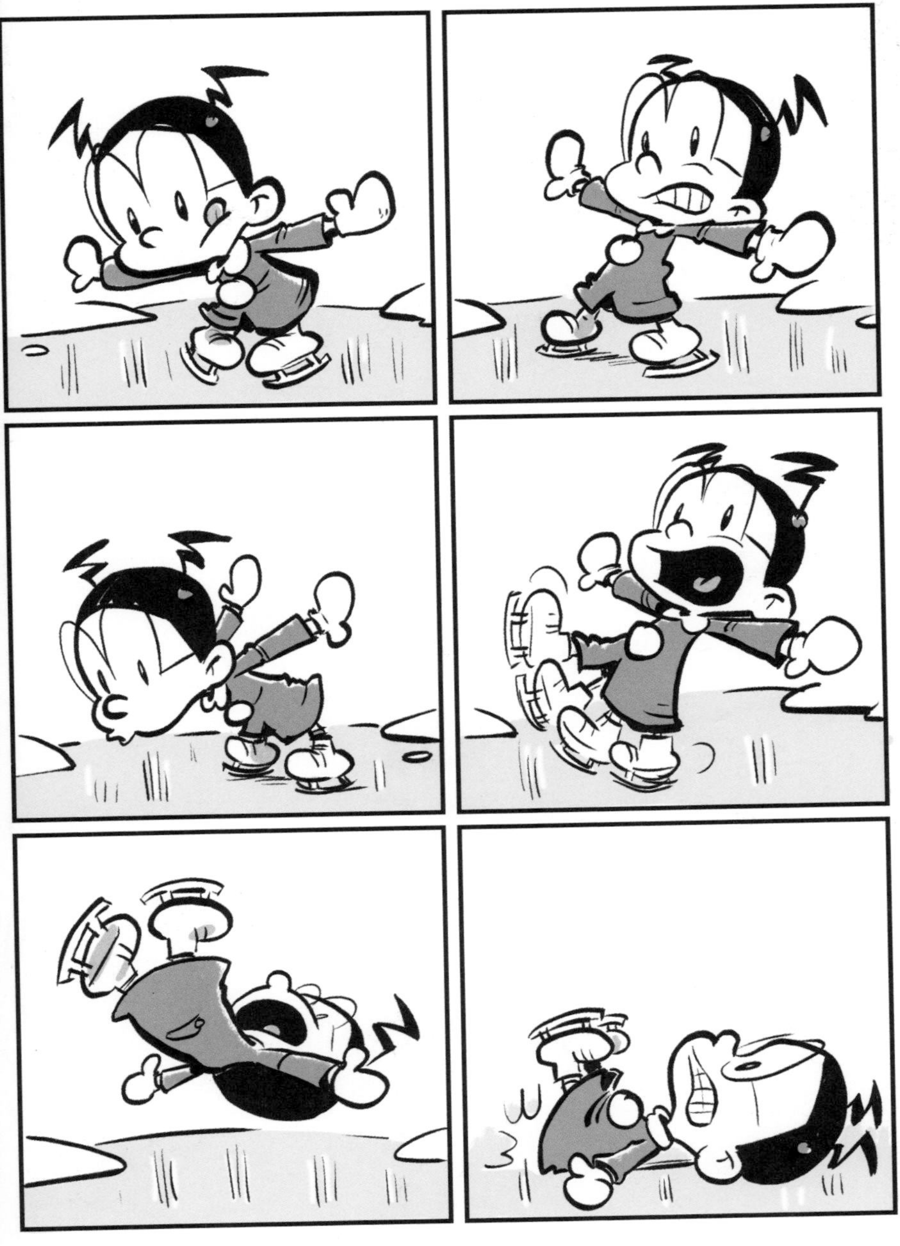

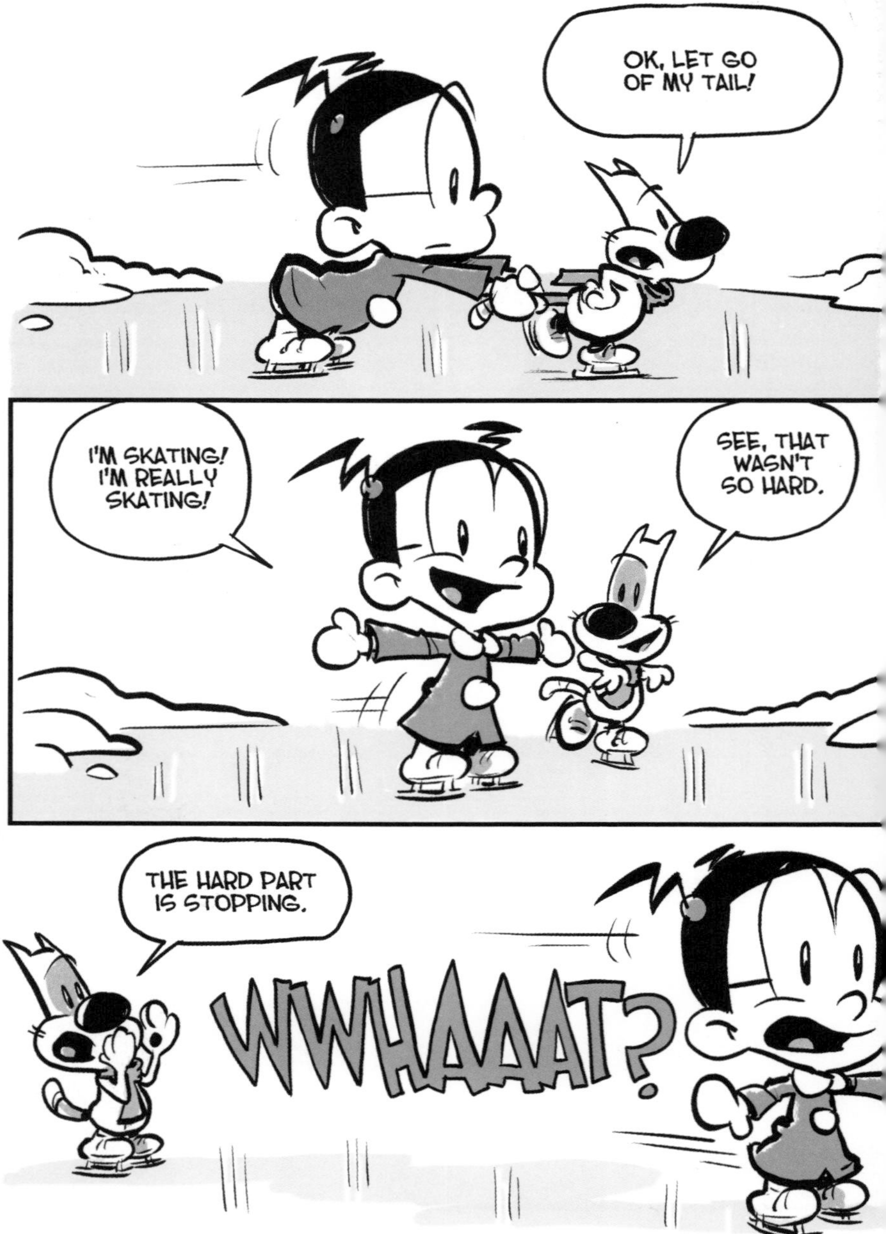
OK, LET GO OF MY TAIL!
I'M SKATING! I'M REALLY SKATING!
SEE, THAT WASN'T SO HARD.
THE HARD PART IS STOPPING.
WWHAAAT?

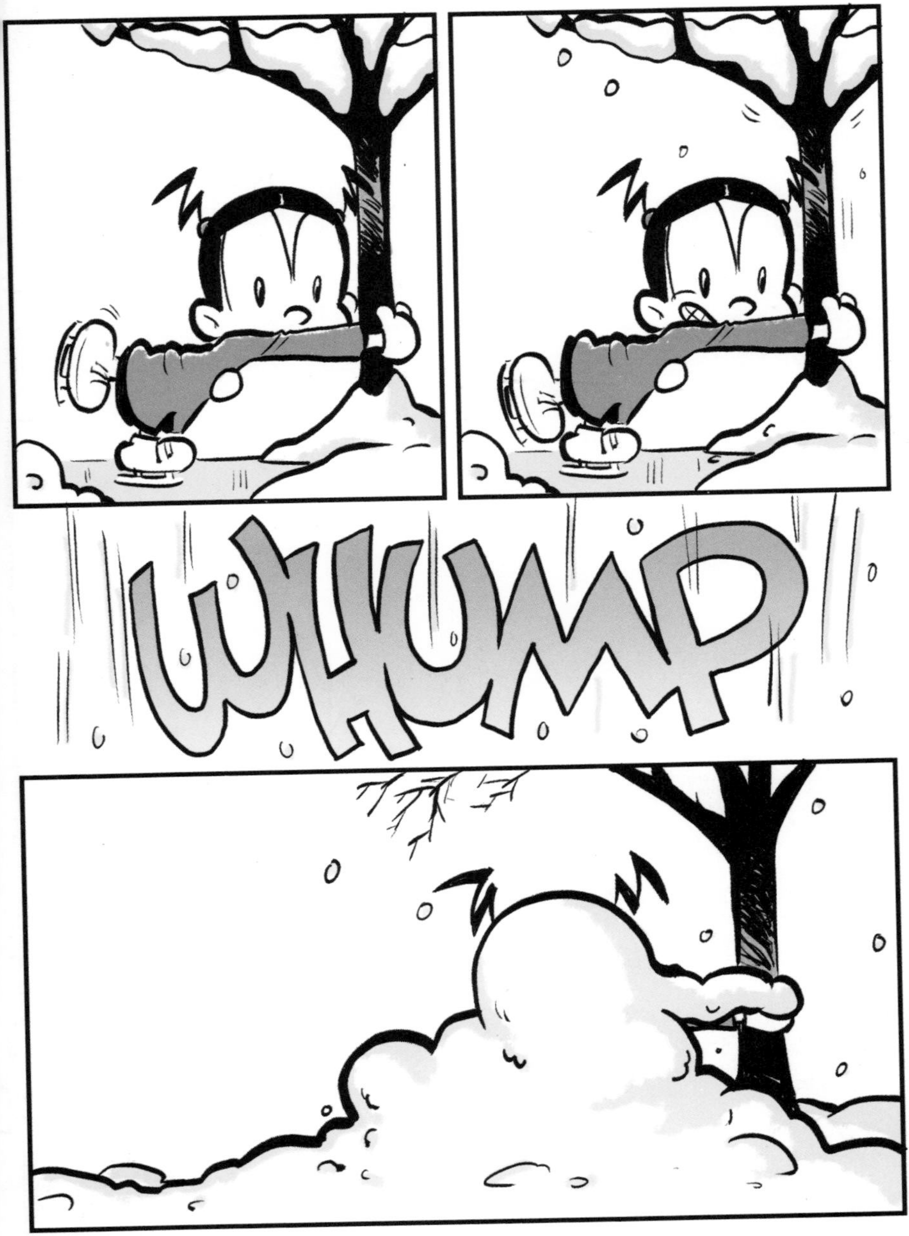
WHUMP

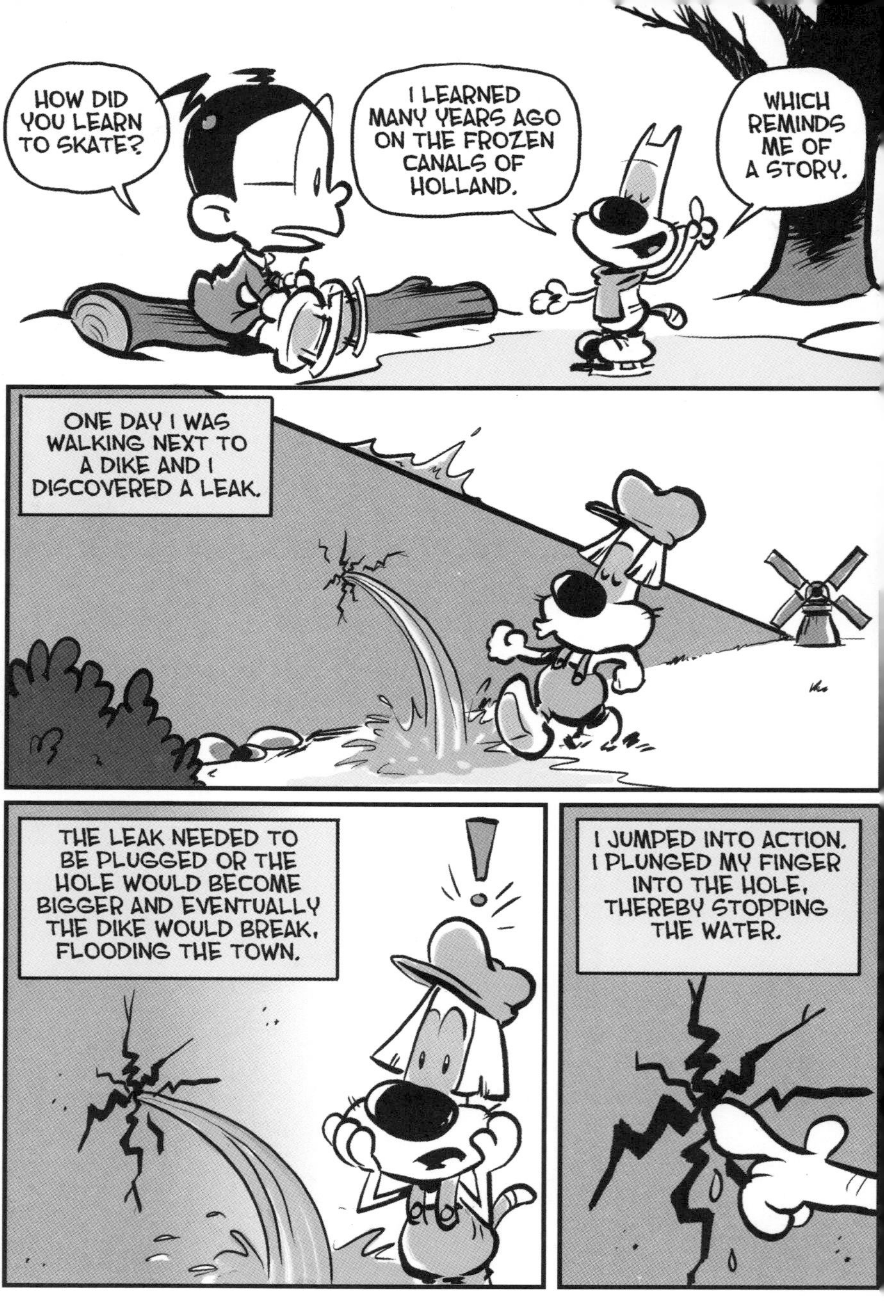
HOW DID YOU LEARN TO SKATE?
I LEARNED MANY YEARS AGO ON THE FROZEN CANALS OF HOLLAND.
WHICH REMINDS ME OF A STORY.
ONE DAY I WAS WALKING NEXT TO A DIKE AND I DISCOVERED A LEAK.
THE LEAK NEEDED TO BE PLUGGED OR THE HOLE WOULD BECOME BIGGER AND EVENTUALLY THE DIKE WOULD BREAK, FLOODING THE TOWN.
!
I JUMPED INTO ACTION. I PLUNGED MY FINGER INTO THE HOLE, THEREBY STOPPING THE WATER.

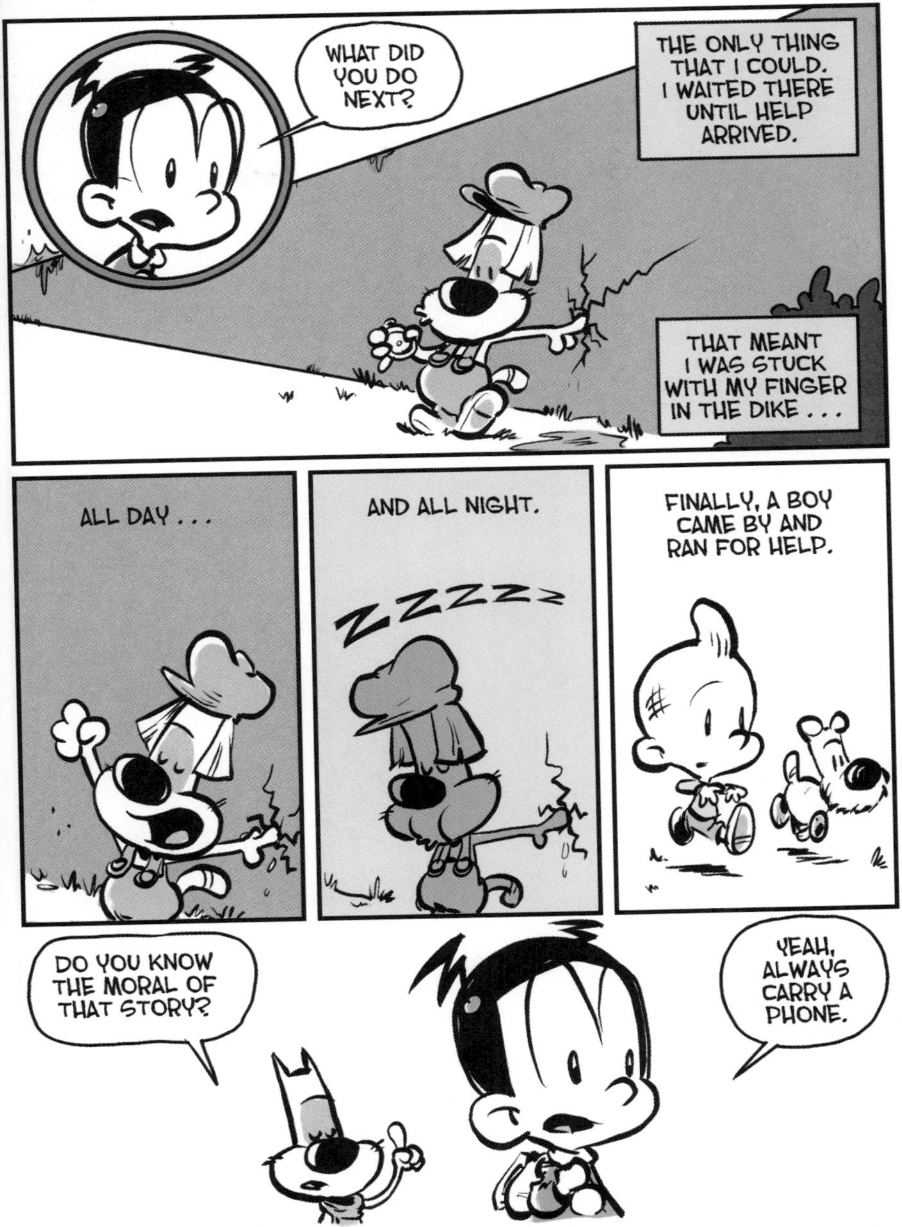
WHAT DID YOU DO NEXT?
THE ONLY THING THAT I COULD. I WAITED THERE UNTIL HELP ARRIVED.
THAT MEANT I WAS STUCK WITH MY FINGER IN THE DIKE . . .
ALL DAY . . .
AND ALL NIGHT.
ZZZZZZ
FINALLY, A BOY CAME BY AND RAN FOR HELP.
DO YOU KNOW THE MORAL OF THAT STORY?
YEAH, ALWAYS CARRY A PHONE.

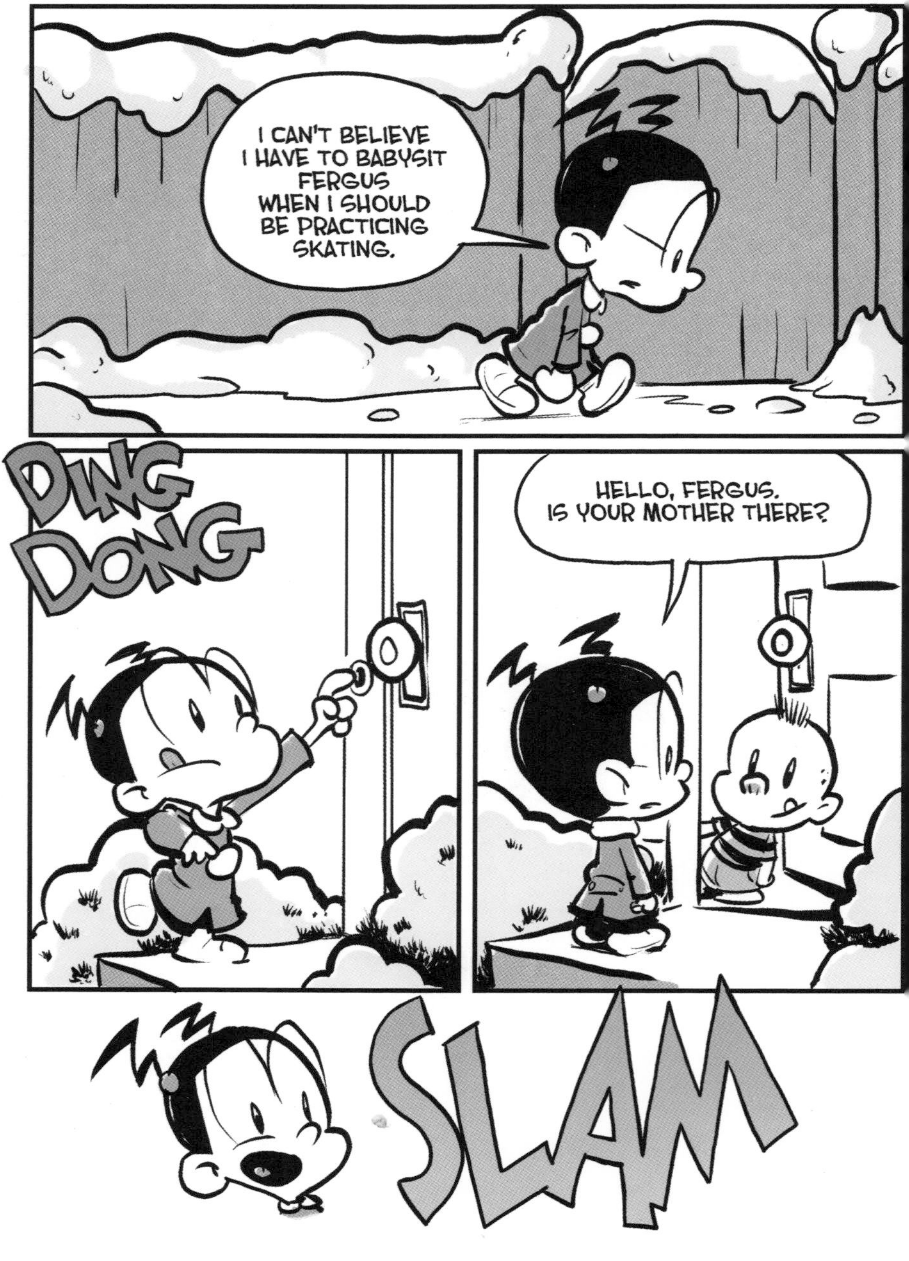
I CAN'T BELIEVE I HAVE TO BABYSIT FERGUS WHEN I SHOULD BE PRACTICING SKATING.
DING DONG
HELLO, FERGUS. IS YOUR MOTHER THERE?
SLAM

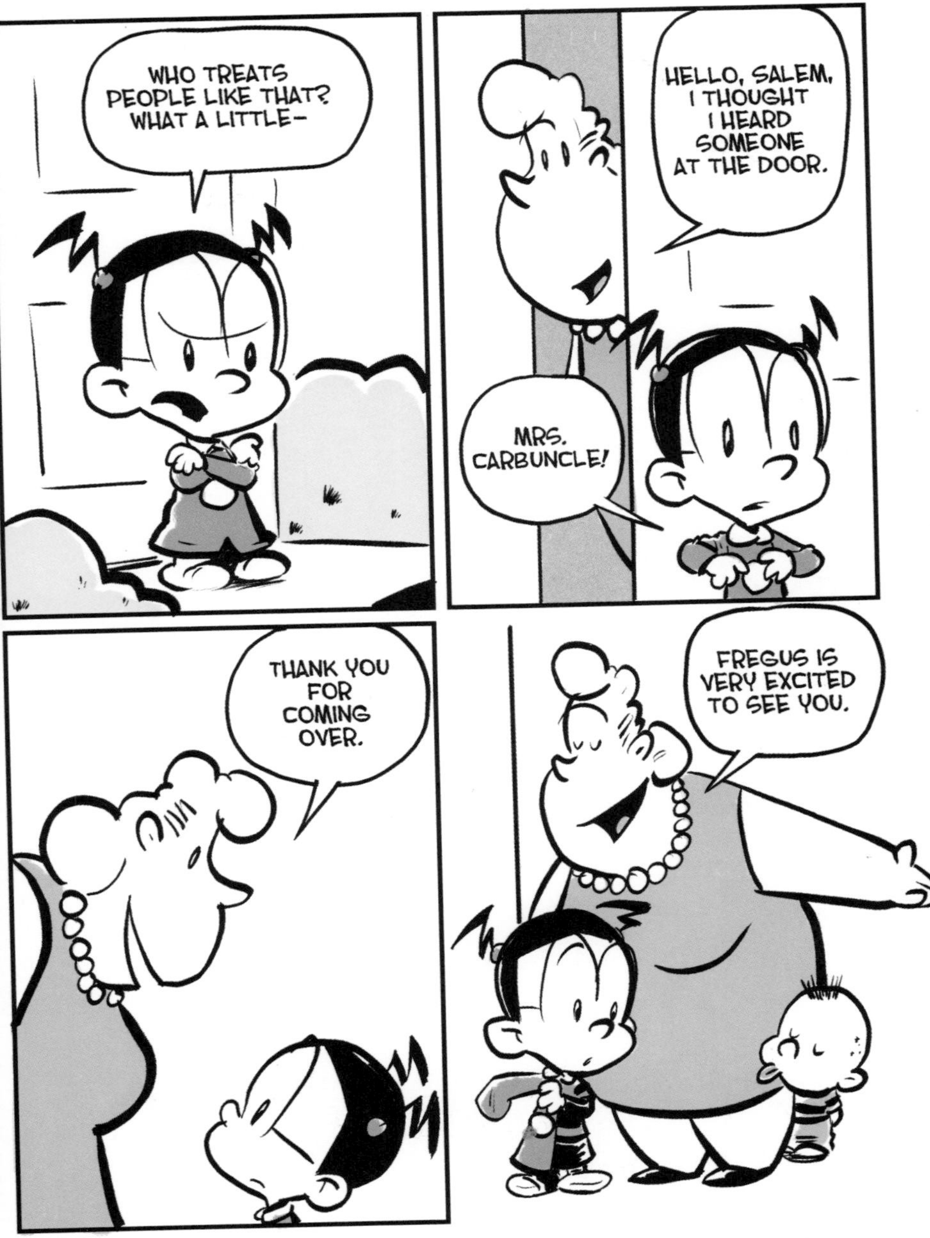
WHO TREATS PEOPLE LIKE THAT? WHAT A LITTLE–
HELLO, SALEM, I THOUGHT I HEARD SOMEONE AT THE DOOR.
MRS. CARBUNCLE!
THANK YOU FOR COMING OVER.
FREGUS IS VERY EXCITED TO SEE YOU.

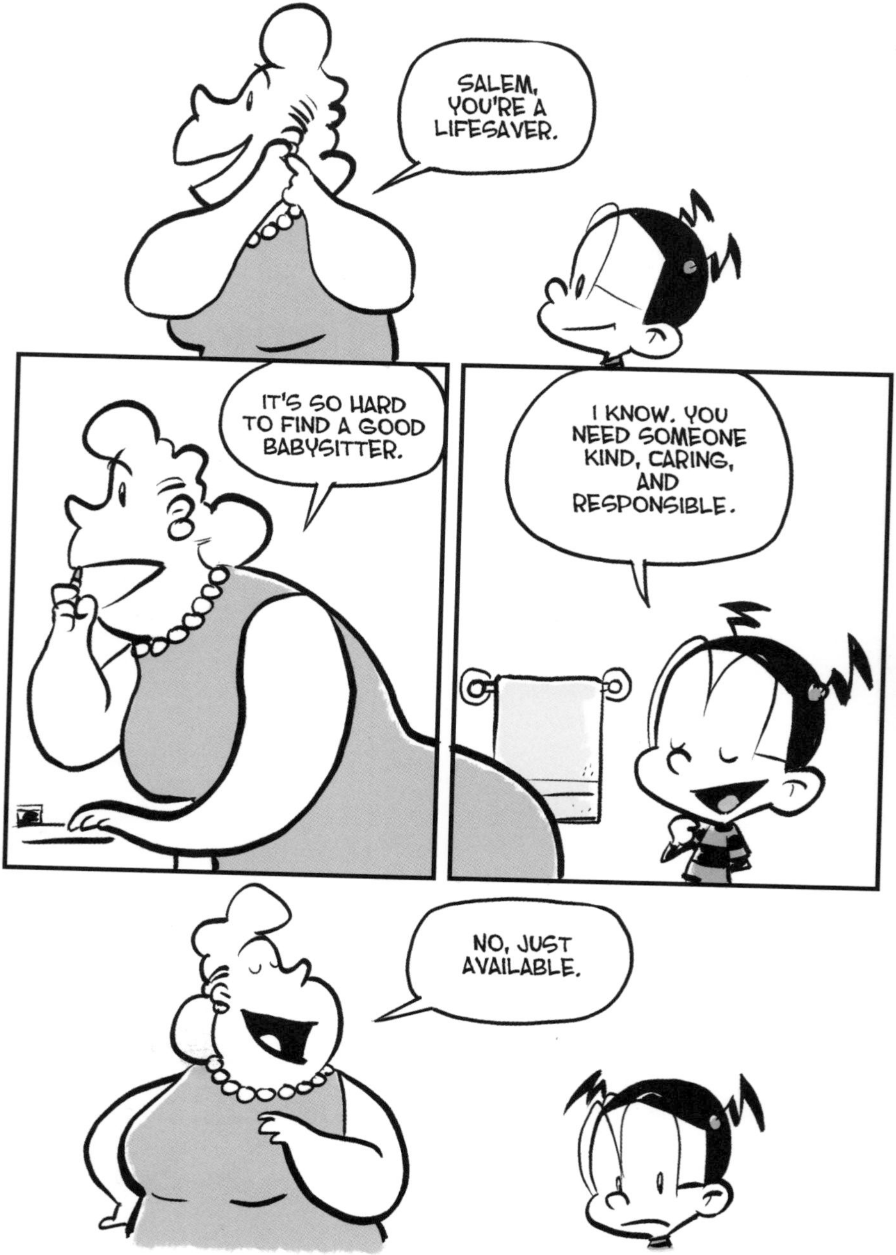
SALEM, YOU'RE A LIFESAVER.
IT'S SO HARD TO FIND A GOOD BABYSITTER.
I KNOW. YOU NEED SOMEONE KIND, CARING, AND RESPONSIBLE.
NO, JUST AVAILABLE.

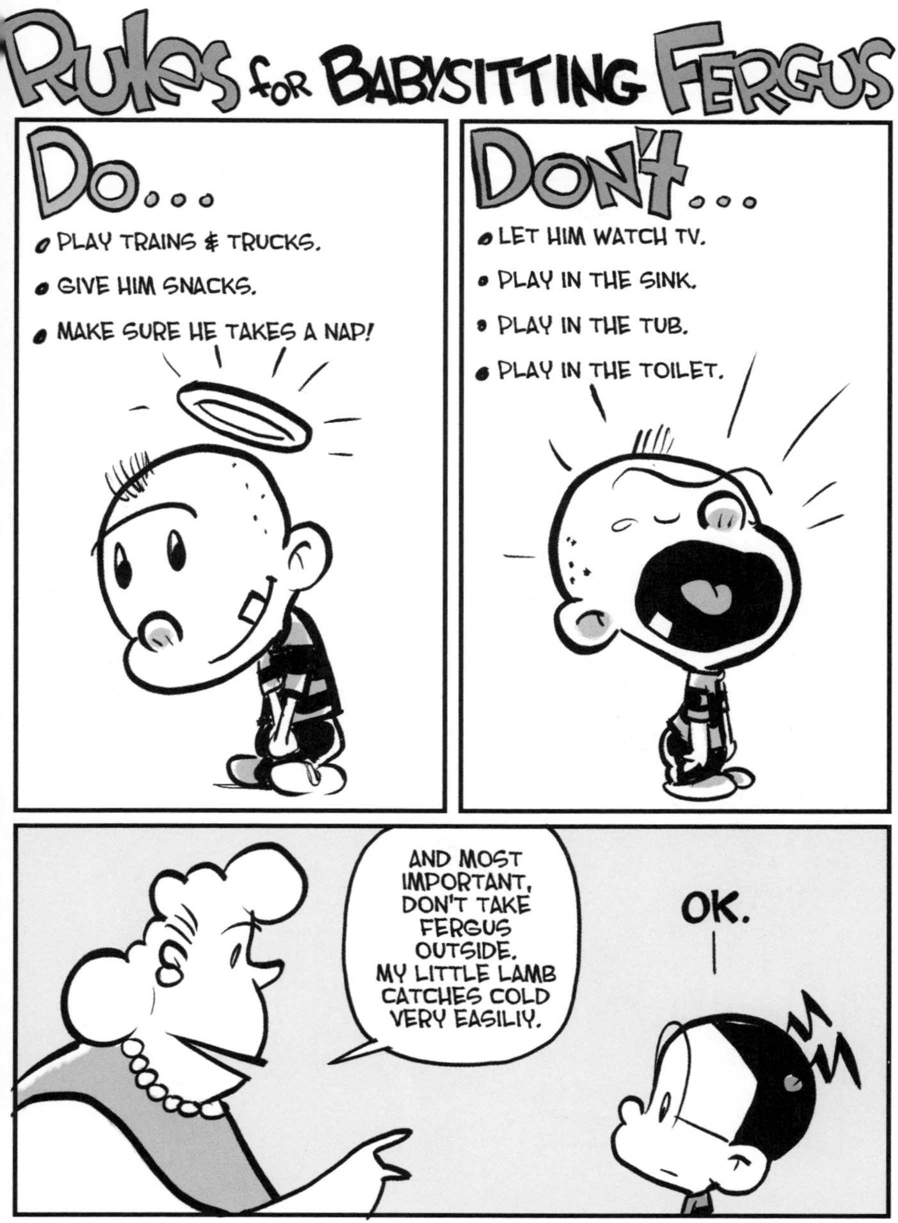
RULES FOR BABYSITTING FERGUS
DO...
PLAY TRAINS & TRUCKS.
GIVE HIM SNACKS.
MAKE SURE HE TAKES A NAP!
DON'T...
LET HIM WATCH TV.
PLAY IN THE SINK.
PLAY IN THE TUB.
PLAY IN THE TOILET.
AND MOST IMPORTANT, DON'T TAKE FERGUS OUTSIDE. MY LITTLE LAMB CATCHES COLD VERY EASILIY.
OK.

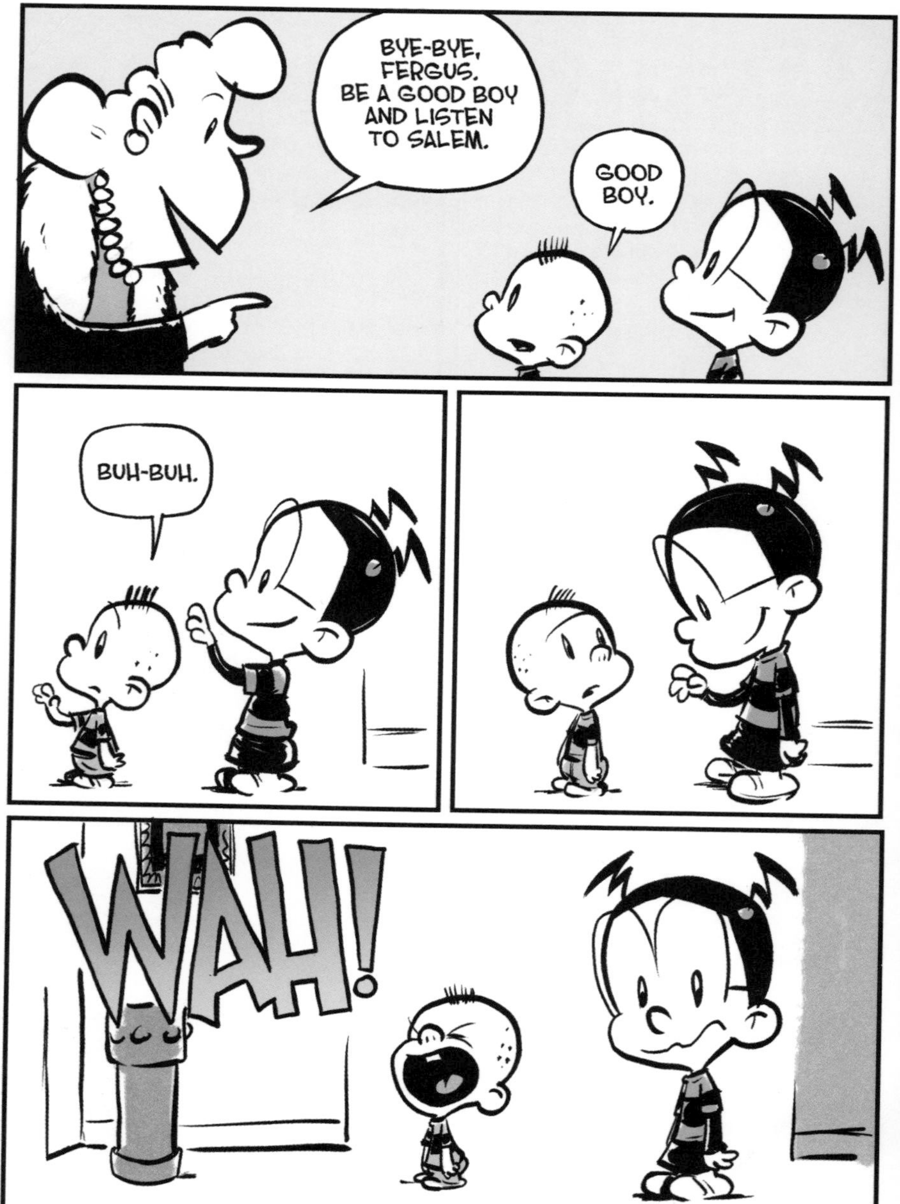
BYE-BYE, FERGUS. BE A GOOD BOY AND LISTEN TO SALEM.
GOOD BOY.
BUH-BUH.
WAH!

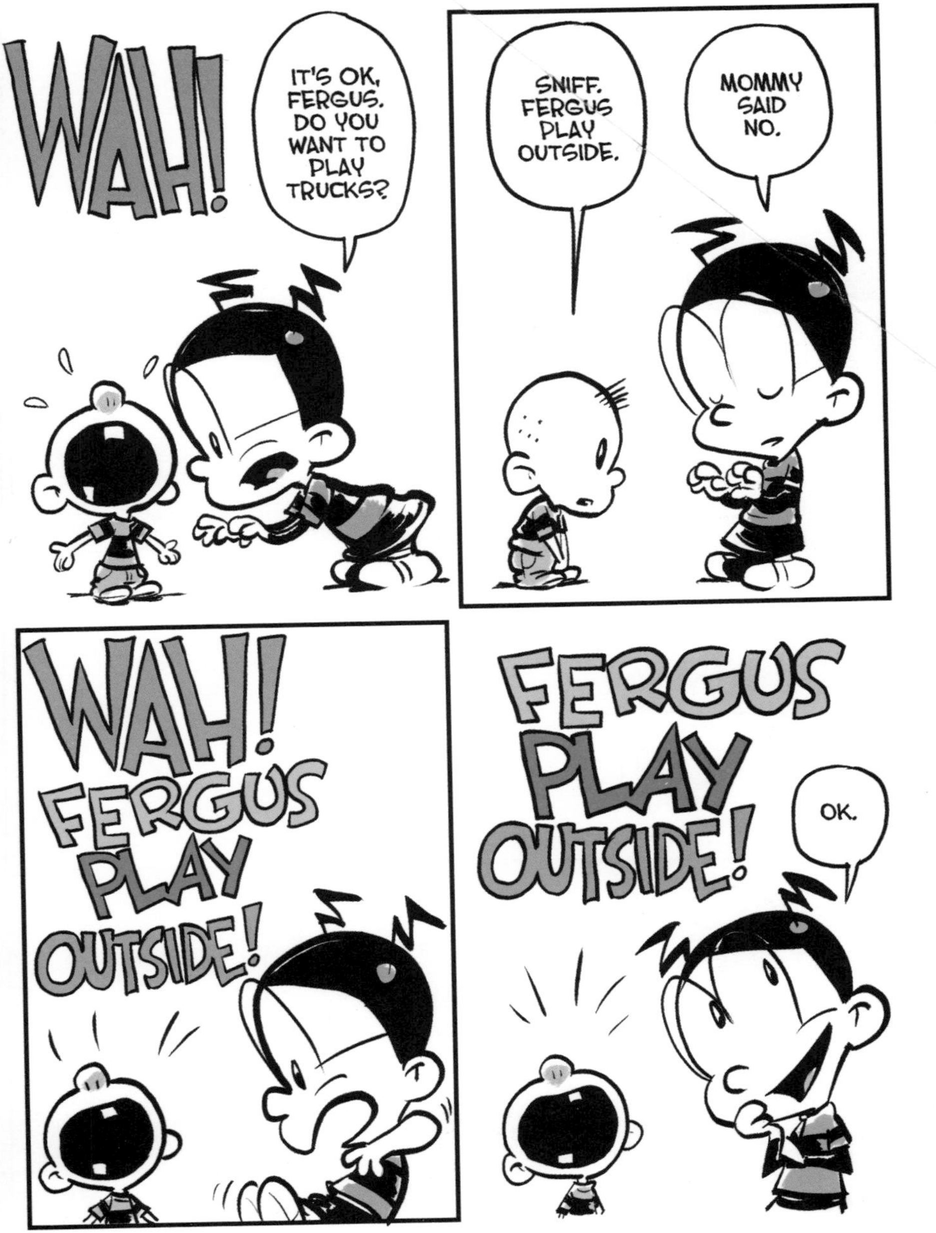
WAH!
IT'S OK, FERGUS. DO YOU WANT TO PLAY TRUCKS?
SNIFF. FERGUS PLAY OUTSIDE.
MOMMY SAID NO.
WAH! FERGUS PLAY OUTSIDE!
FERGUS PLAY OUTSIDE!
OK.

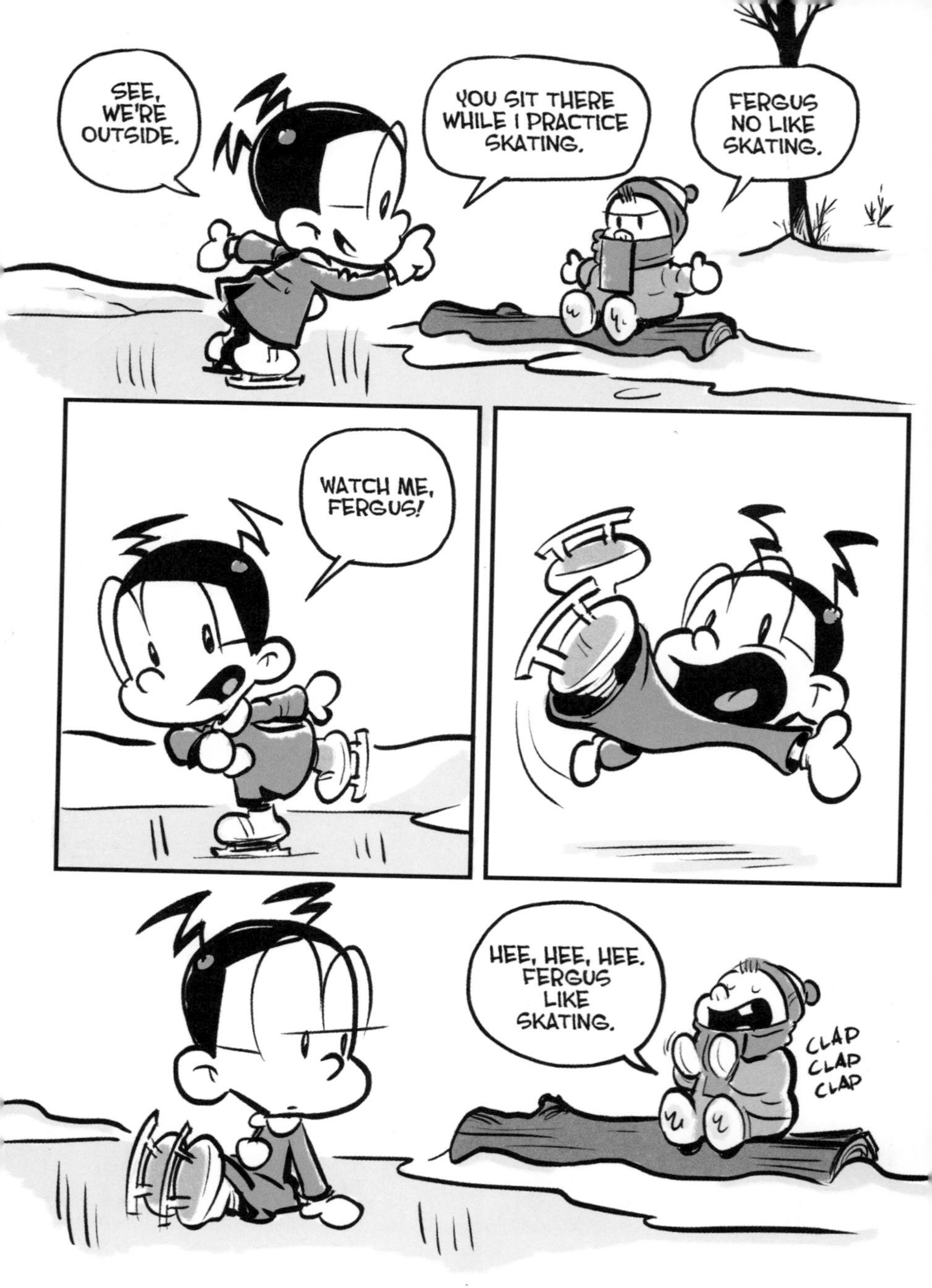
SEE, WE'RE OUTSIDE.
YOU SIT THERE WHILE I PRACTICE SKATING.
FERGUS NO LIKE SKATING.
WATCH ME, FERGUS!
HEE, HEE, HEE. FERGUS LIKE SKATING.
CLAP CLAP CLAP

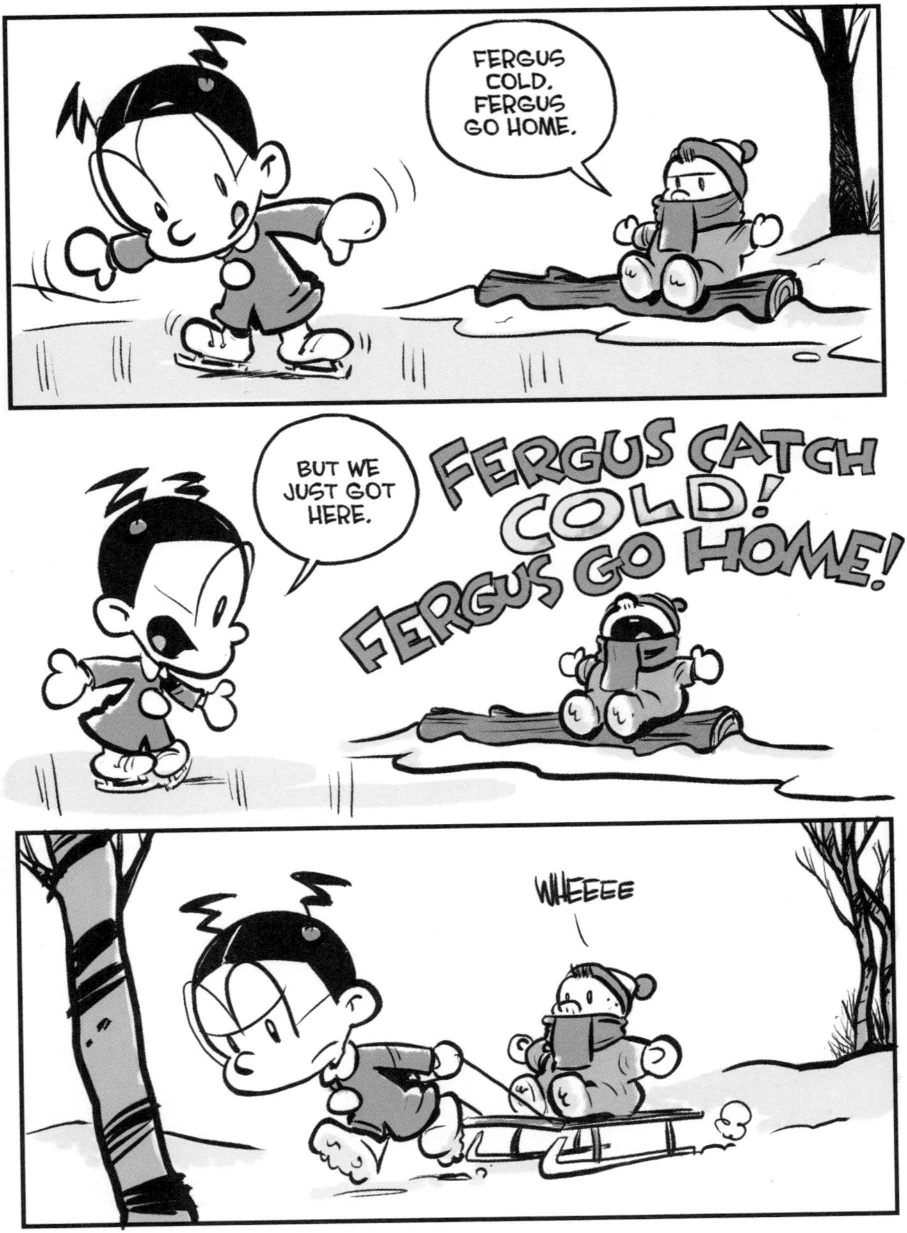
FERGUS COLD. FERGUS GO HOME.
BUT WE JUST GOT HERE.
FERGUS CATCH COLD! FERGUS GO HOME!
WHEEEE

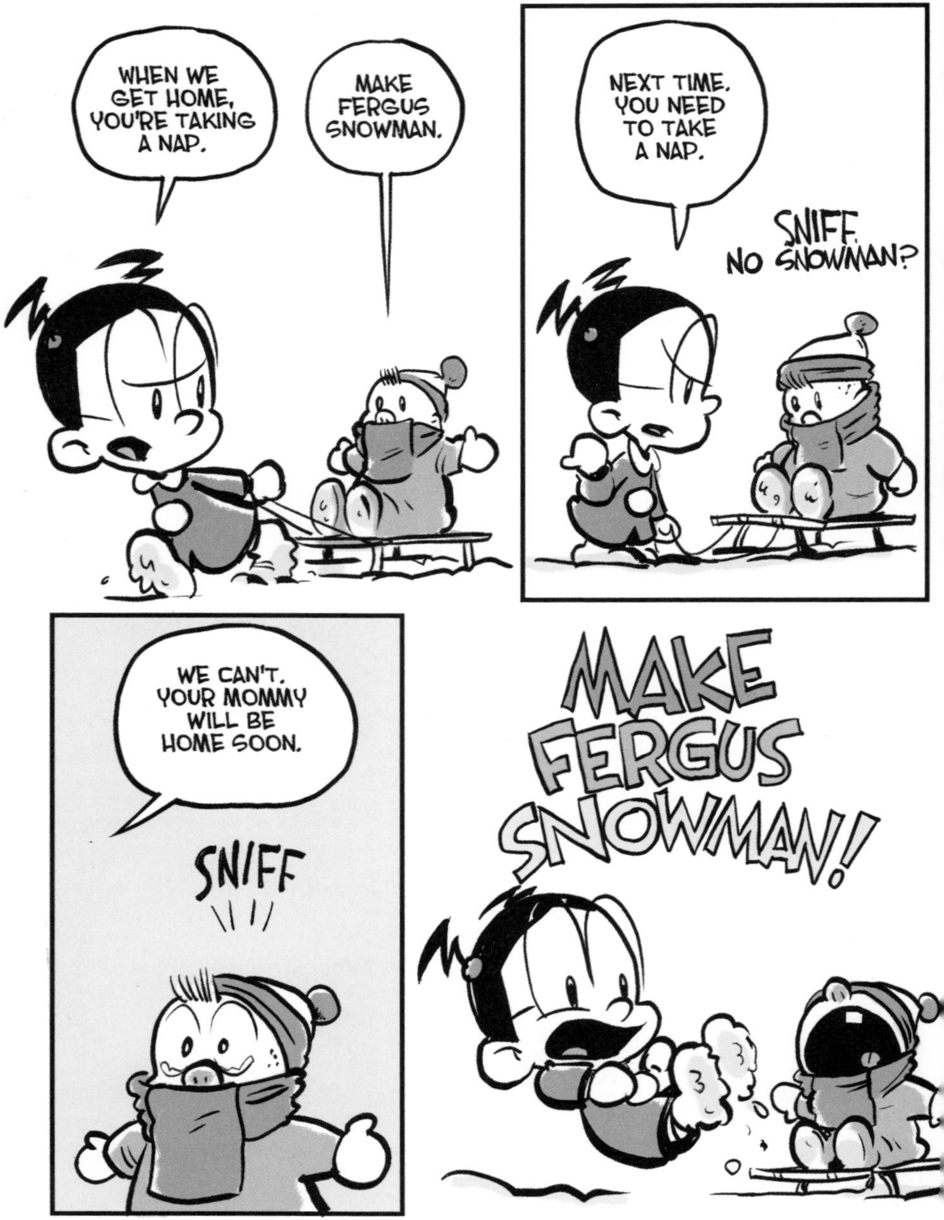

WHEN WE GET HOME, YOU'RE TAKING A NAP.
MAKE FERGUS SNOWMAN.
NEXT TIME, YOU NEED TO TAKE A NAP.
SNIFF. NO SNOWMAN?
WE CAN'T. YOUR MOMMY WILL BE HOME SOON.
SNIFF
MAKE FERGUS SNOWMAN!

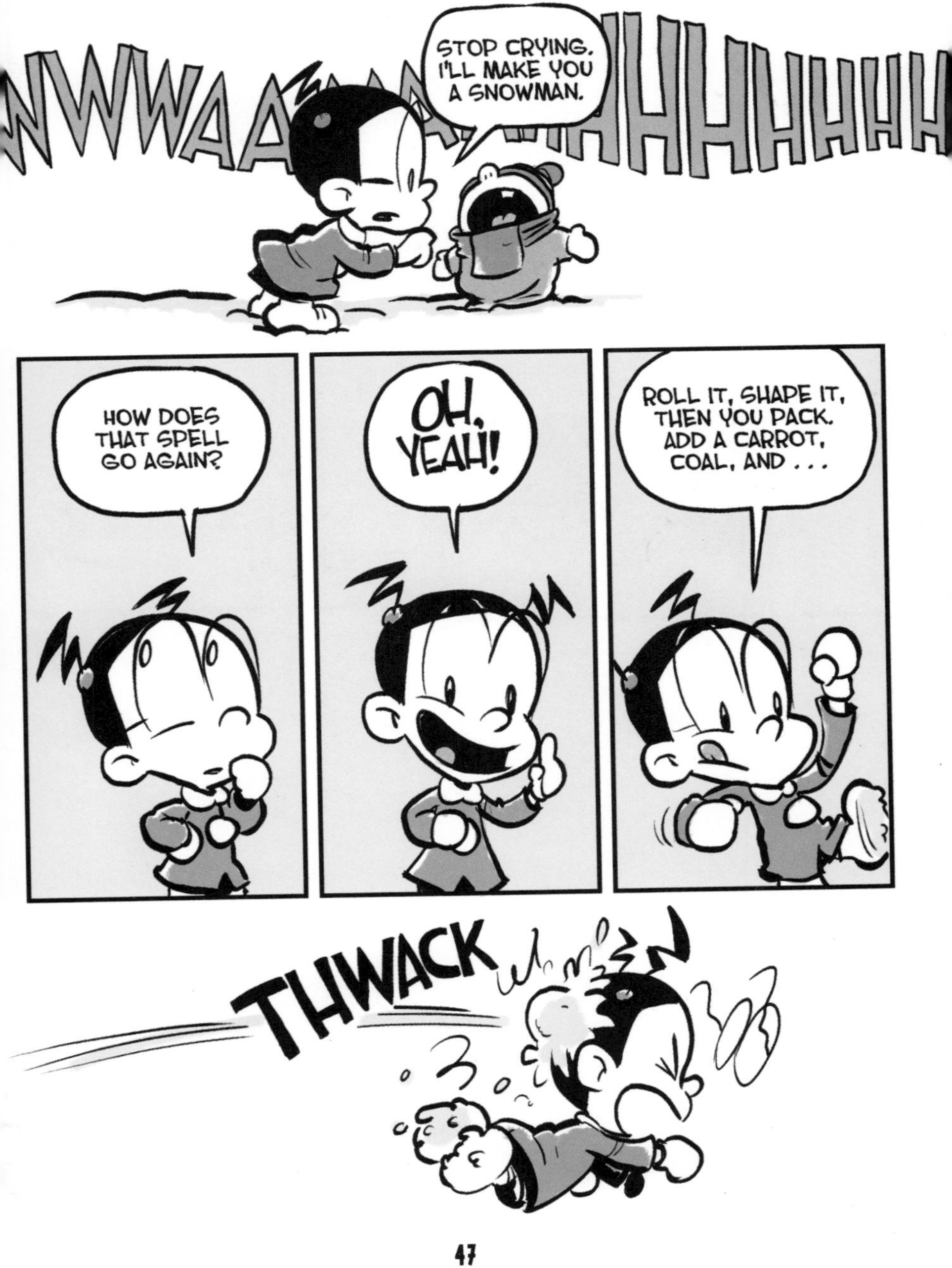
NWWAAAAAAAHHHHHHHH
STOP CRYING. I'LL MAKE YOU A SNOWMAN.
HOW DOES THAT SPELL GO AGAIN?
OH, YEAH!
ROLL IT, SHAPE IT, THEN YOU PACK. ADD A CARROT, COAL, AND . . .
THWACK

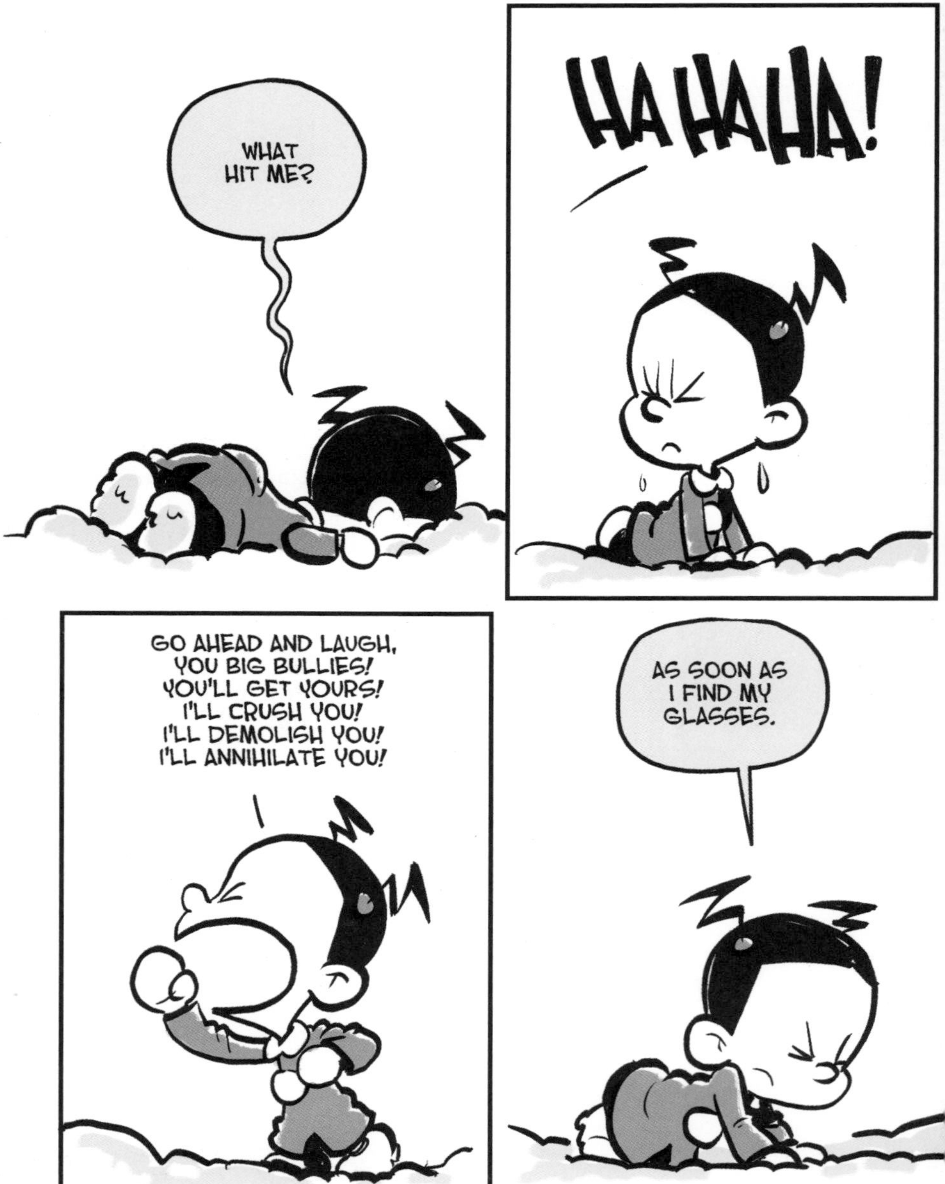
WHAT HIT ME?
HA HA HA HA!
GO AHEAD AND LAUGH, YOU BIG BULLIES! YOU'LL GET YOURS! I'LL CRUSH YOU! I'LL DEMOLISH YOU! I'LL ANNIHILATE YOU!
AS SOON AS I FIND MY GLASSES.

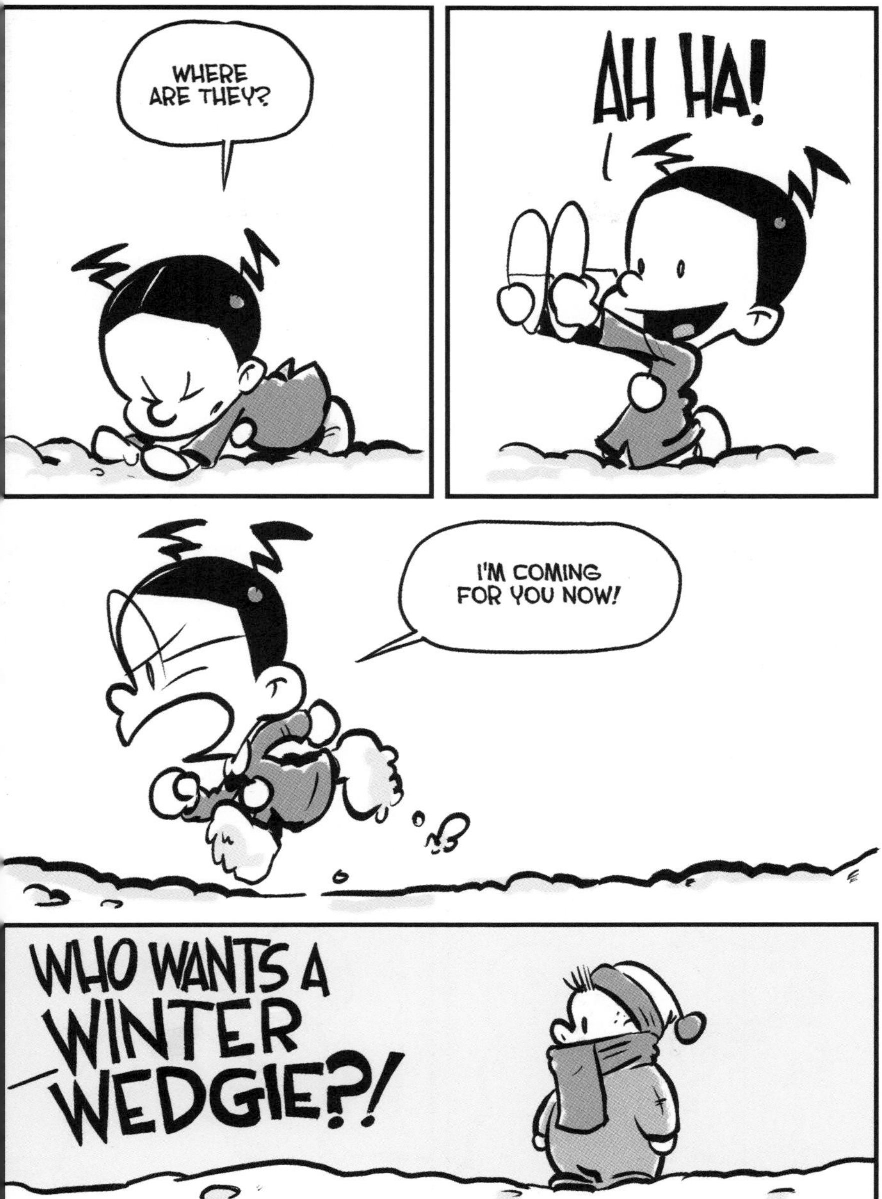
WHERE ARE THEY?
AH HA!
I'M COMING FOR YOU NOW!
WHO WANTS A WINTER WEDGIE?!

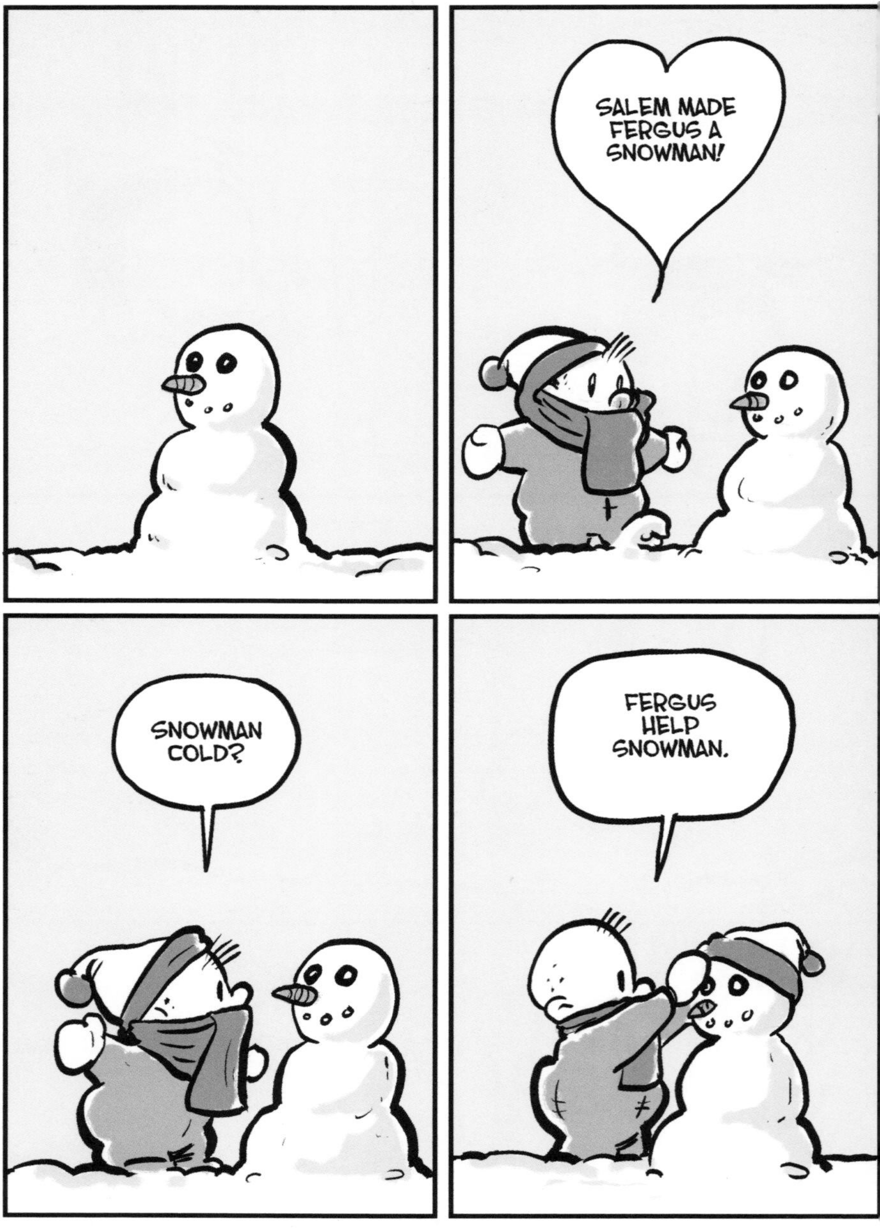
SALEM MADE FERGUS A SNOWMAN!
SNOWMAN COLD?
FERGUS HELP SNOWMAN.

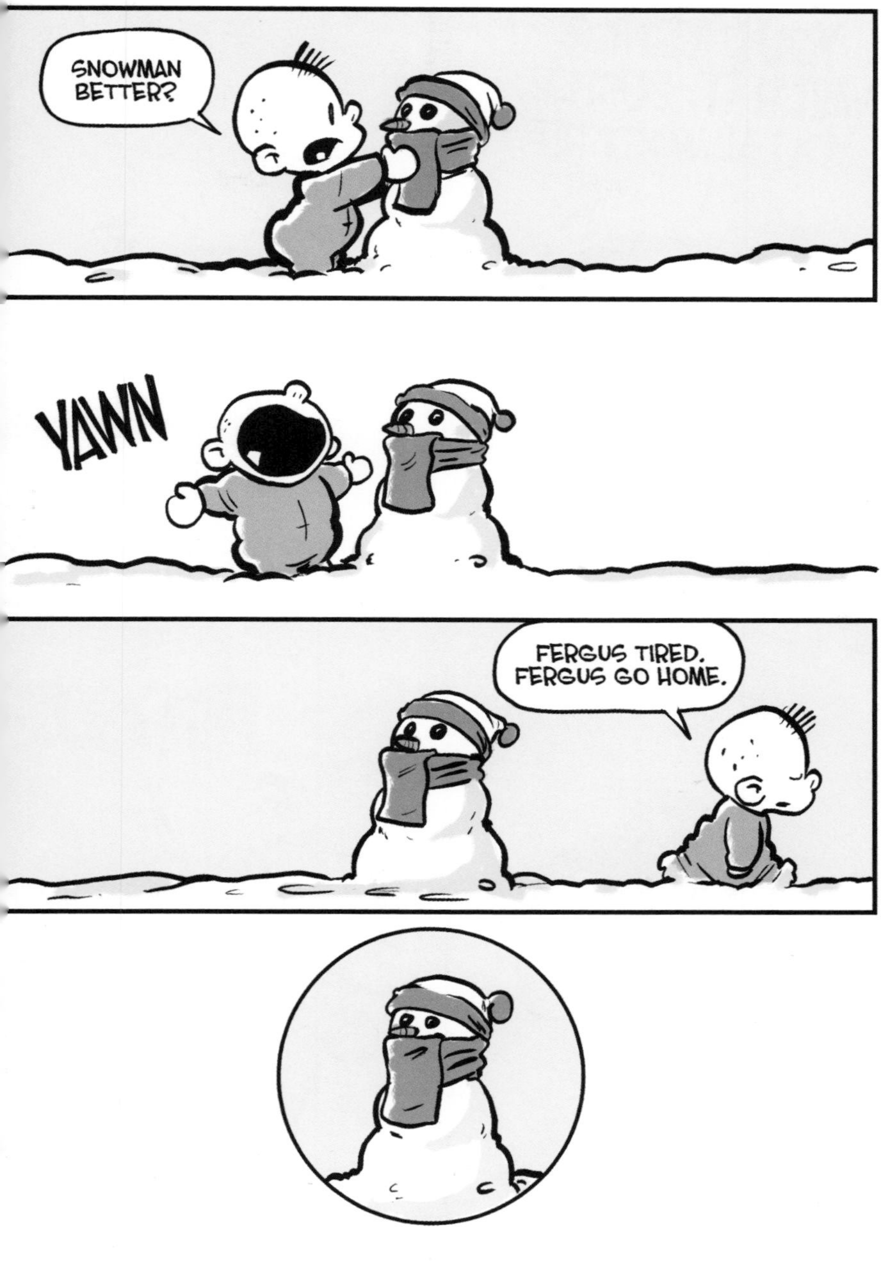

SNOWMAN BETTER?
YAWN
FERGUS TIRED. FERGUS GO HOME.

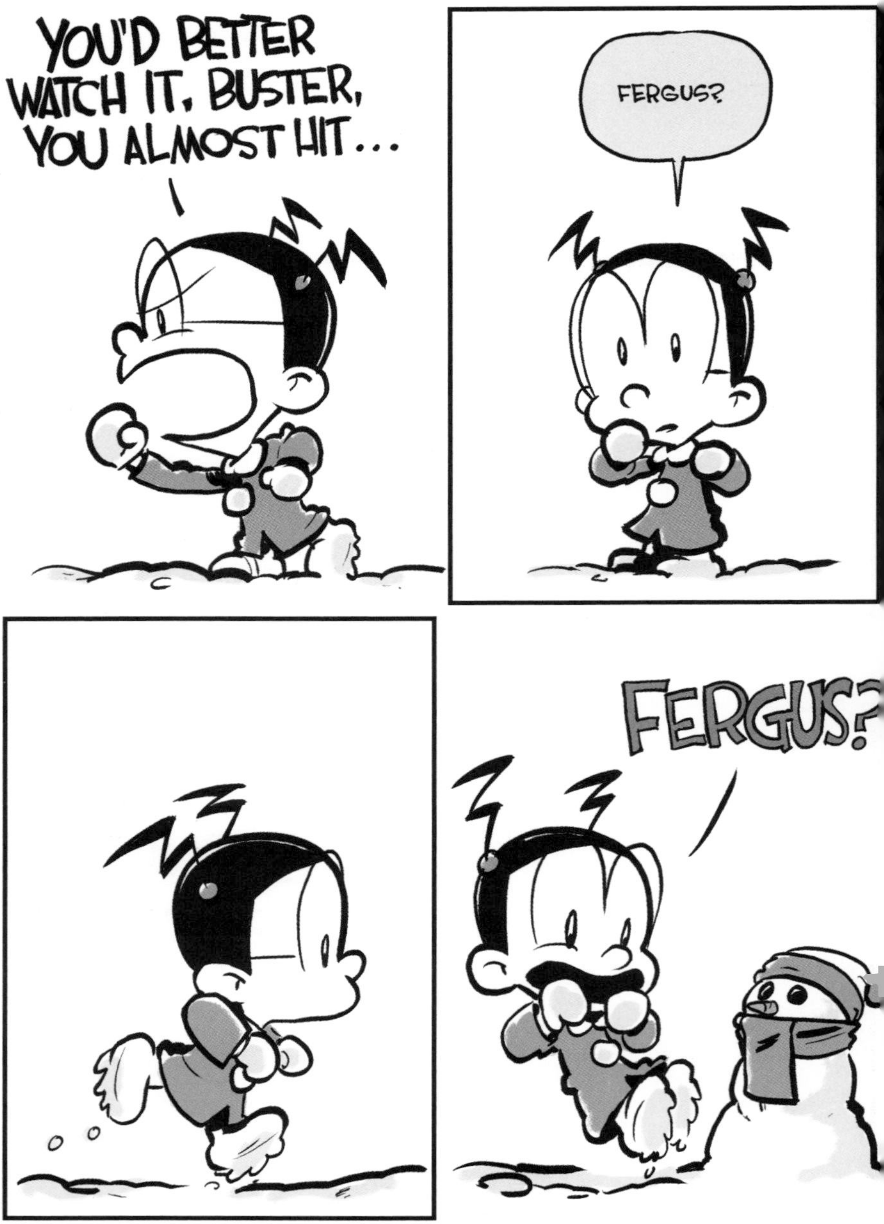
YOU'D BETTER WATCH IT, BUSTER, YOU ALMOST HIT...
FERGUS?
FERGUS?

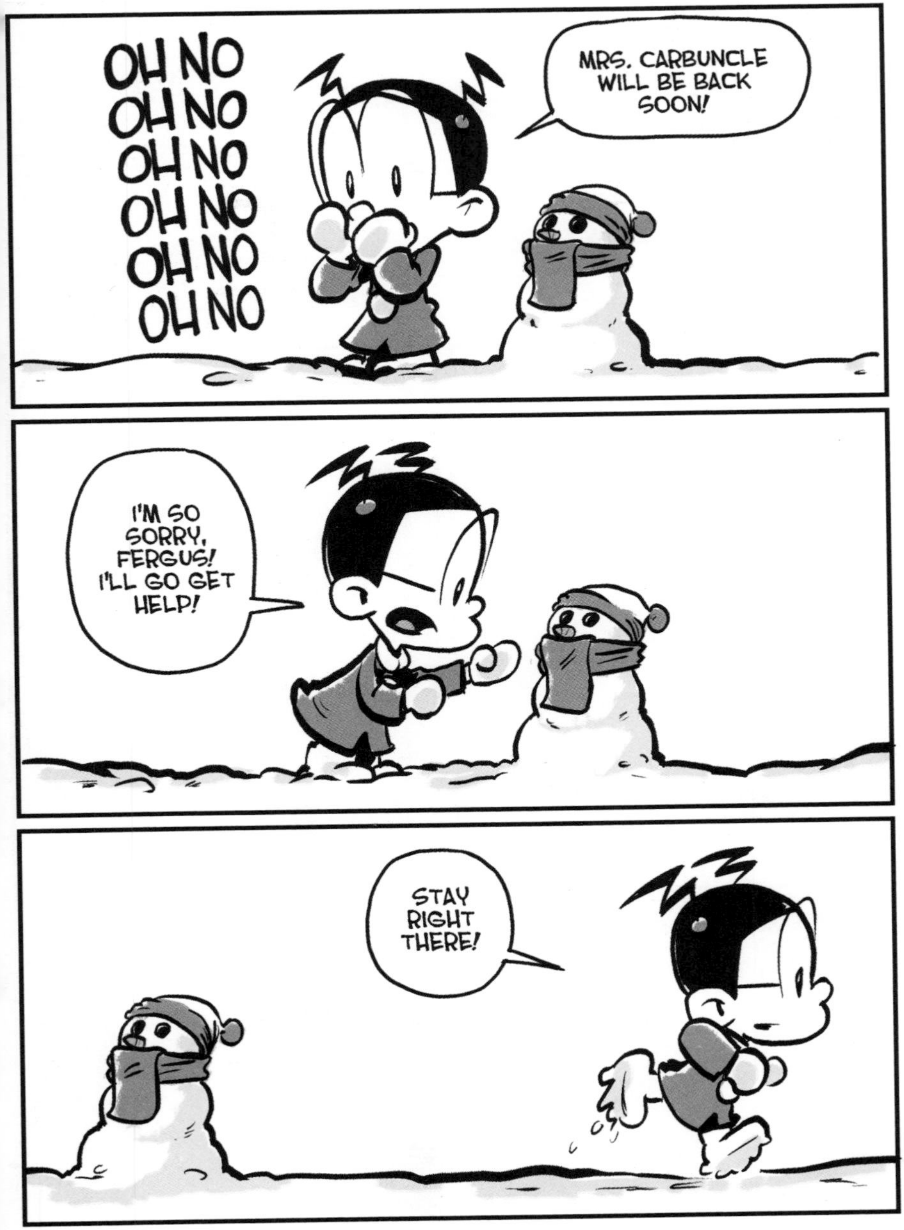
OH NO
OH NO
OH NO
OH NO
OH NO
OH NO
MRS. CARBUNCLE WILL BE BACK SOON!
I'M SO SORRY, FERGUS! I'LL GO GET HELP!
STAY RIGHT THERE!

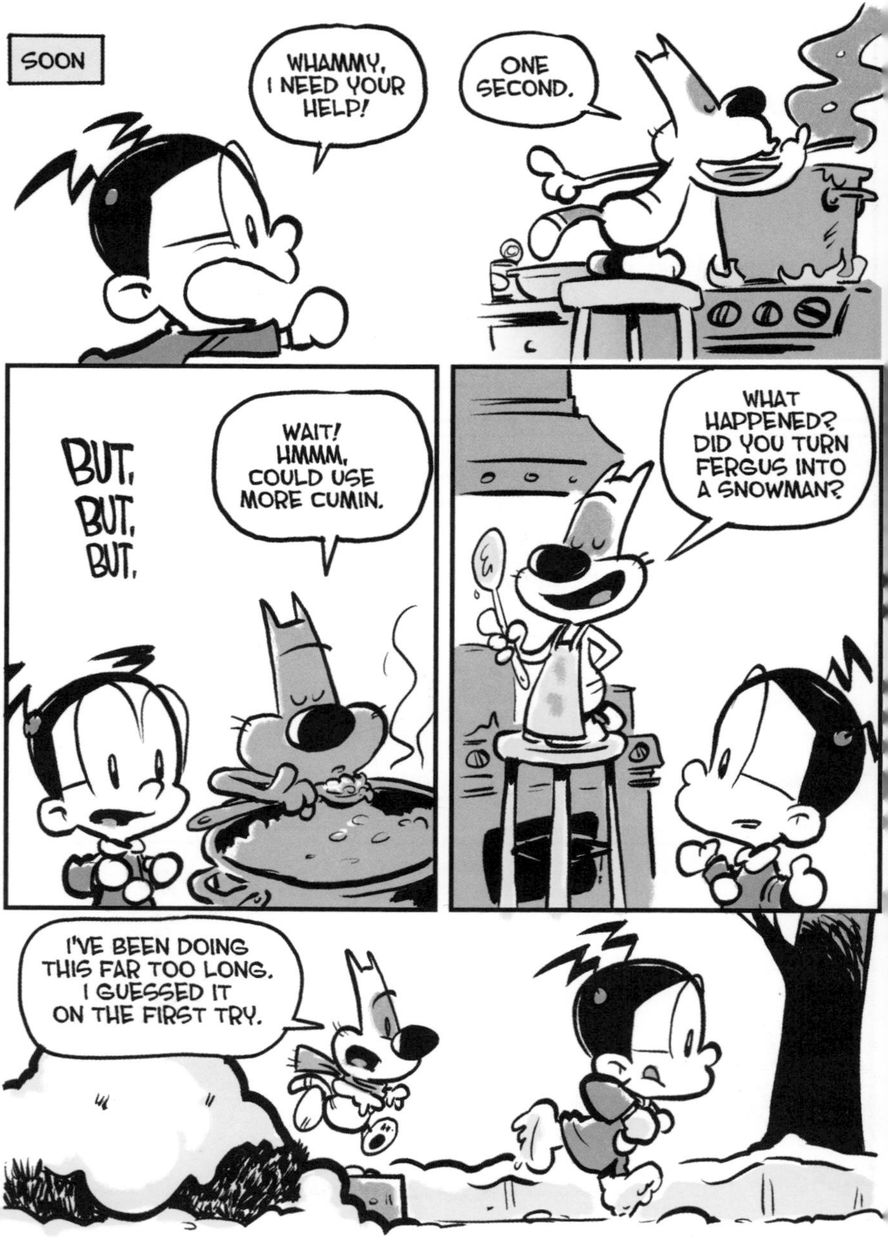
SOON
WHAMMY, I NEED YOUR HELP!
ONE SECOND.
BUT, BUT, BUT,
WAIT! HMMM, COULD USE MORE CUMIN.
WHAT HAPPENED? DID YOU TURN FERGUS INTO A SNOWMAN?
I'VE BEEN DOING THIS FAR TOO LONG. I GUESSED IT ON THE FIRST TRY.

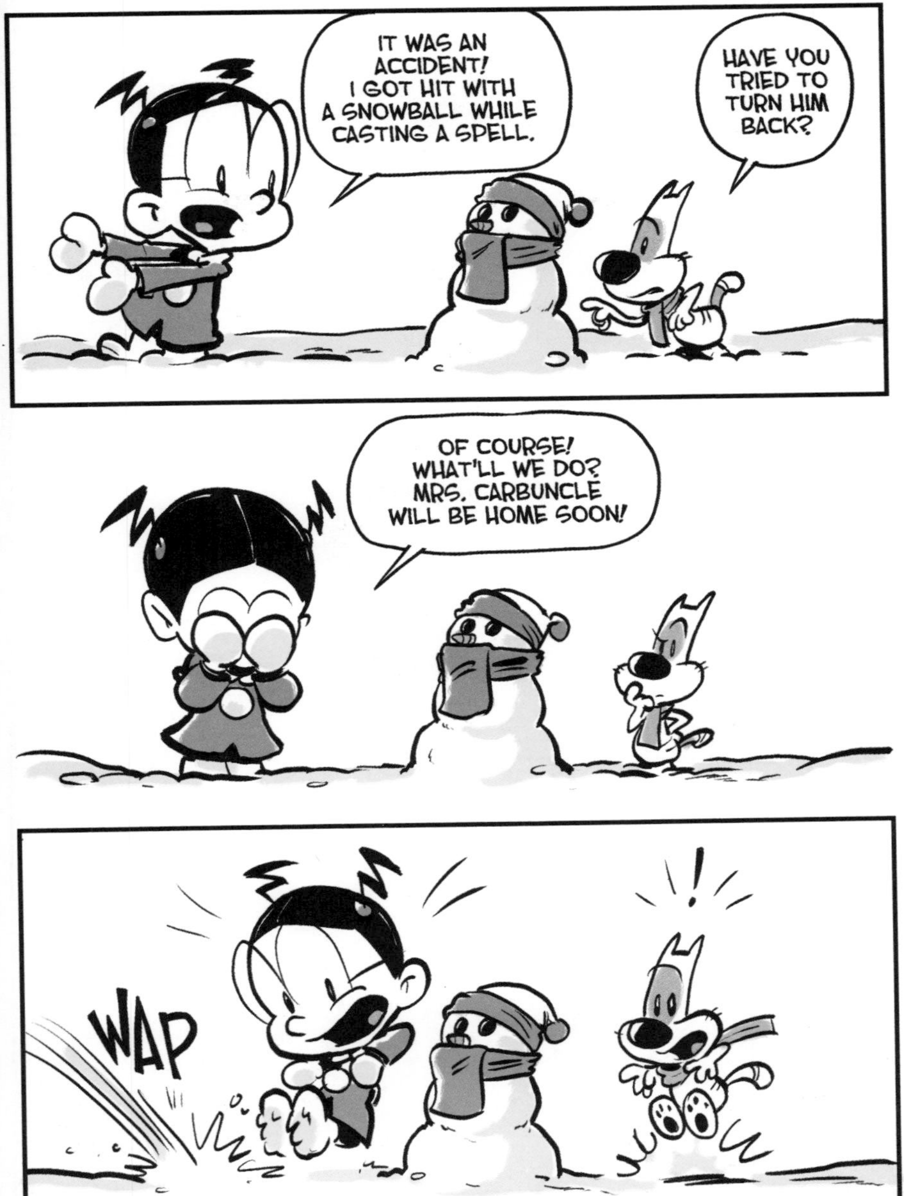
IT WAS AN ACCIDENT! I GOT HIT WITH A SNOWBALL WHILE CASTING A SPELL.
HAVE YOU TRIED TO TURN HIM BACK?
OF COURSE! WHAT'LL WE DO? MRS. CARBUNCLE WILL BE HOME SOON!
WAP
!

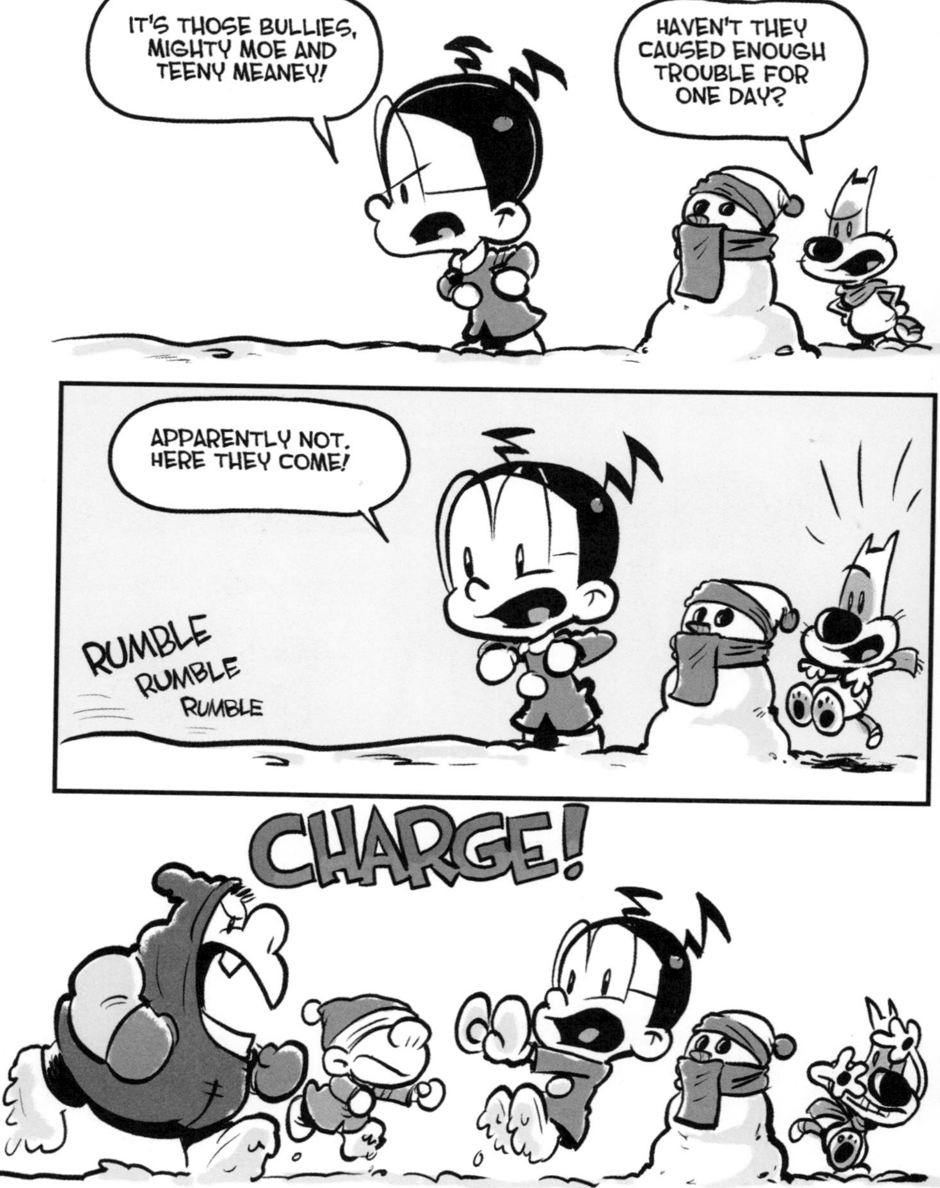
IT'S THOSE BULLIES, MIGHTY MOE AND TEENY MEANEY!
HAVEN'T THEY CAUSED ENOUGH TROUBLE FOR ONE DAY?
APPARENTLY NOT. HERE THEY COME!
RUMBLE
RUMBLE
RUMBLE
CHARGE!

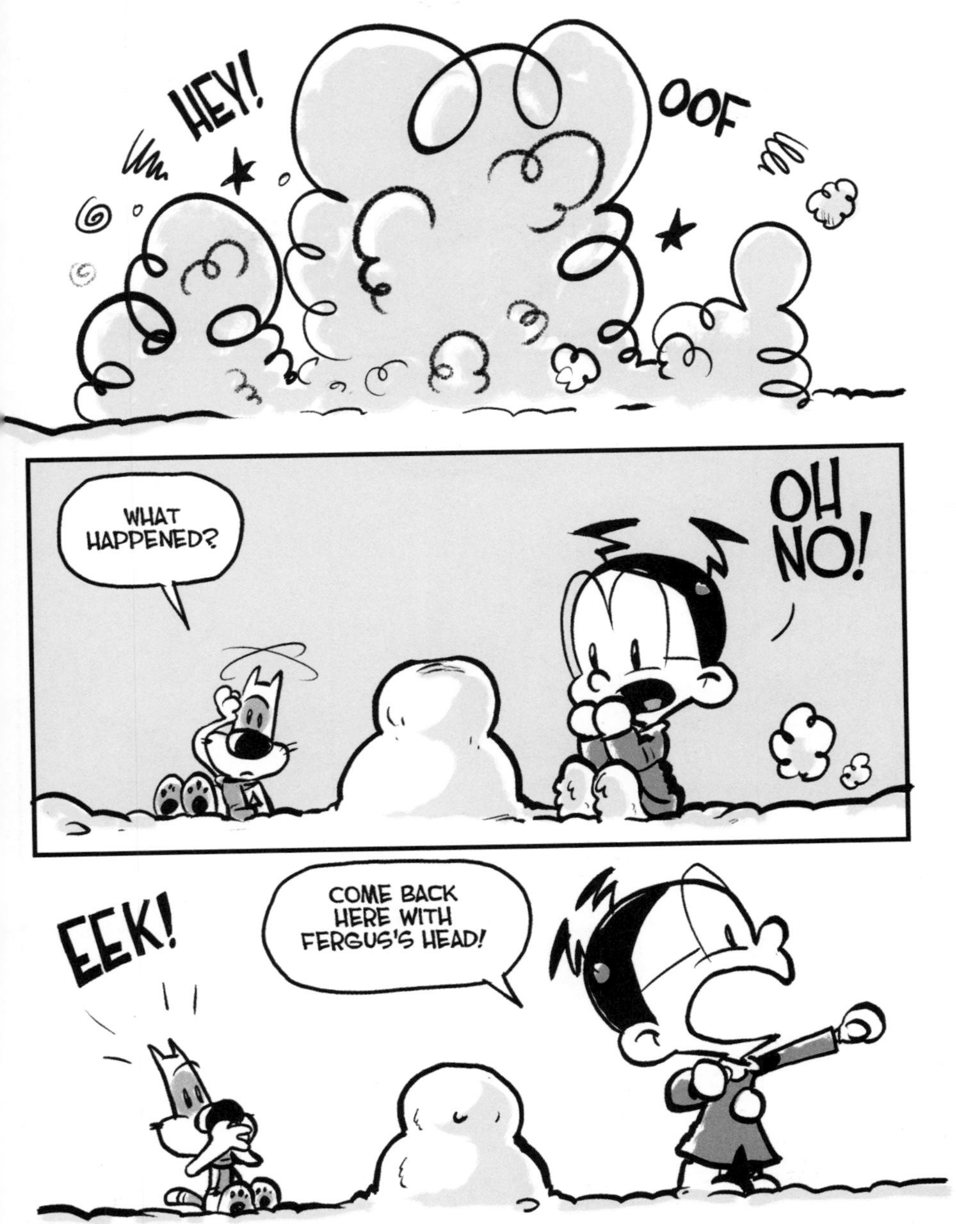
HEY!
OOF
WHAT HAPPENED?
OH NO!
EEK!
COME BACK HERE WITH FERGUS'S HEAD!

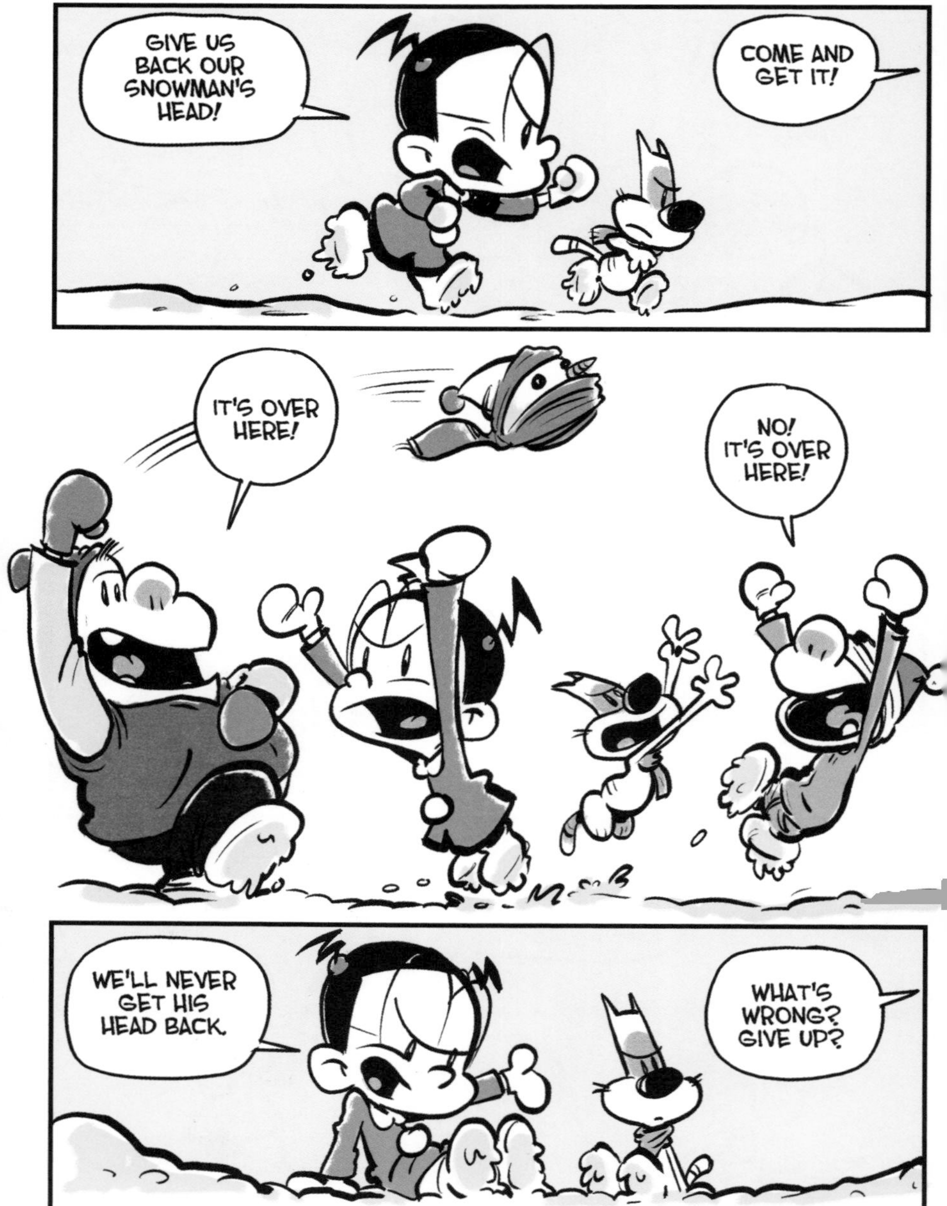
GIVE US BACK OUR SNOWMAN'S HEAD!
COME AND GET IT!
IT'S OVER HERE!
NO! IT'S OVER HERE!
WE'LL NEVER GET HIS HEAD BACK.
WHAT'S WRONG? GIVE UP?

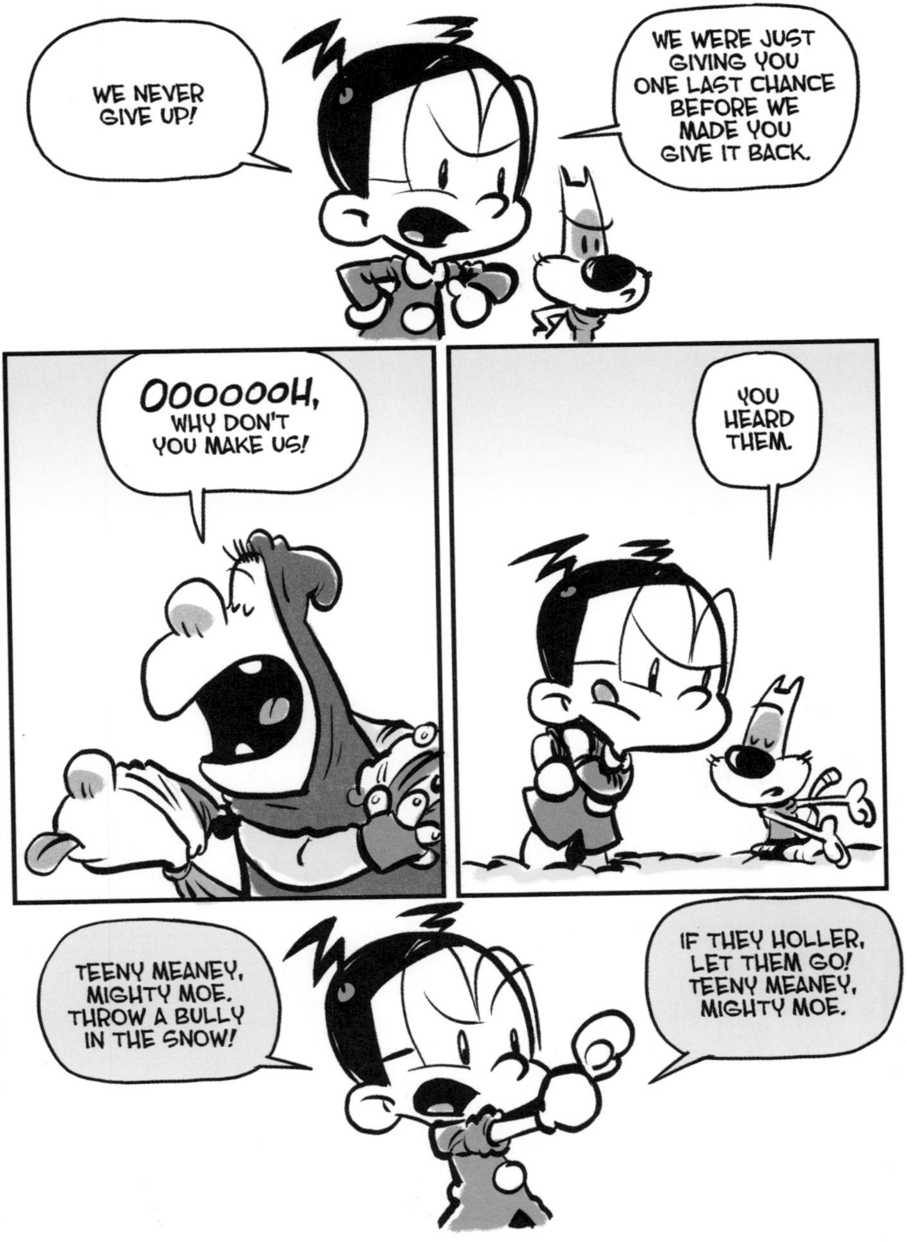
WE NEVER GIVE UP!
WE WERE JUST GIVING YOU ONE LAST CHANCE BEFORE WE MADE YOU GIVE IT BACK.
OOOOOOH, WHY DON'T YOU MAKE US!
YOU HEARD THEM.
TEENY MEANEY, MIGHTY MOE. THROW A BULLY IN THE SNOW!
IF THEY HOLLER, LET THEM GO! TEENY MEANEY, MIGHTY MOE.

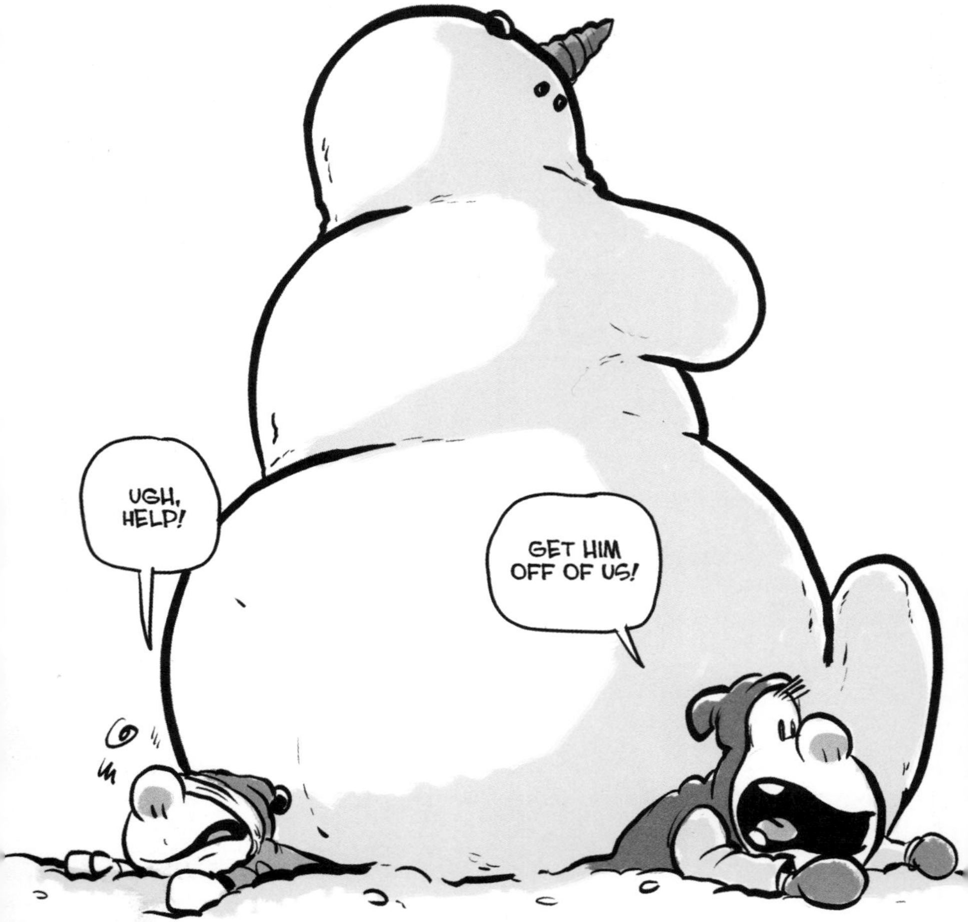
UGH, HELP!
GET HIM OFF OF US!

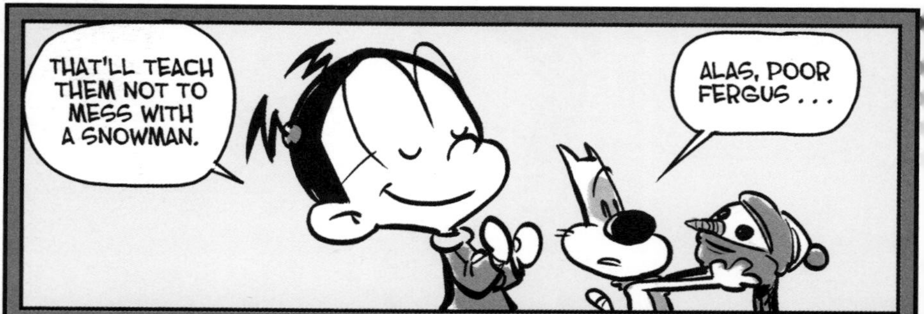
THAT'LL TEACH THEM NOT TO MESS WITH A SNOWMAN.
ALAS, POOR FERGUS . . .

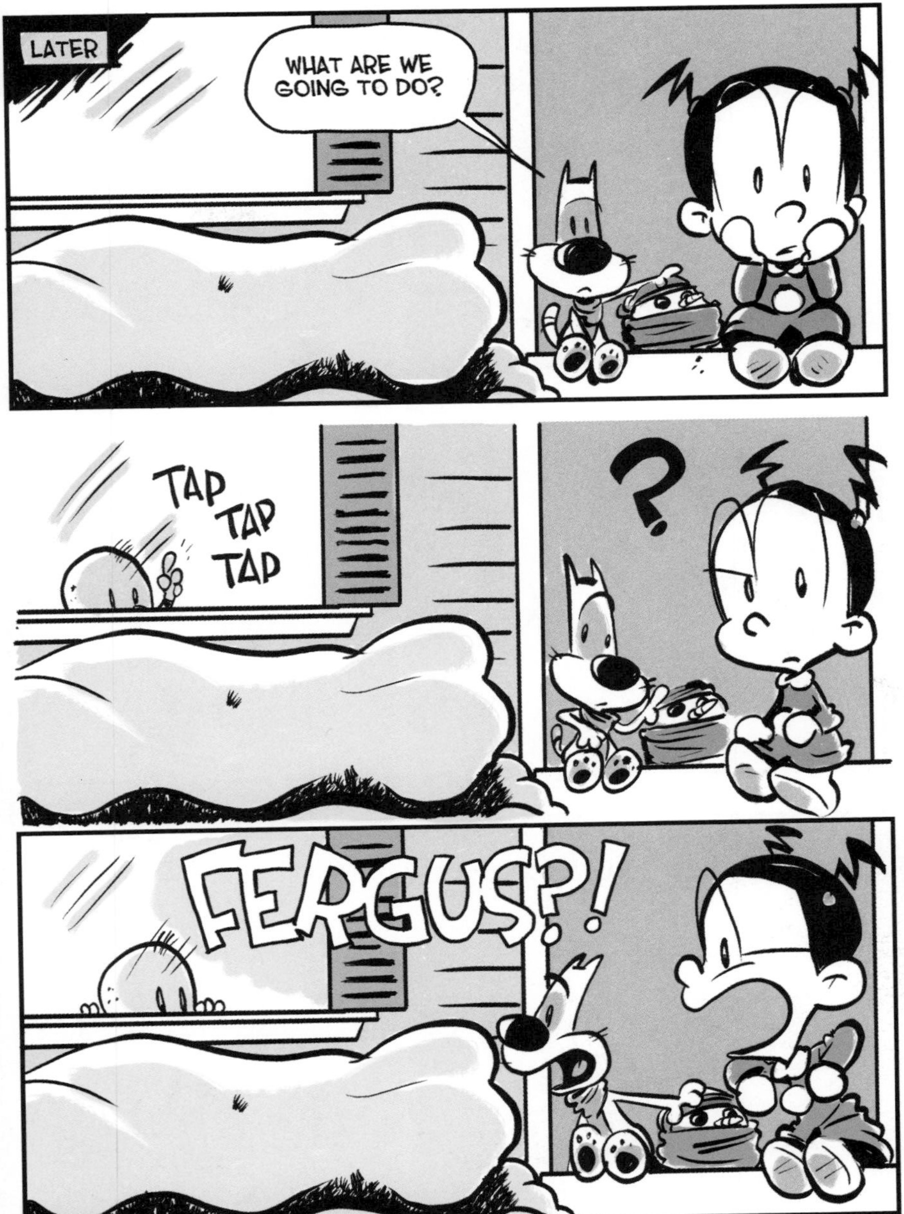
LATER
WHAT ARE WE GOING TO DO?
TAP TAP TAP
?
FERGUS?!

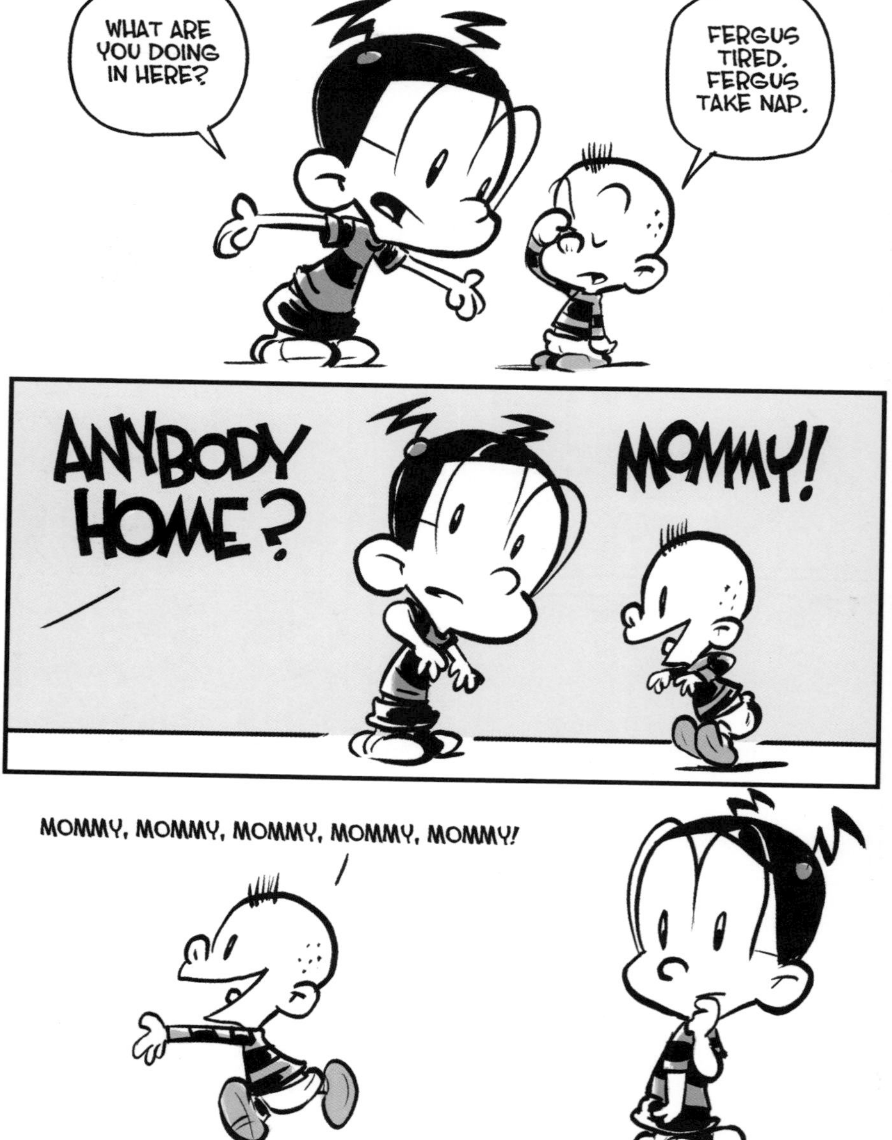
WHAT ARE YOU DOING IN HERE?
FERGUS TIRED. FERGUS TAKE NAP.
ANYBODY HOME?
MOMMY!
MOMMY, MOMMY, MOMMY, MOMMY, MOMMY!

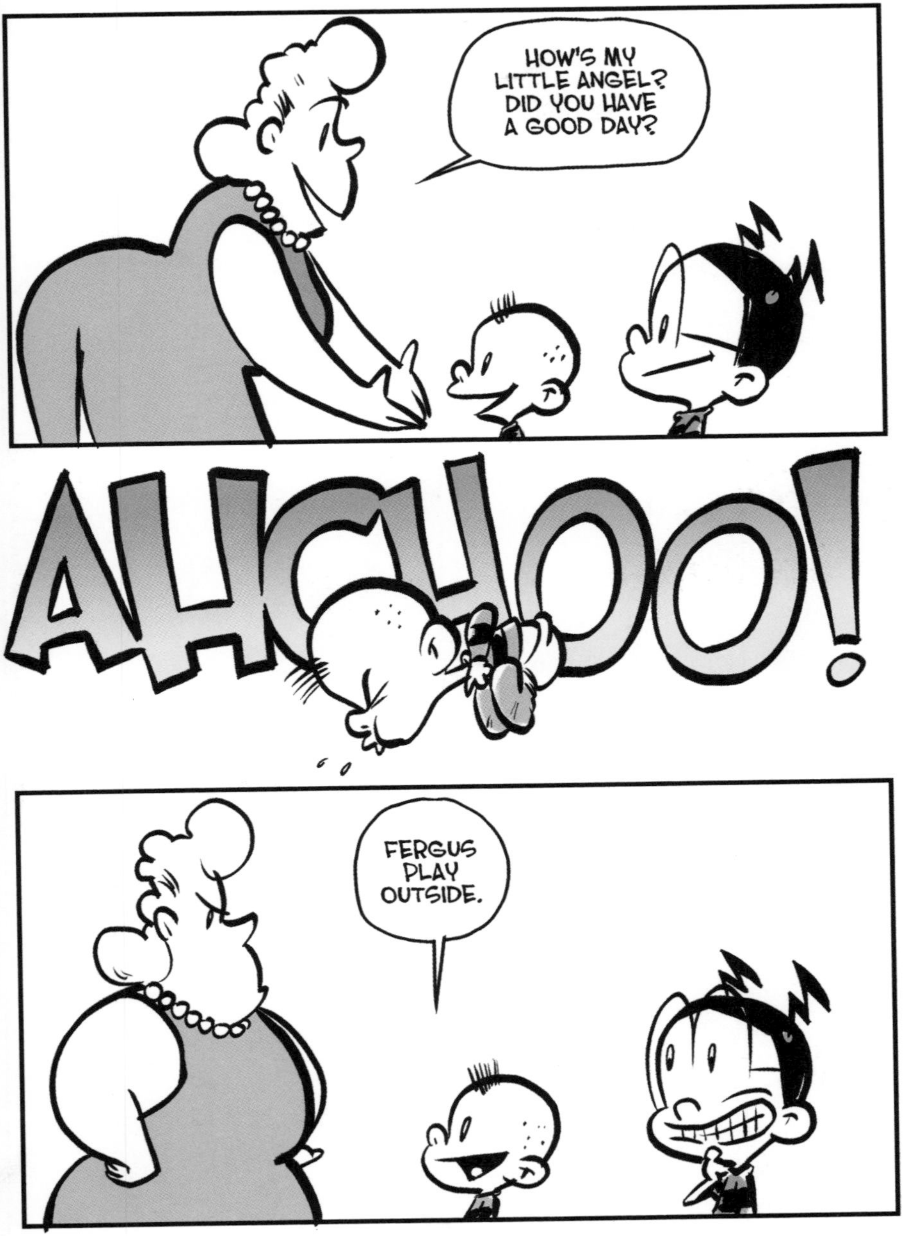
HOW'S MY LITTLE ANGEL? DID YOU HAVE A GOOD DAY?
AHCHOO!
FERGUS PLAY OUTSIDE.

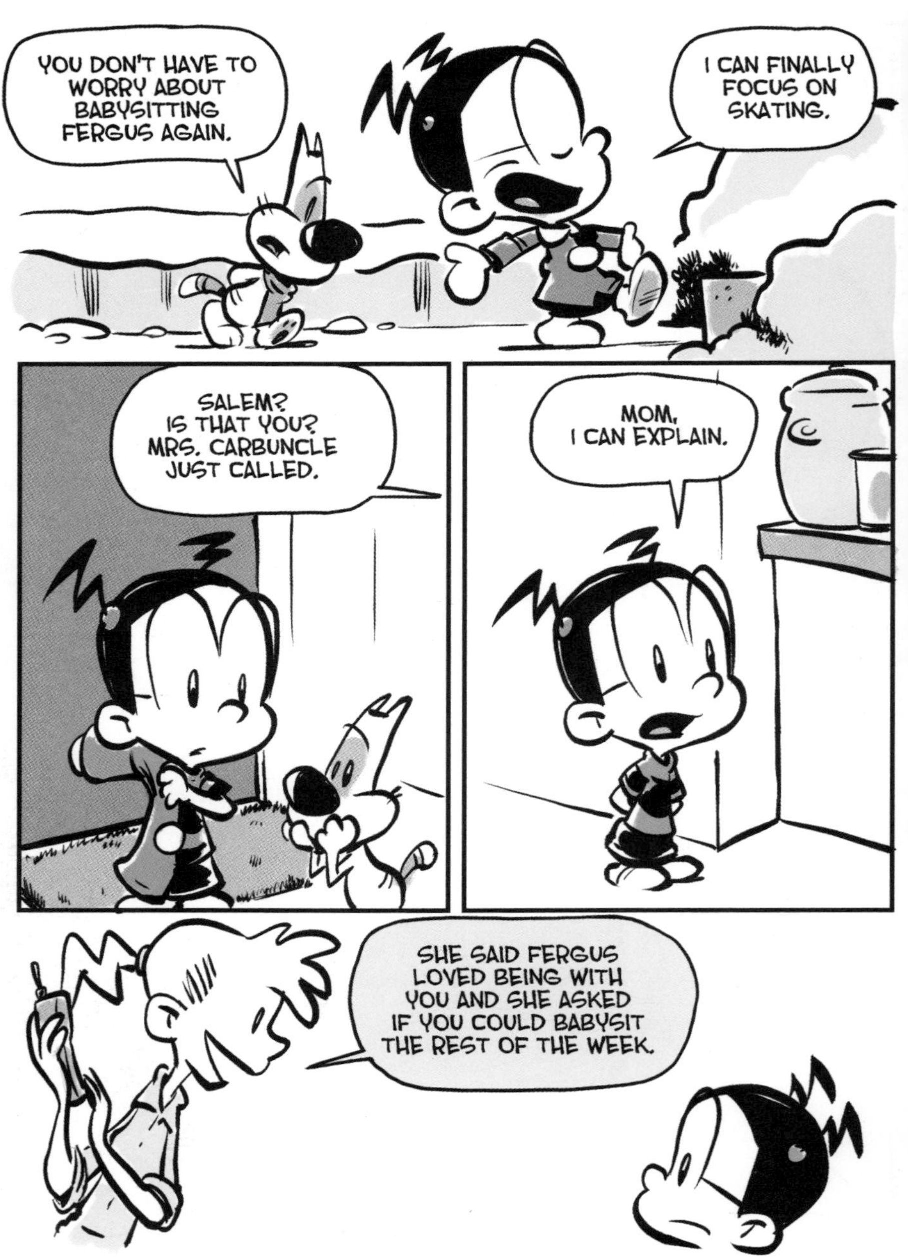
YOU DON'T HAVE TO WORRY ABOUT BABYSITTING FERGUS AGAIN.
I CAN FINALLY FOCUS ON SKATING.
SALEM? IS THAT YOU? MRS. CARBUNCLE JUST CALLED.
MOM, I CAN EXPLAIN.
SHE SAID FERGUS LOVED BEING WITH YOU AND SHE ASKED IF YOU COULD BABYSIT THE REST OF THE WEEK.

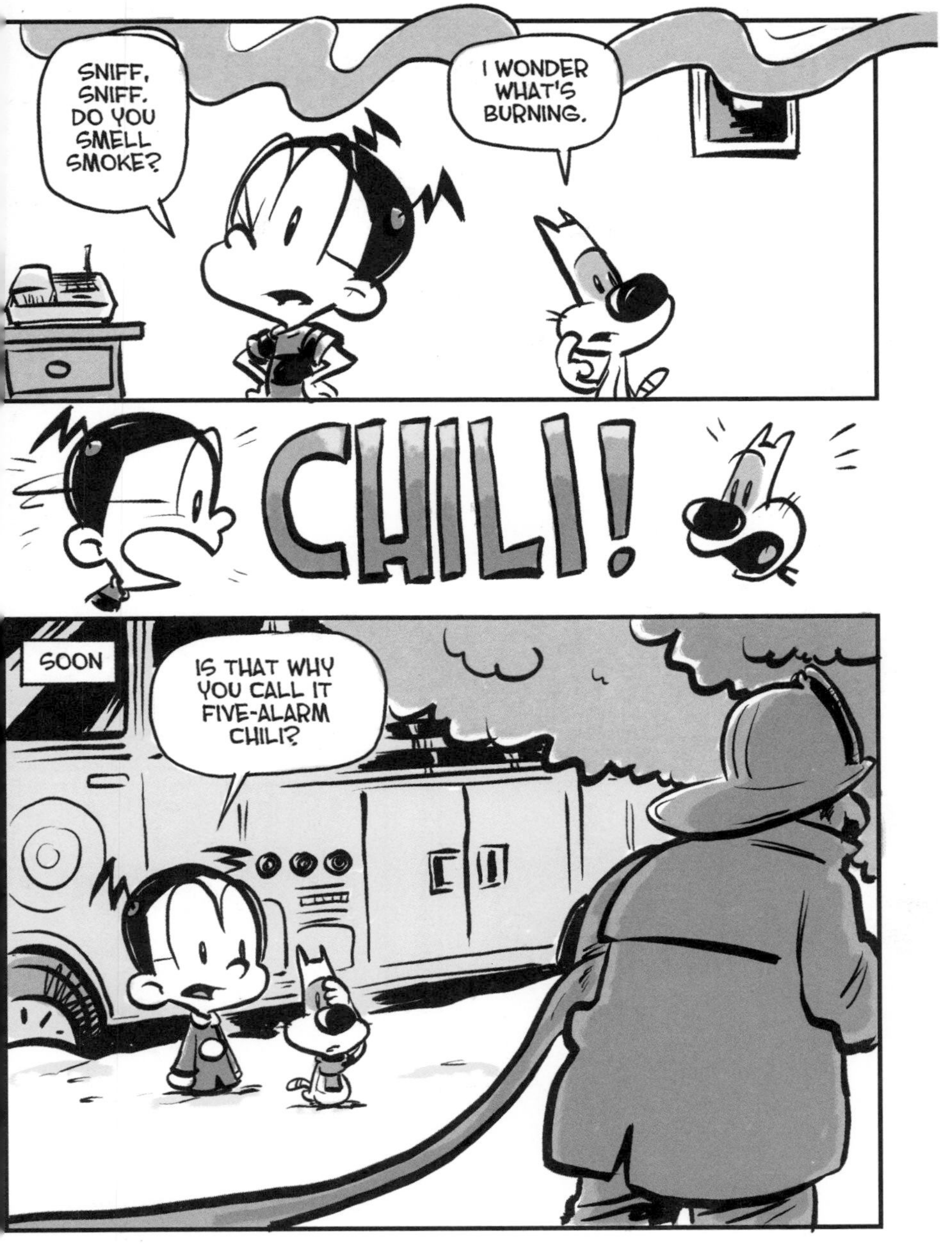
SNIFF, SNIFF. DO YOU SMELL SMOKE?
I WONDER WHAT'S BURNING.
CHILI!
SOON
IS THAT WHY YOU CALL IT FIVE-ALARM CHILI?

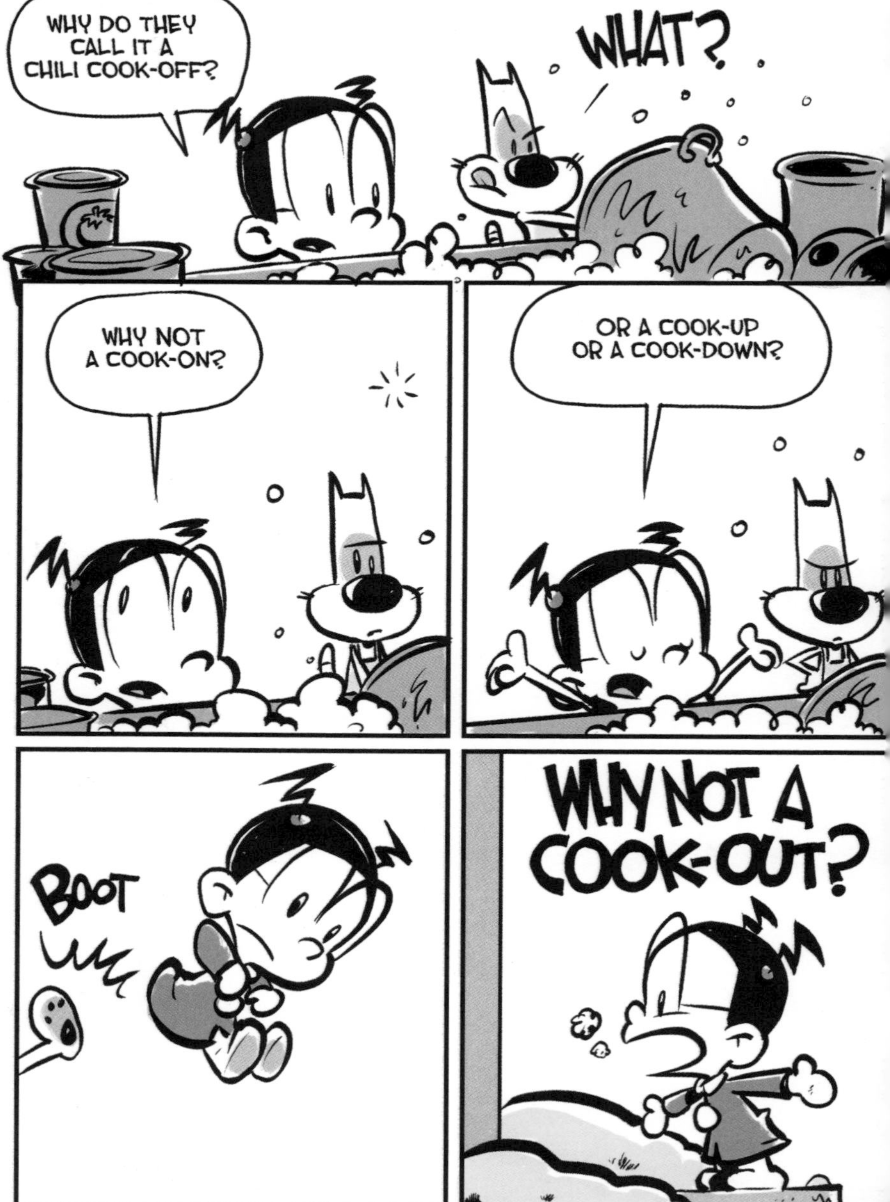
WHY DO THEY CALL IT A CHILI COOK-OFF?
WHAT?
WHY NOT A COOK-ON?
OR A COOK-UP OR A COOK-DOWN?
BOOT
WHY NOT A COOK-OUT?

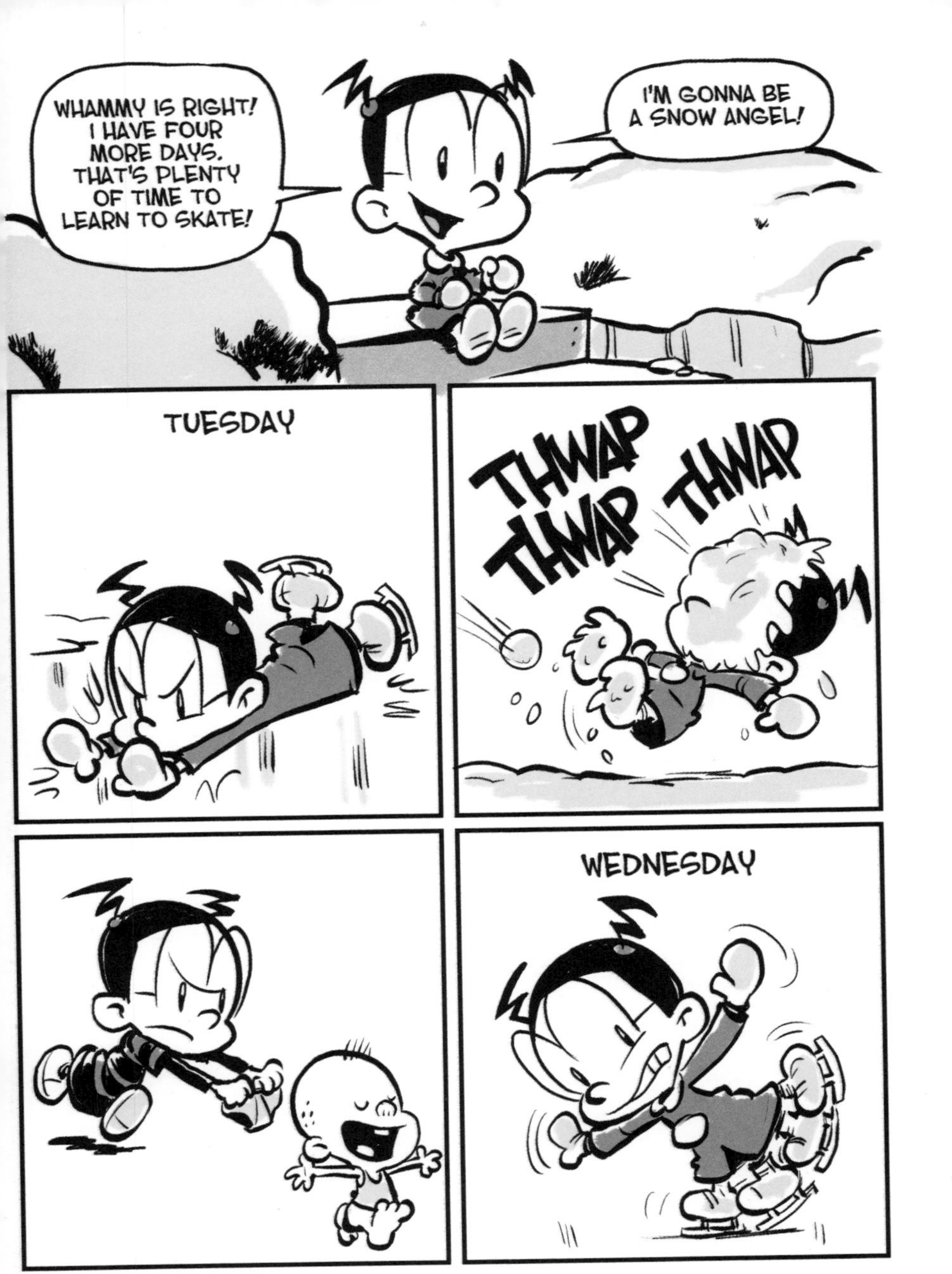
WHAMMY IS RIGHT! I HAVE FOUR MORE DAYS. THAT'S PLENTY OF TIME TO LEARN TO SKATE!
I'M GONNA BE A SNOW ANGEL!
TUESDAY
THWAP THWAP THWAP
WEDNESDAY

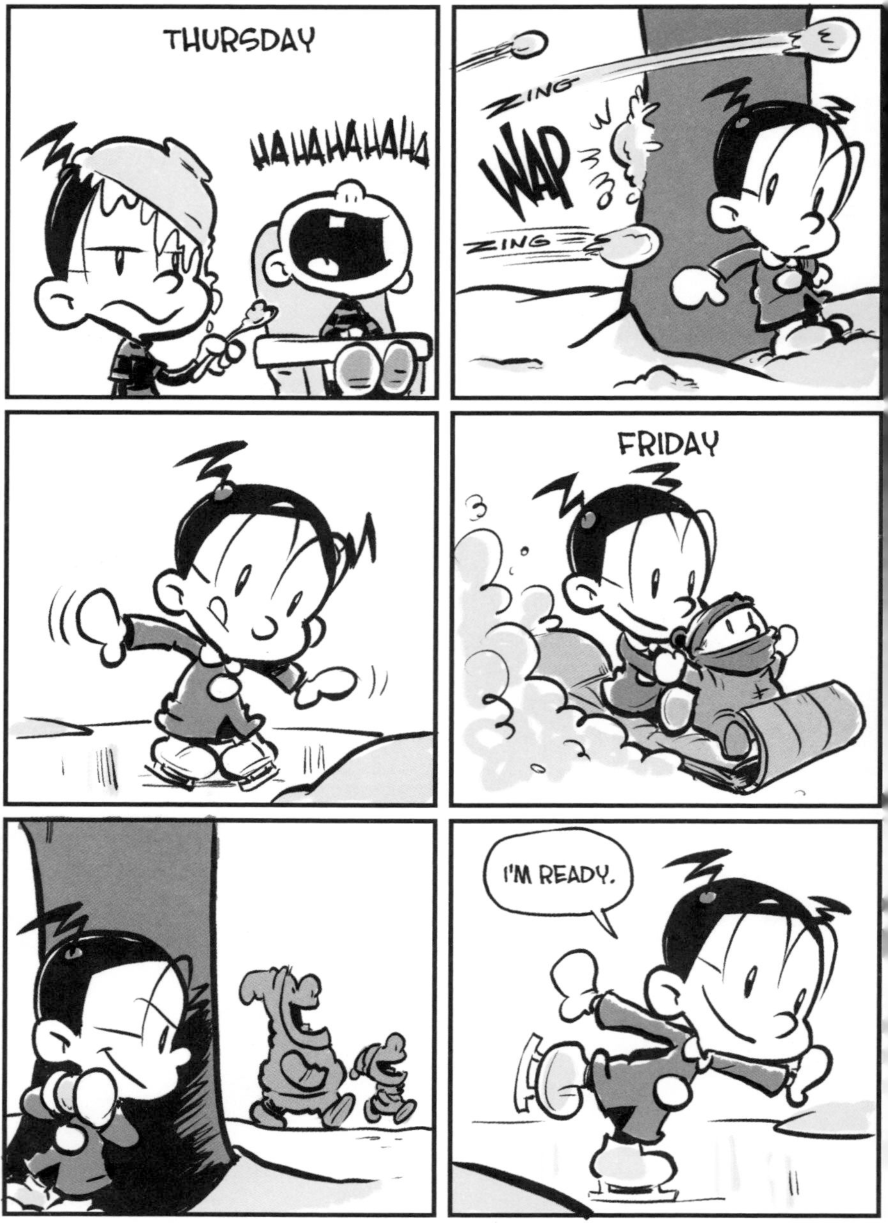
THURSDAY
HAHAHAHAHA
ZING
WAP
ZING
FRIDAY
I'M READY.

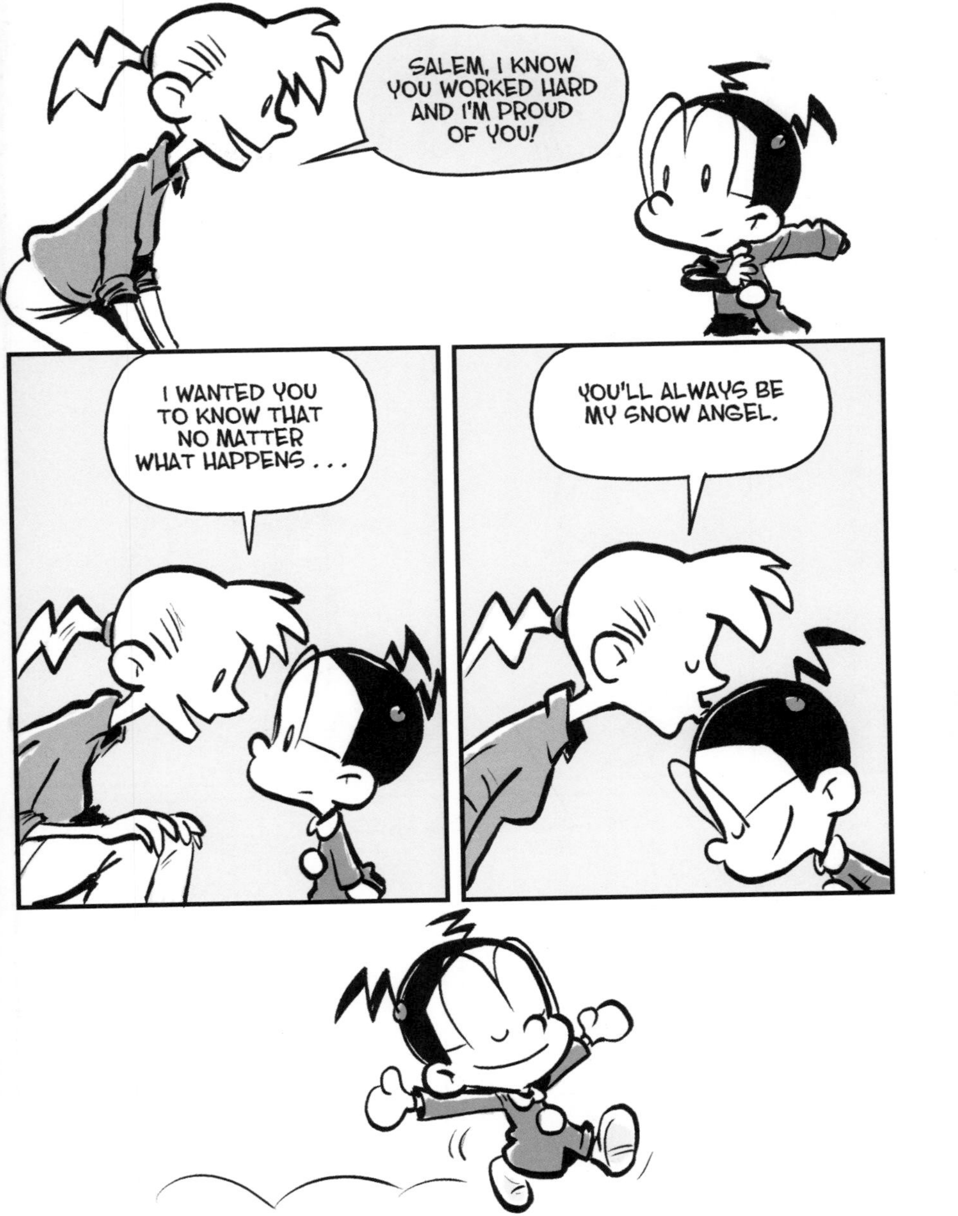
SALEM, I KNOW YOU WORKED HARD AND I'M PROUD OF YOU!
I WANTED YOU TO KNOW THAT NO MATTER WHAT HAPPENS . . .
YOU'LL ALWAYS BE MY SNOW ANGEL.

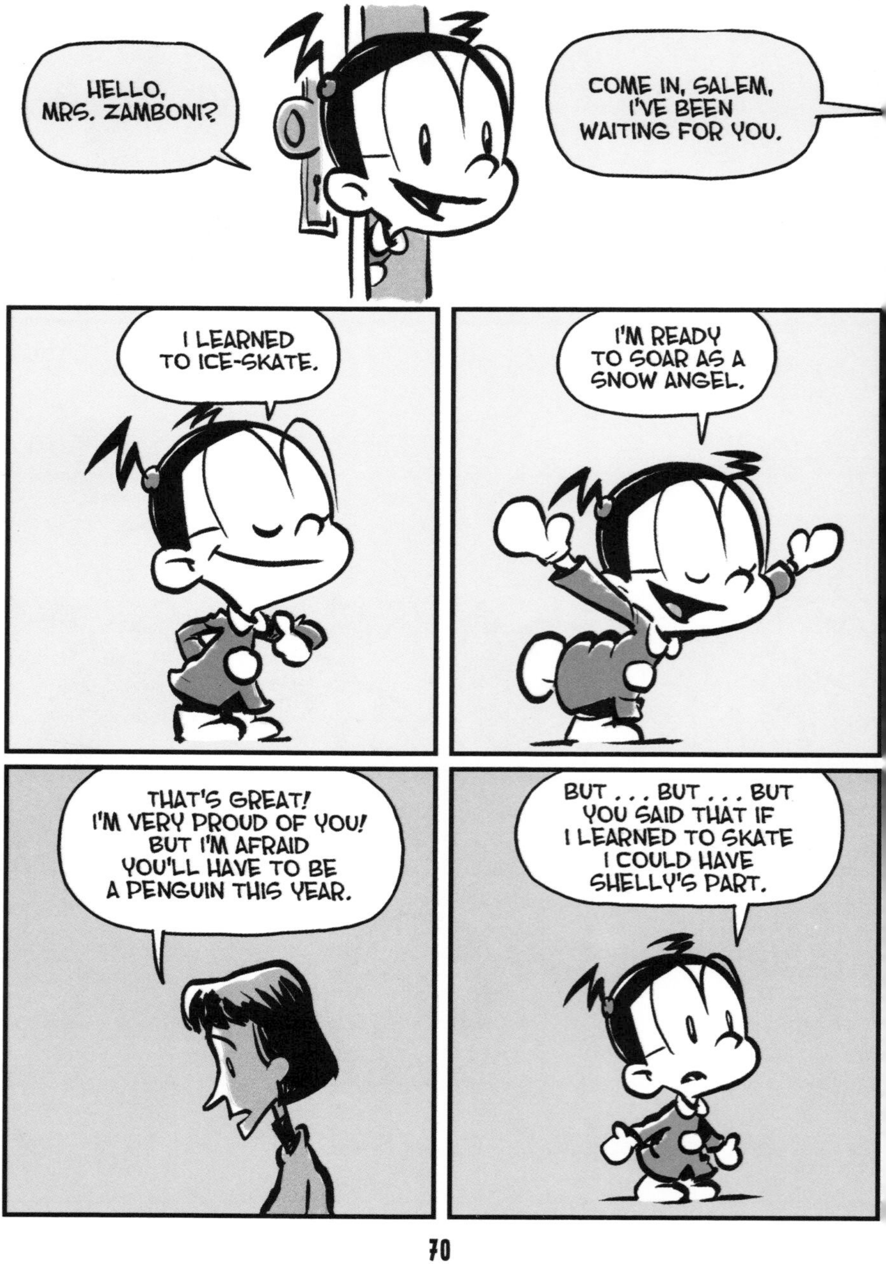
HELLO, MRS. ZAMBONI?
COME IN, SALEM, I'VE BEEN WAITING FOR YOU.
I LEARNED TO ICE-SKATE.
I'M READY TO SOAR AS A SNOW ANGEL.
THAT'S GREAT! I'M VERY PROUD OF YOU! BUT I'M AFRAID YOU'LL HAVE TO BE A PENGUIN THIS YEAR.
BUT . . . BUT . . . BUT YOU SAID THAT IF I LEARNED TO SKATE I COULD HAVE SHELLY'S PART.

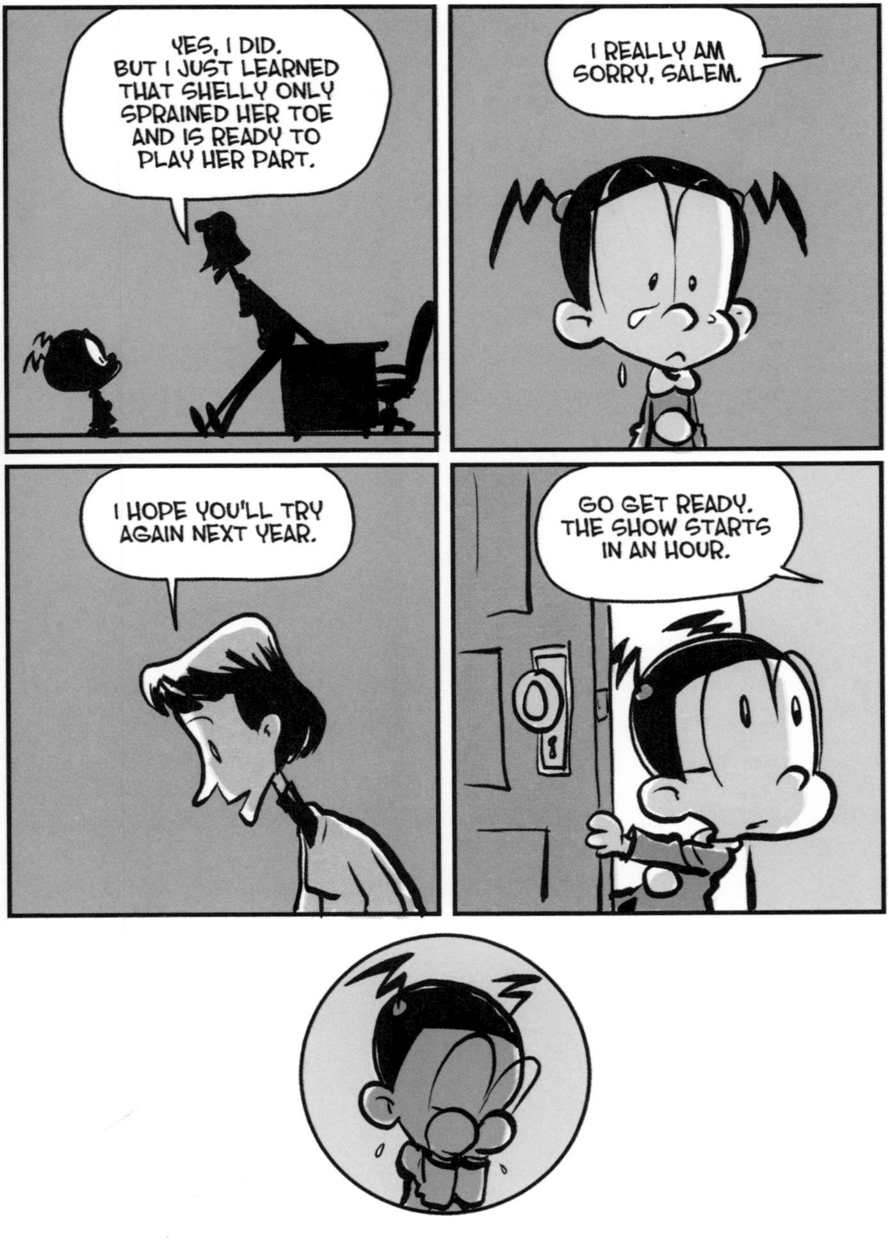
YES, I DID. BUT I JUST LEARNED THAT SHELLY ONLY SPRAINED HER TOE AND IS READY TO PLAY HER PART.
I REALLY AM SORRY, SALEM.
I HOPE YOU'LL TRY AGAIN NEXT YEAR.
GO GET READY. THE SHOW STARTS IN AN HOUR.

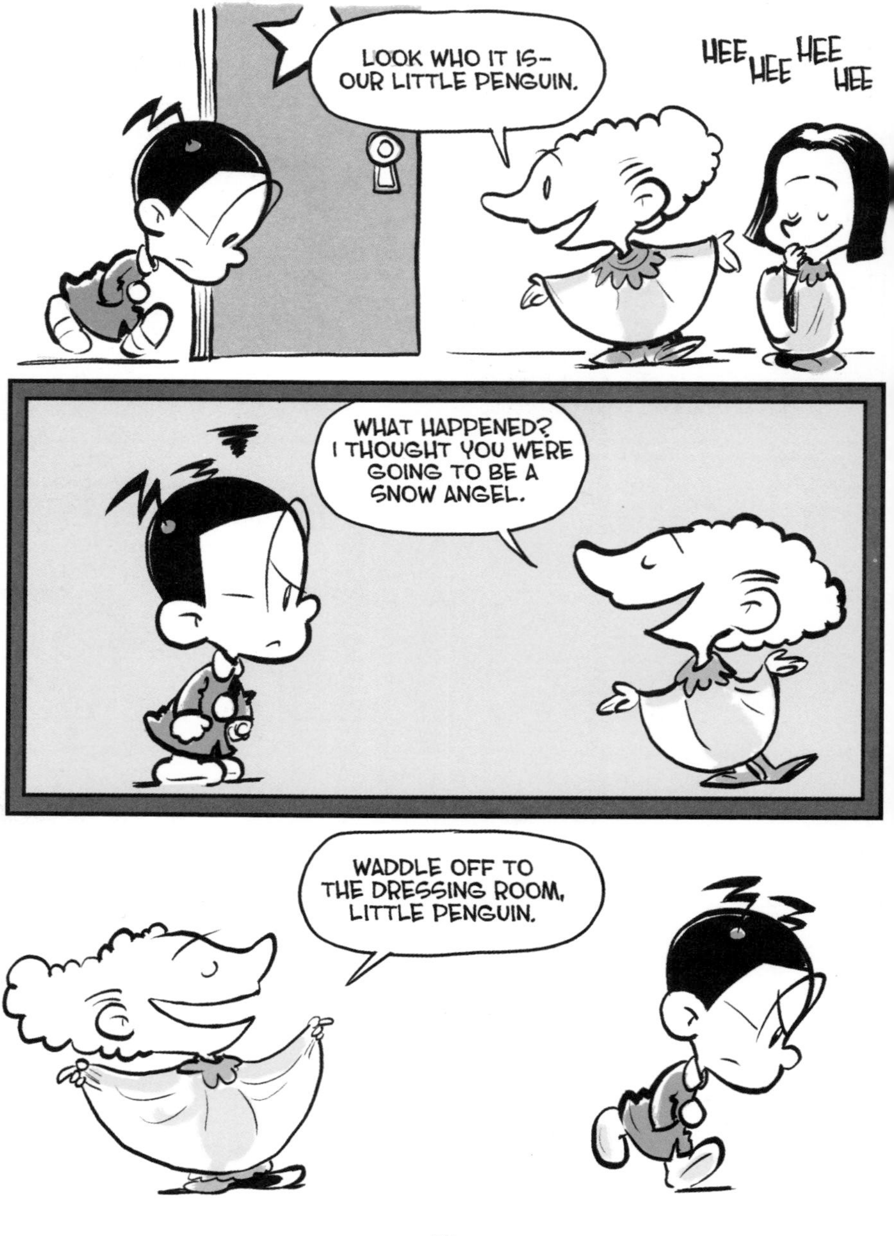
LOOK WHO IT IS-
OUR LITTLE PENGUIN.
HEE HEE HEE HEE
WHAT HAPPENED?
I THOUGHT YOU WERE
GOING TO BE A
SNOW ANGEL.
WADDLE OFF TO
THE DRESSING ROOM,
LITTLE PENGUIN.

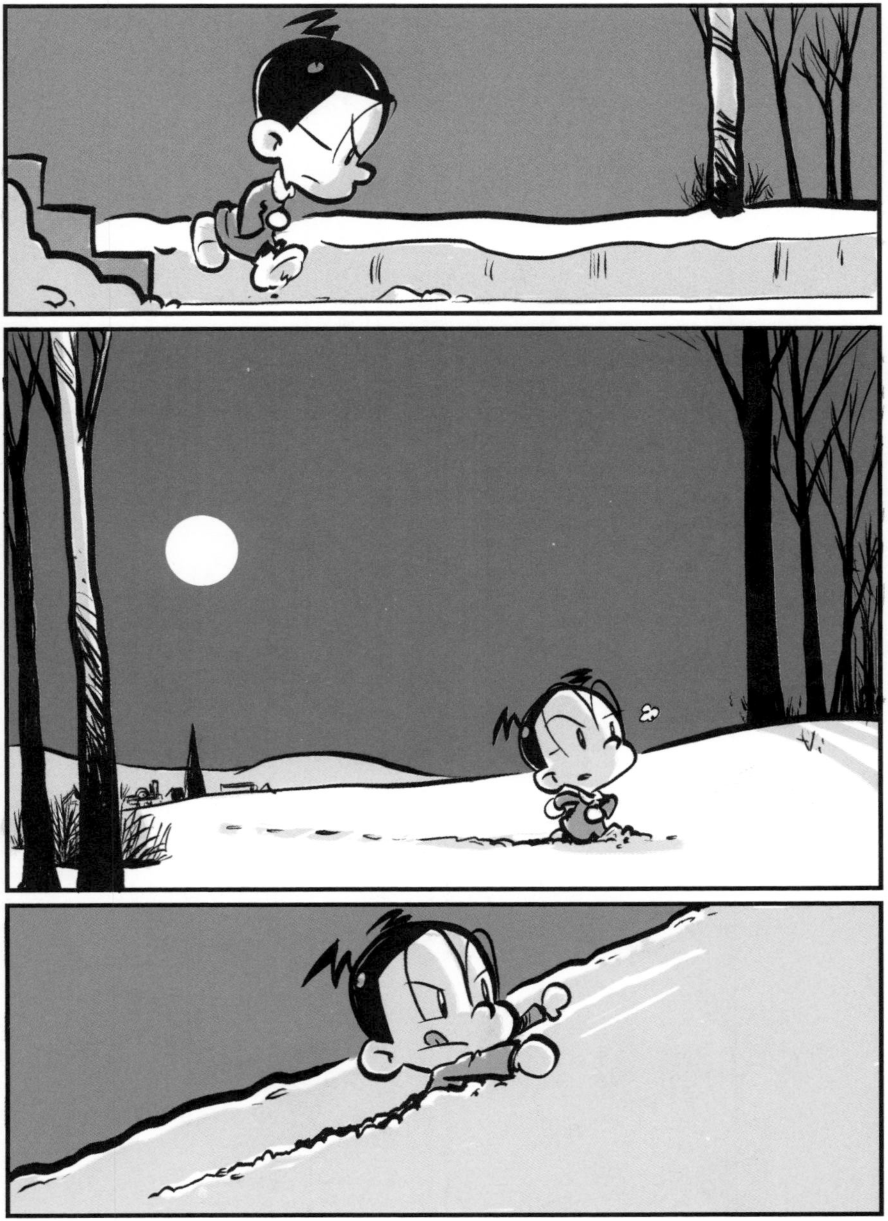

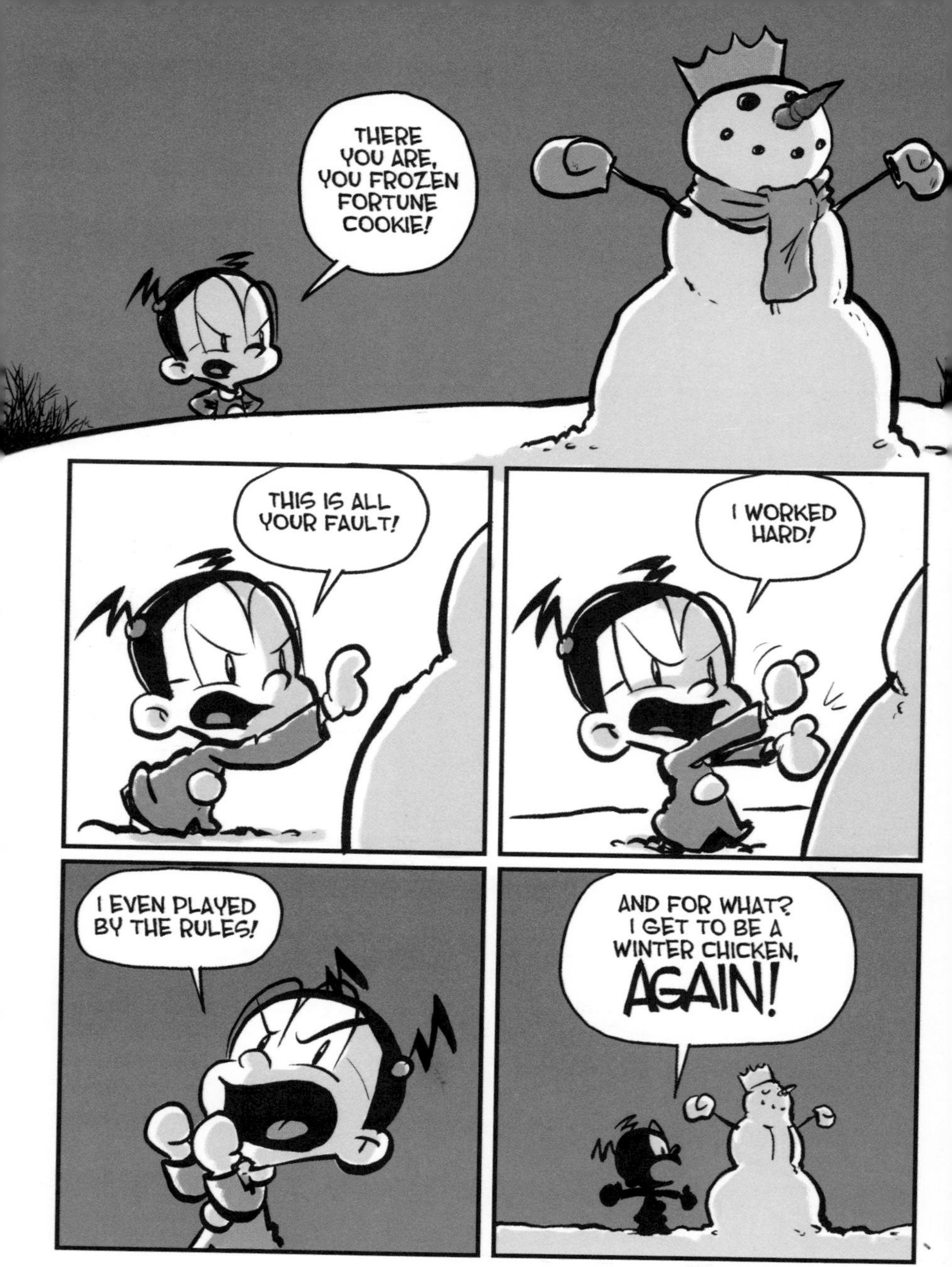
THERE YOU ARE, YOU FROZEN FORTUNE COOKIE!
THIS IS ALL YOUR FAULT!
I WORKED HARD!
I EVEN PLAYED BY THE RULES!
AND FOR WHAT? I GET TO BE A WINTER CHICKEN, AGAIN!

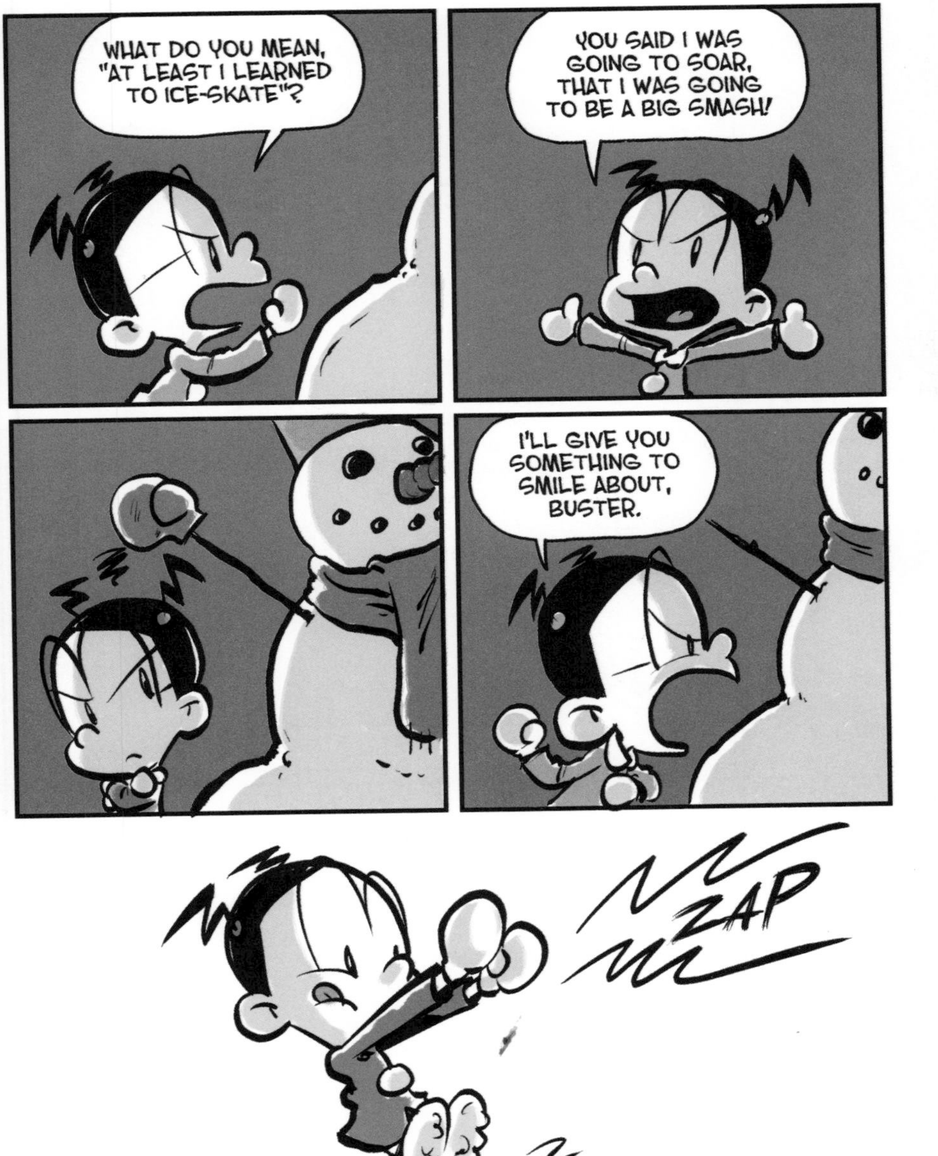
WHAT DO YOU MEAN, "AT LEAST I LEARNED TO ICE-SKATE"?
YOU SAID I WAS GOING TO SOAR, THAT I WAS GOING TO BE A BIG SMASH!
I'LL GIVE YOU SOMETHING TO SMILE ABOUT, BUSTER.
ZAP

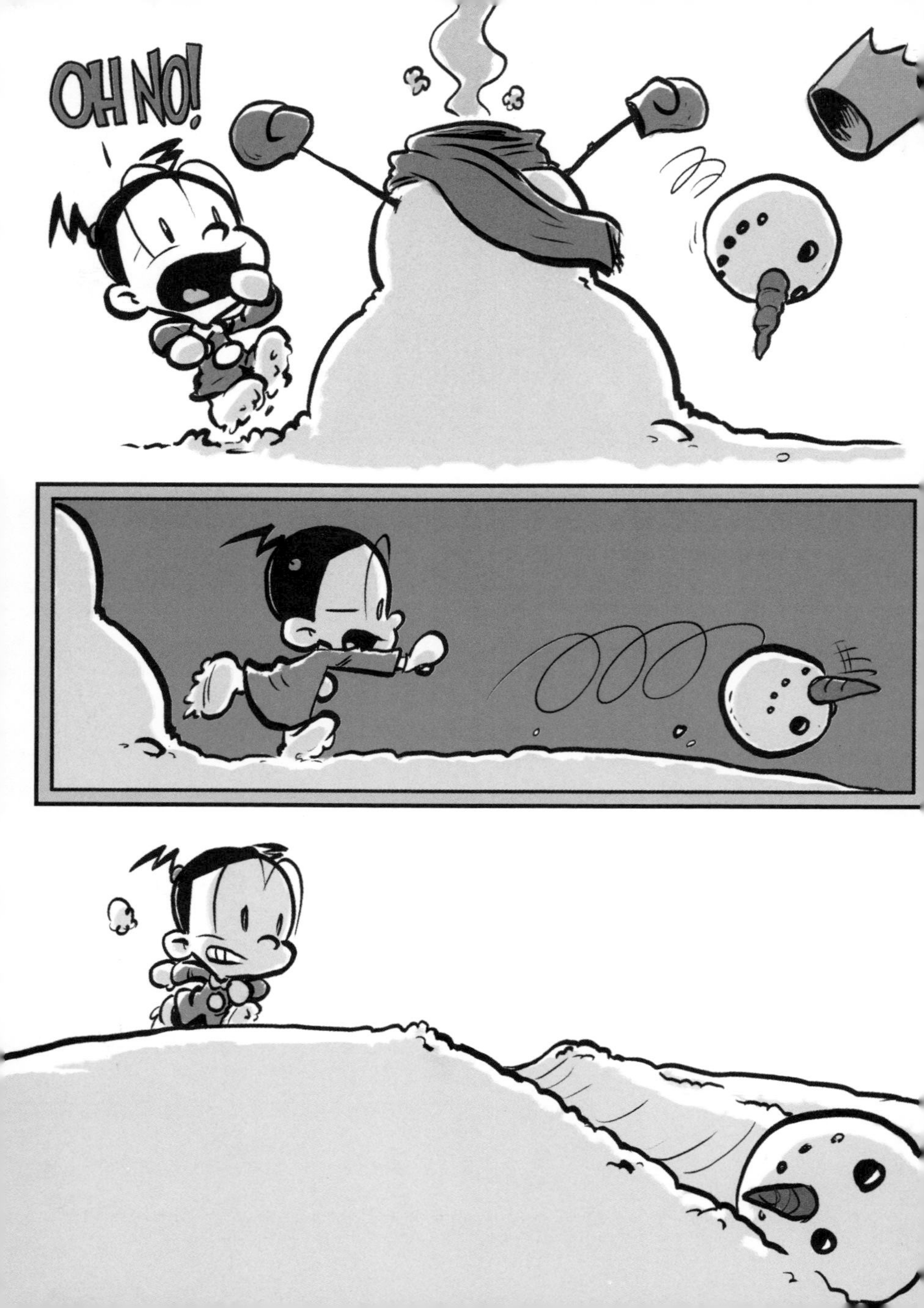
OH NO!

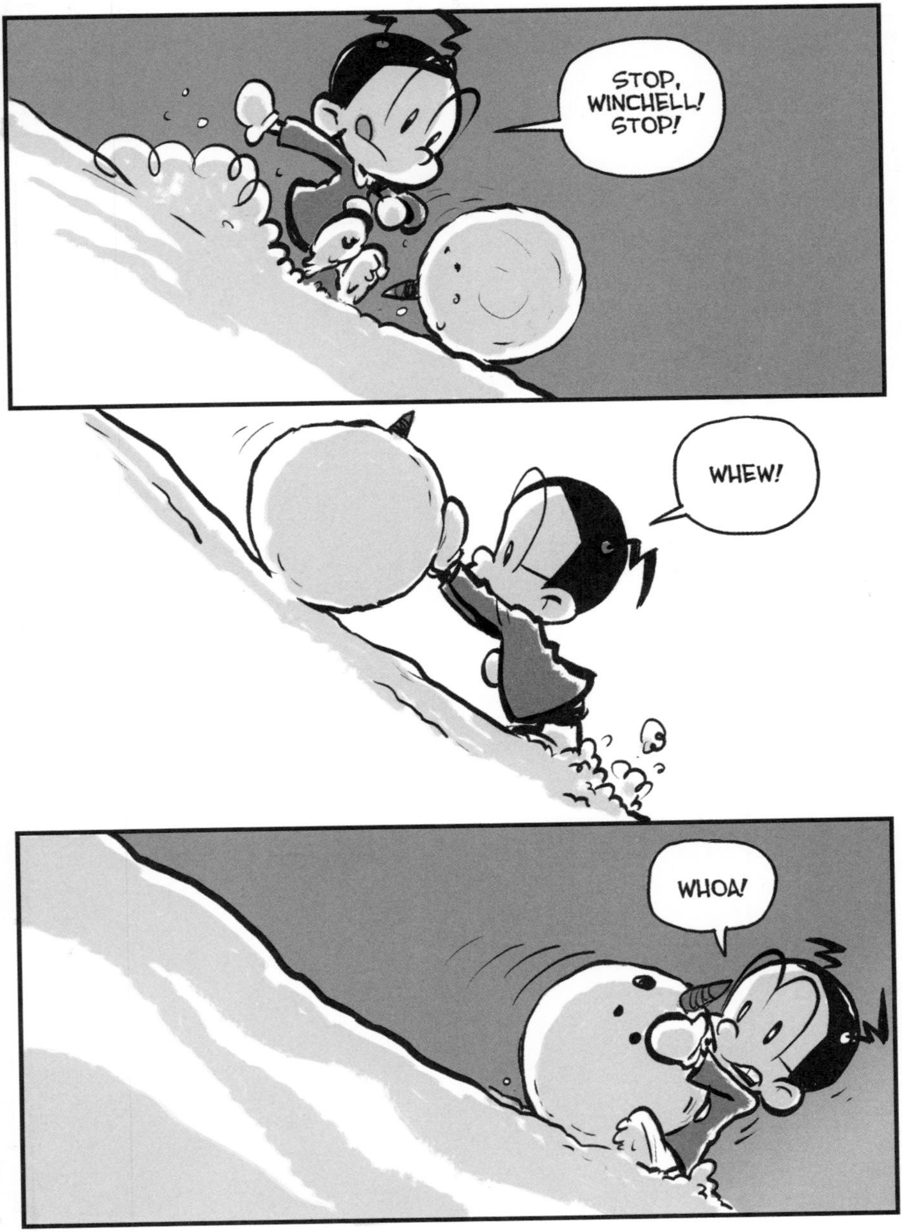
STOP, WINCHELL! STOP!
WHEW!
WHOA!

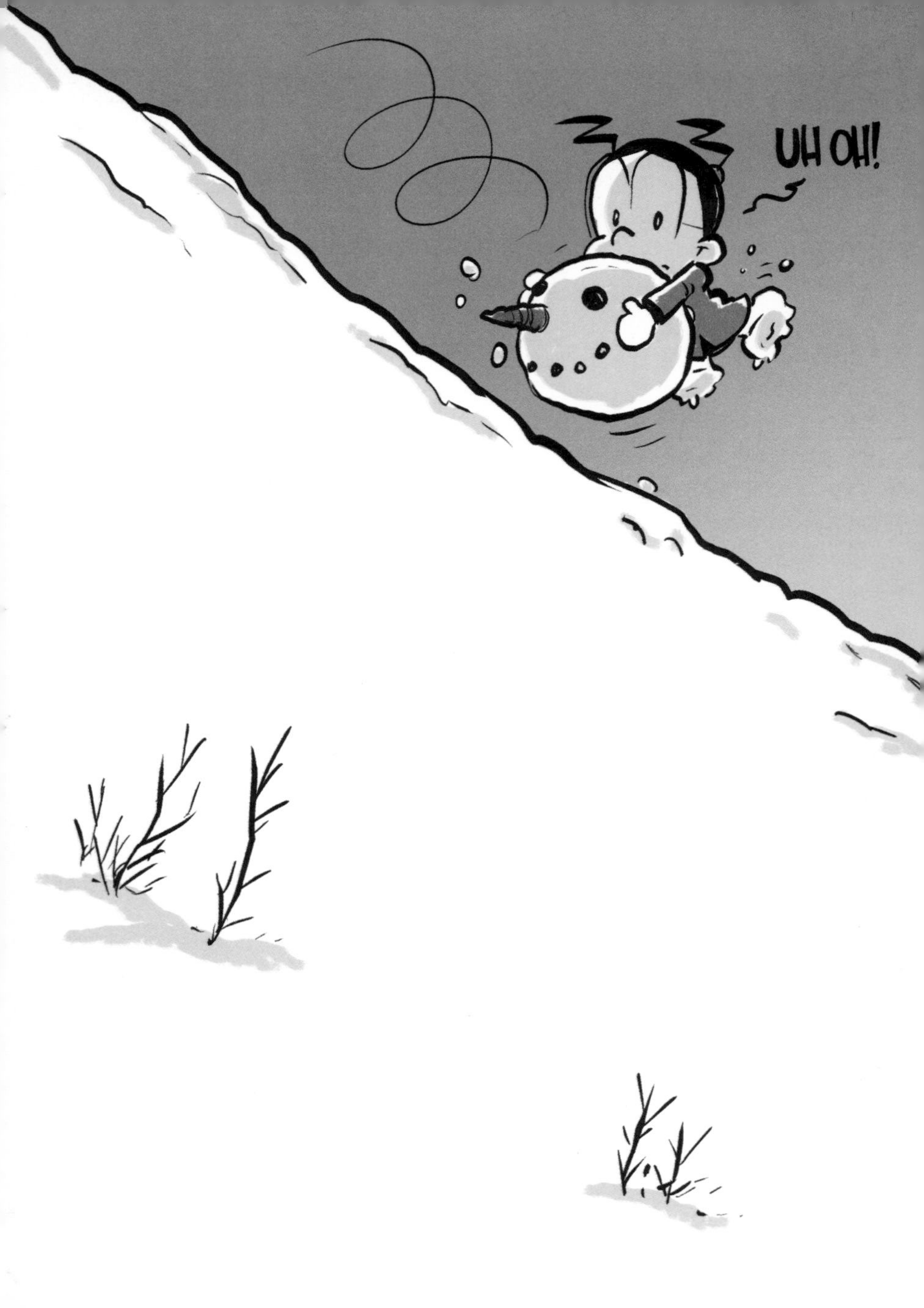
UH OH!

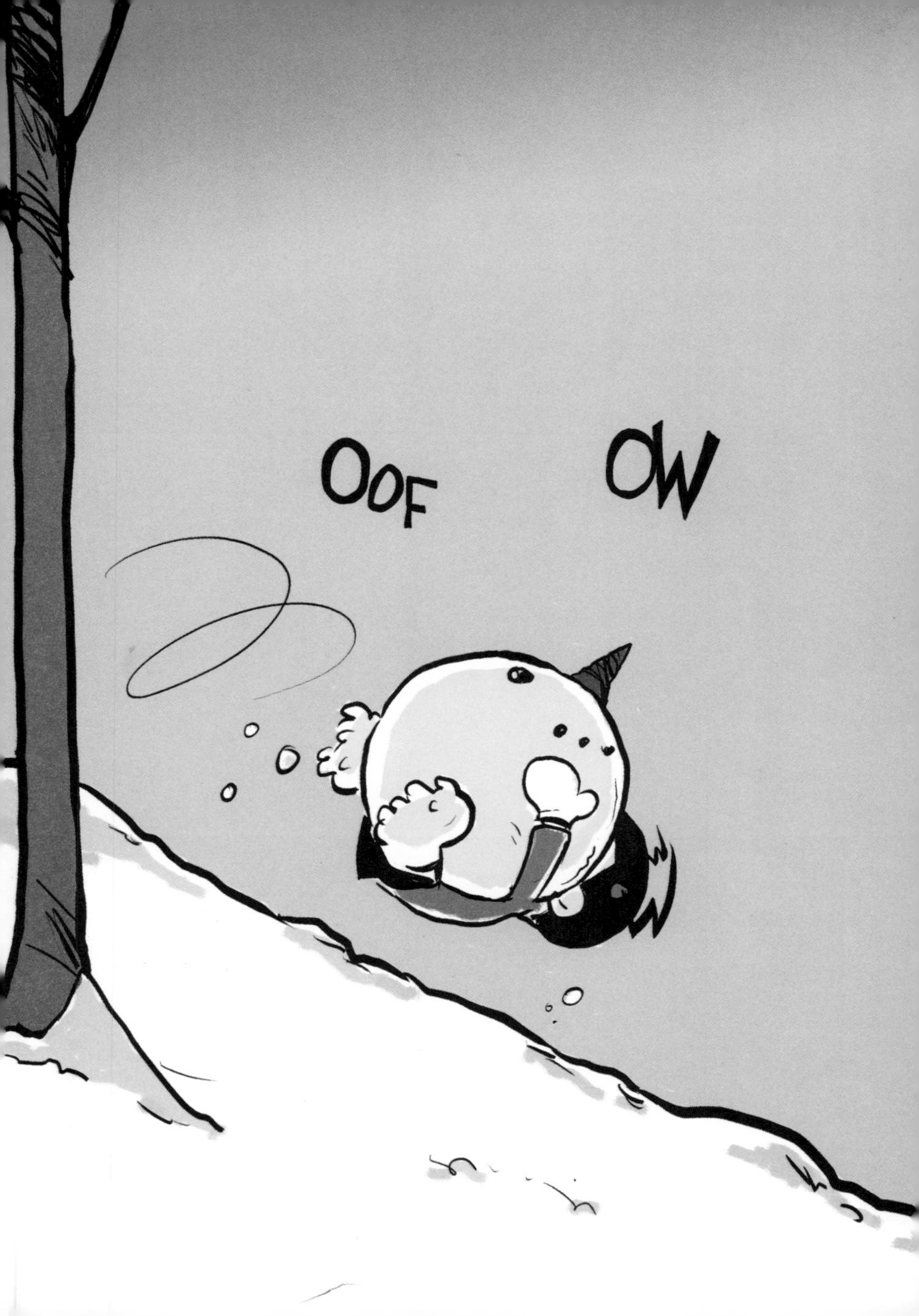
OOF
OW

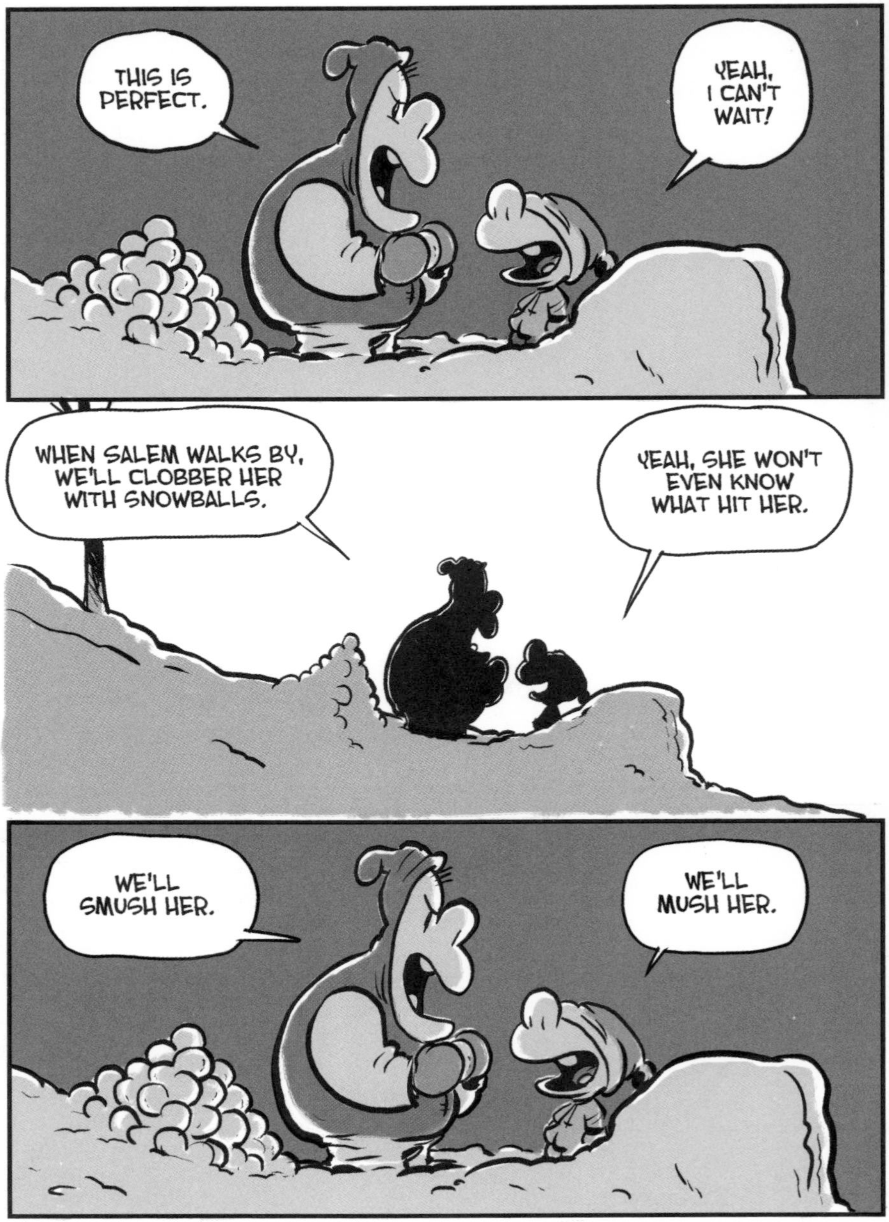
THIS IS PERFECT.
YEAH, I CAN'T WAIT!
WHEN SALEM WALKS BY, WE'LL CLOBBER HER WITH SNOWBALLS.
YEAH, SHE WON'T EVEN KNOW WHAT HIT HER.
WE'LL SMUSH HER.
WE'LL MUSH HER.

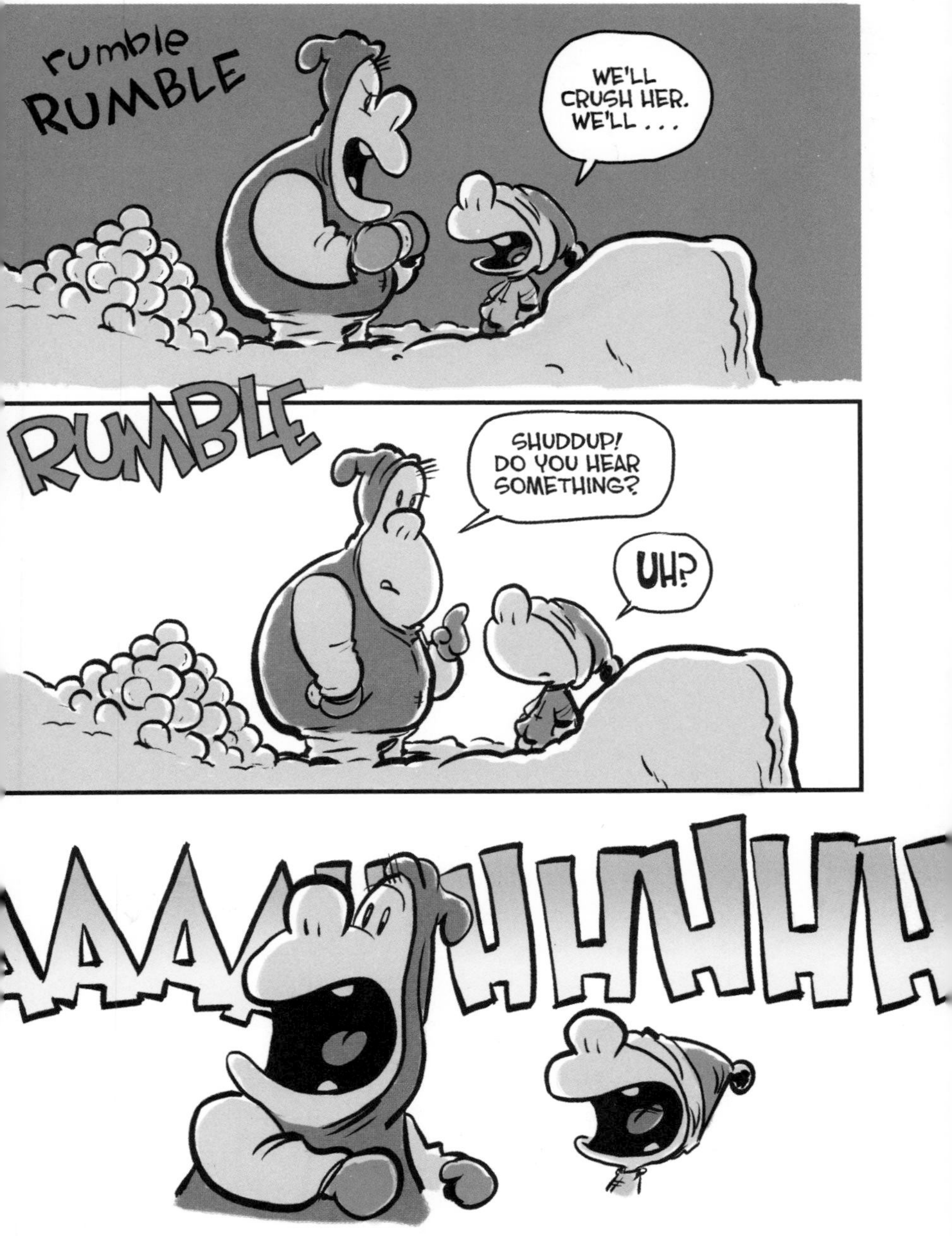
rumble
RUMBLE
WE'LL CRUSH HER. WE'LL . . .
RUMBLE
SHUDDUP! DO YOU HEAR SOMETHING?
UH?
AAAAHHHHHHHH

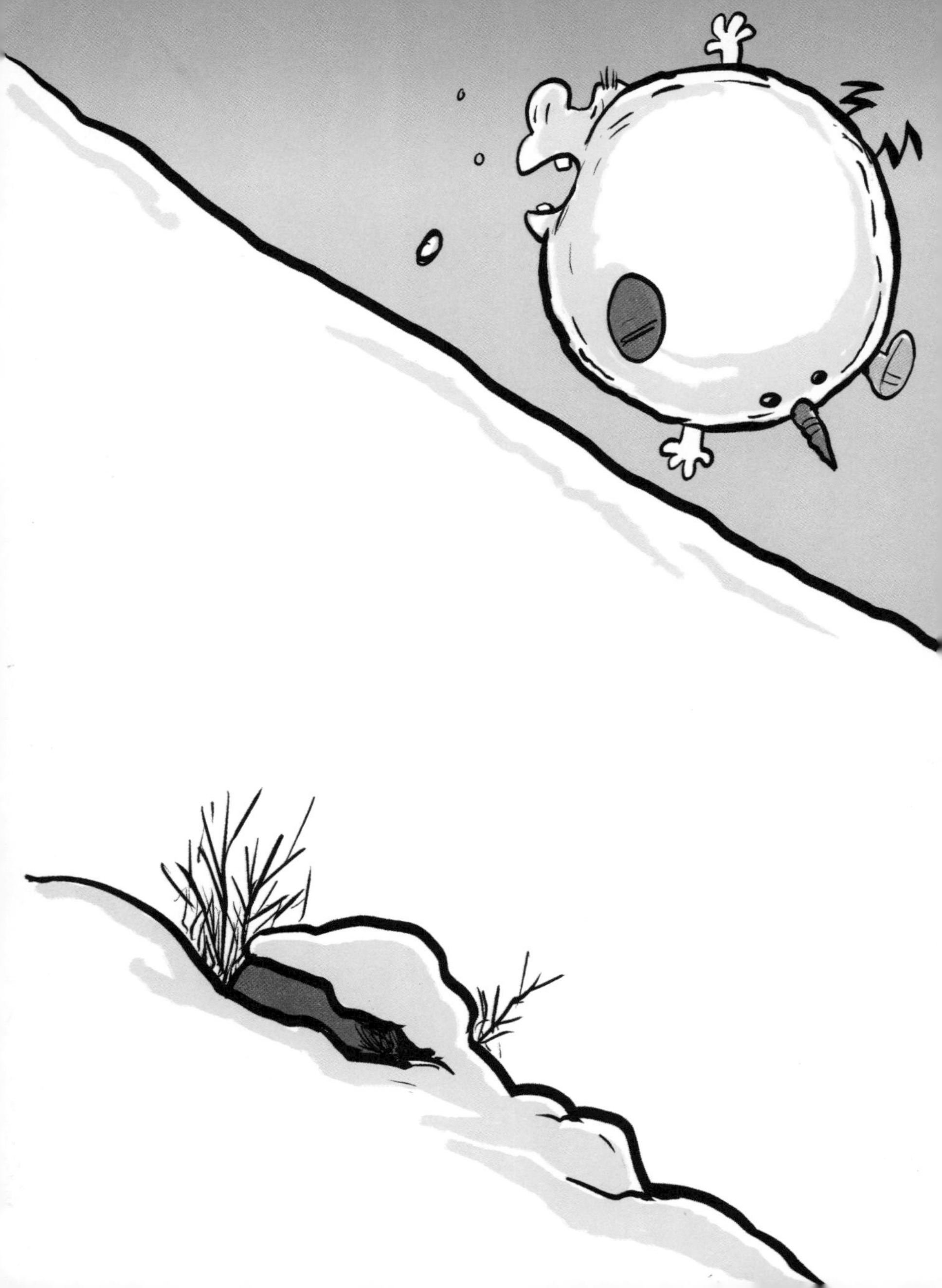

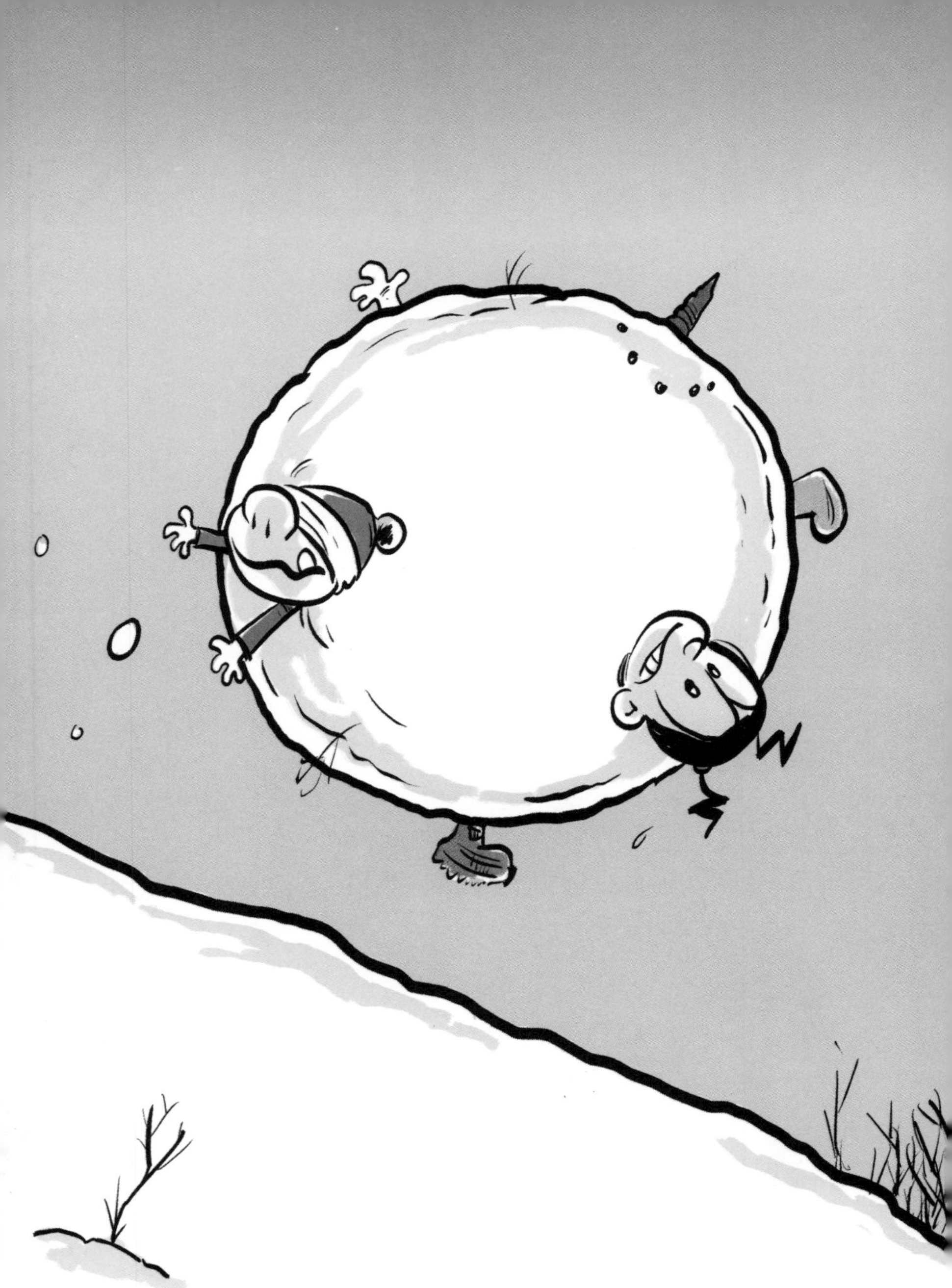

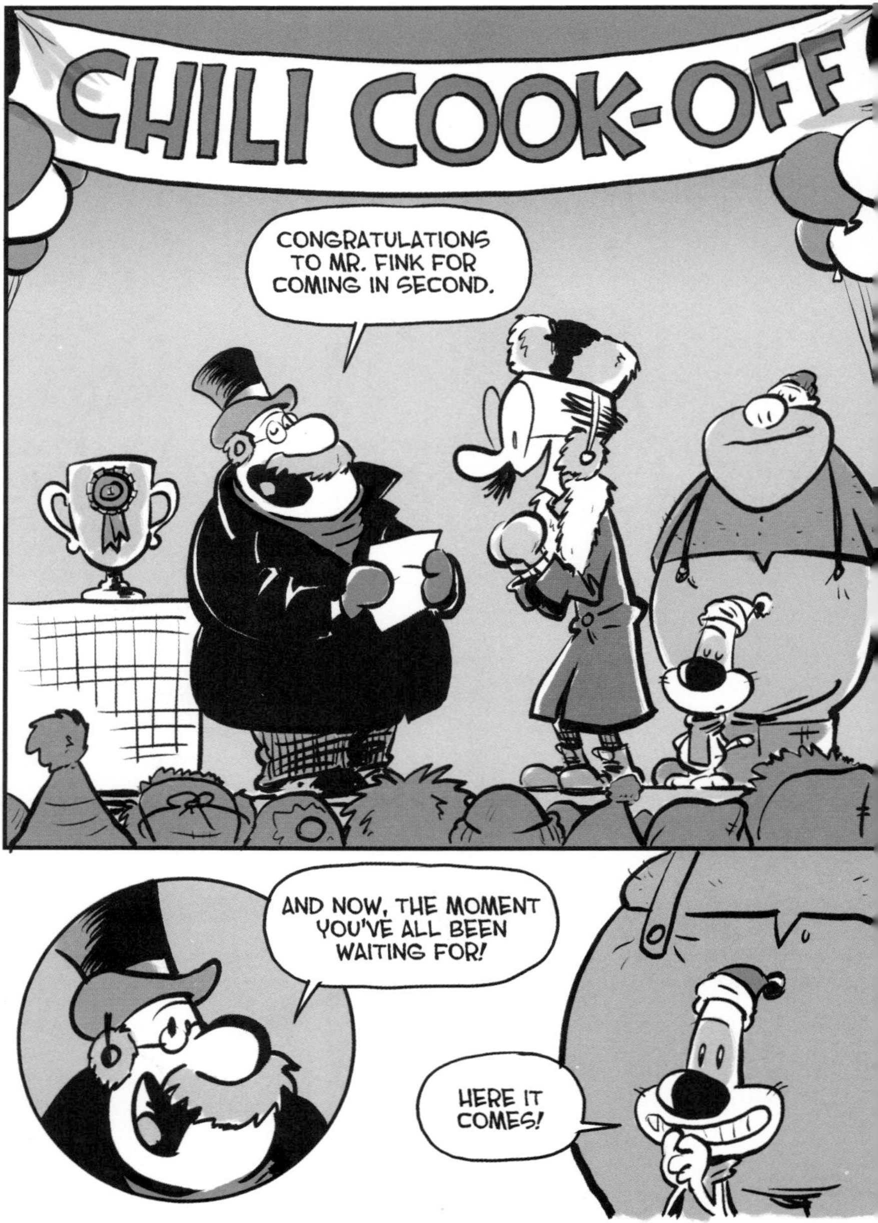
CHILI COOK-OFF
CONGRATULATIONS TO MR. FINK FOR COMING IN SECOND.
AND NOW, THE MOMENT YOU'VE ALL BEEN WAITING FOR!
HERE IT COMES!

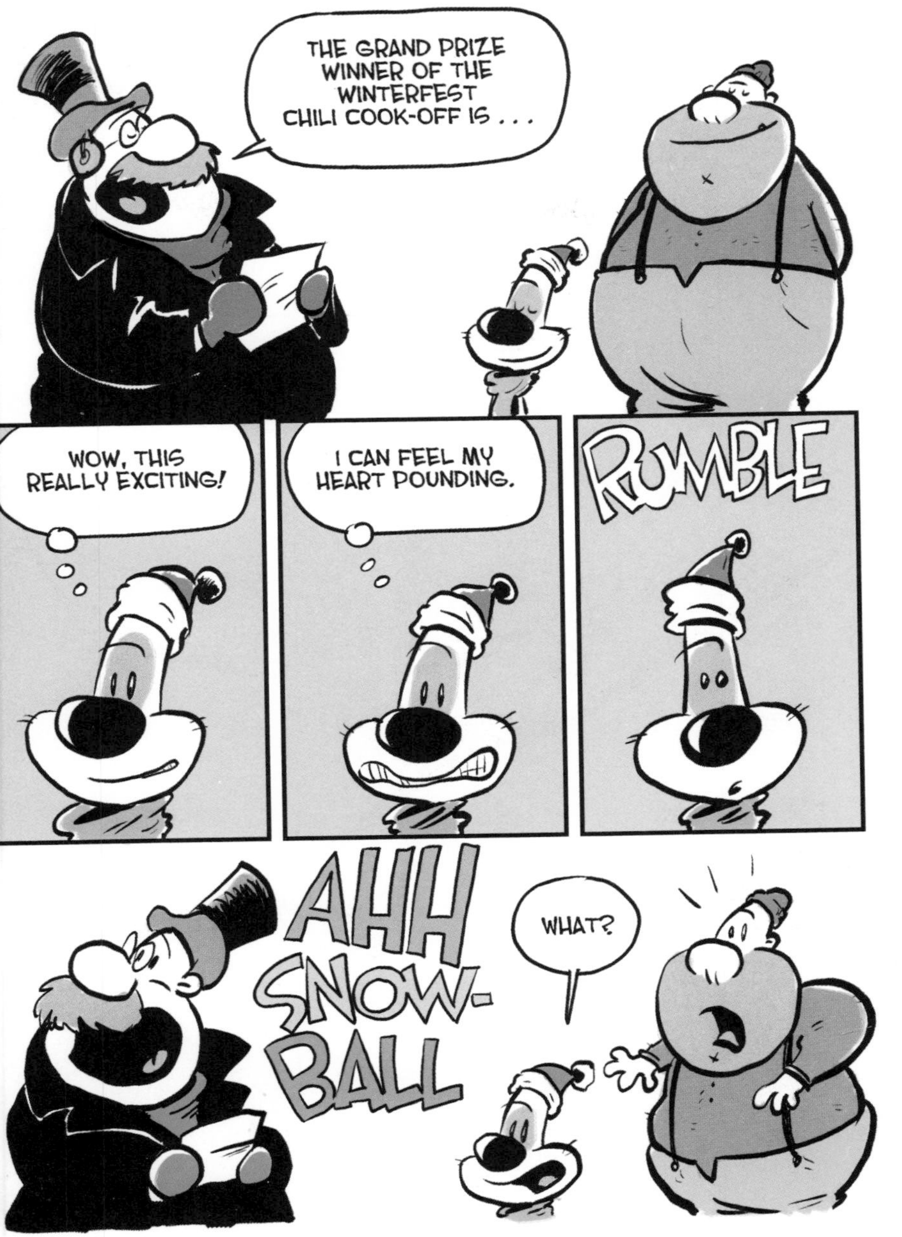
THE GRAND PRIZE WINNER OF THE WINTERFEST CHILI COOK-OFF IS . . .
WOW, THIS REALLY EXCITING!
I CAN FEEL MY HEART POUNDING.
RUMBLE
AHH SNOW-BALL
WHAT?

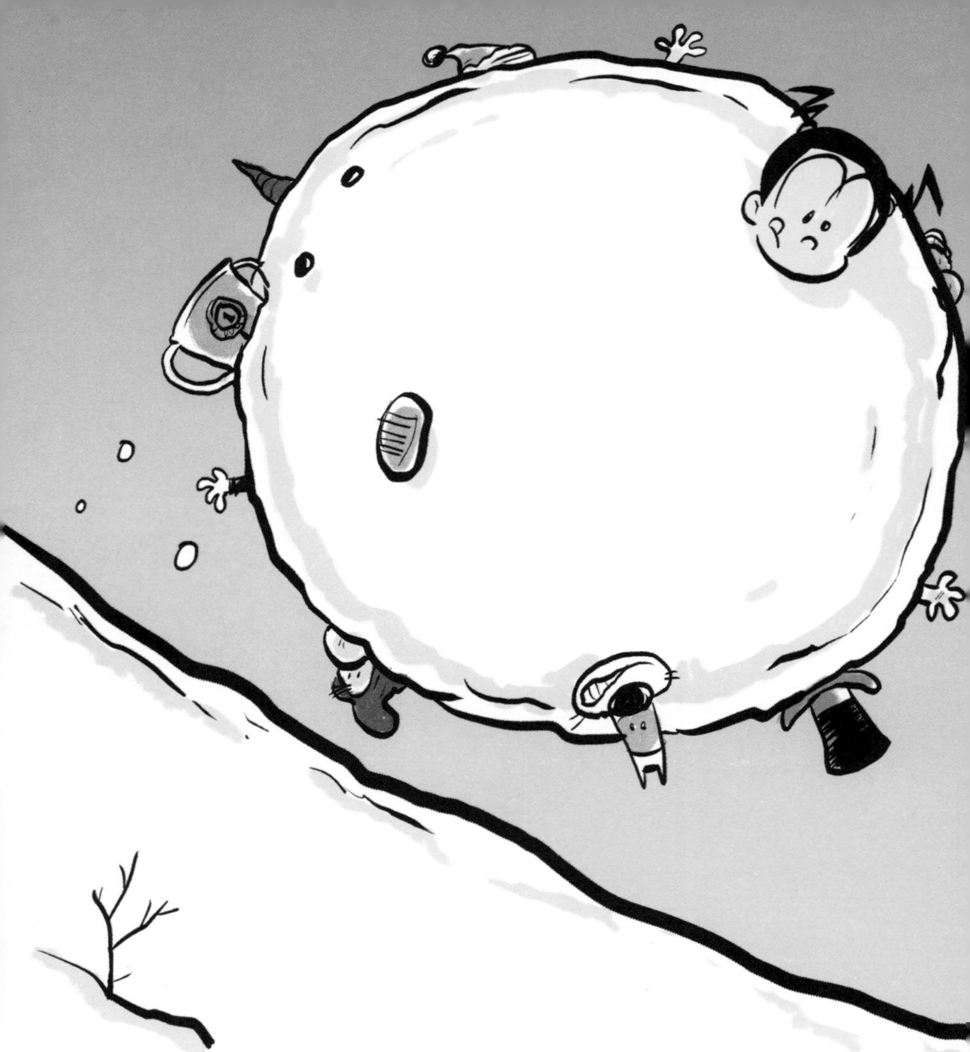

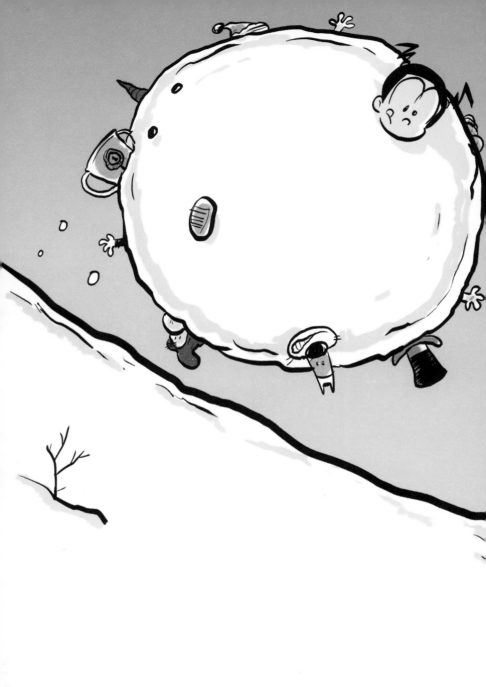

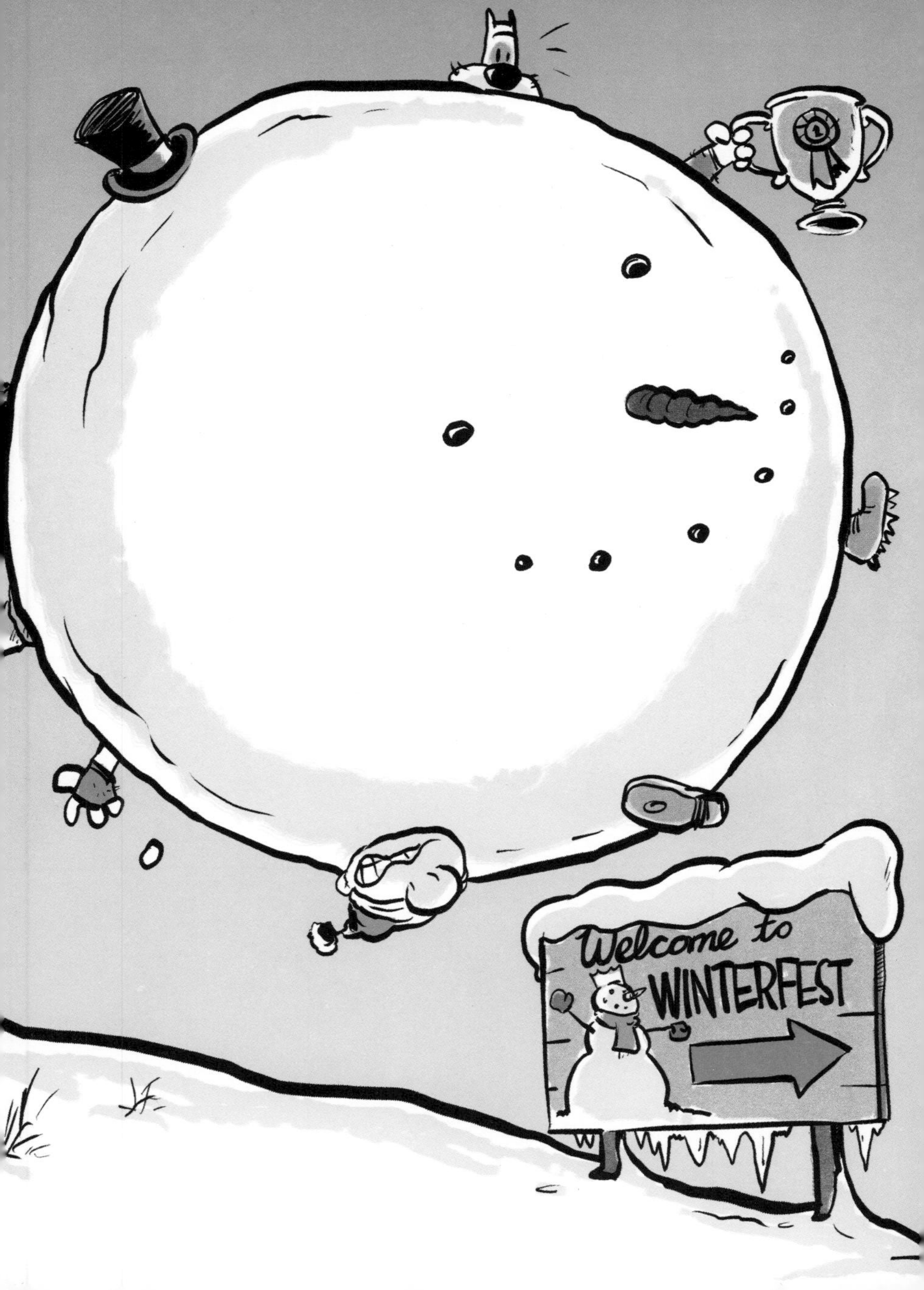
Welcome to
WINTERFEST

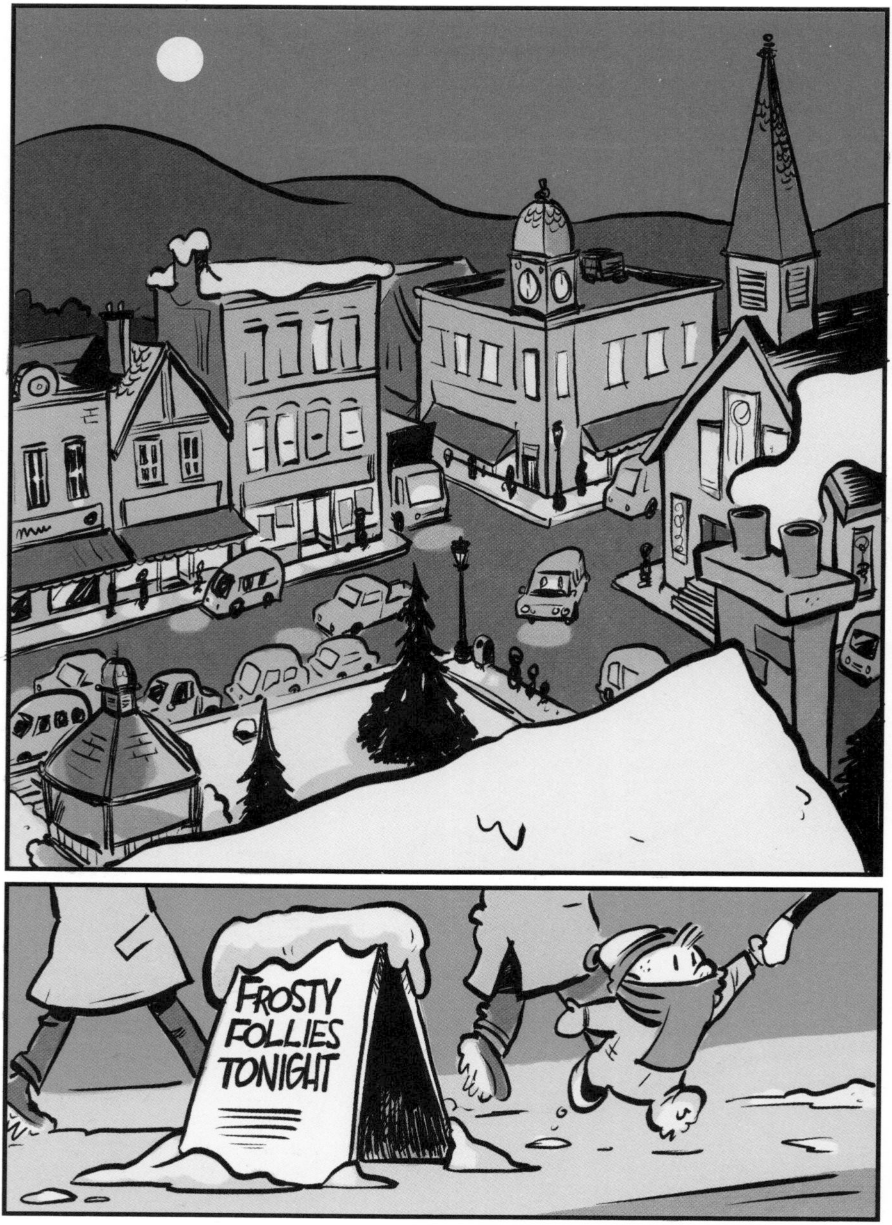
FROSTY FOLLIES TONIGHT

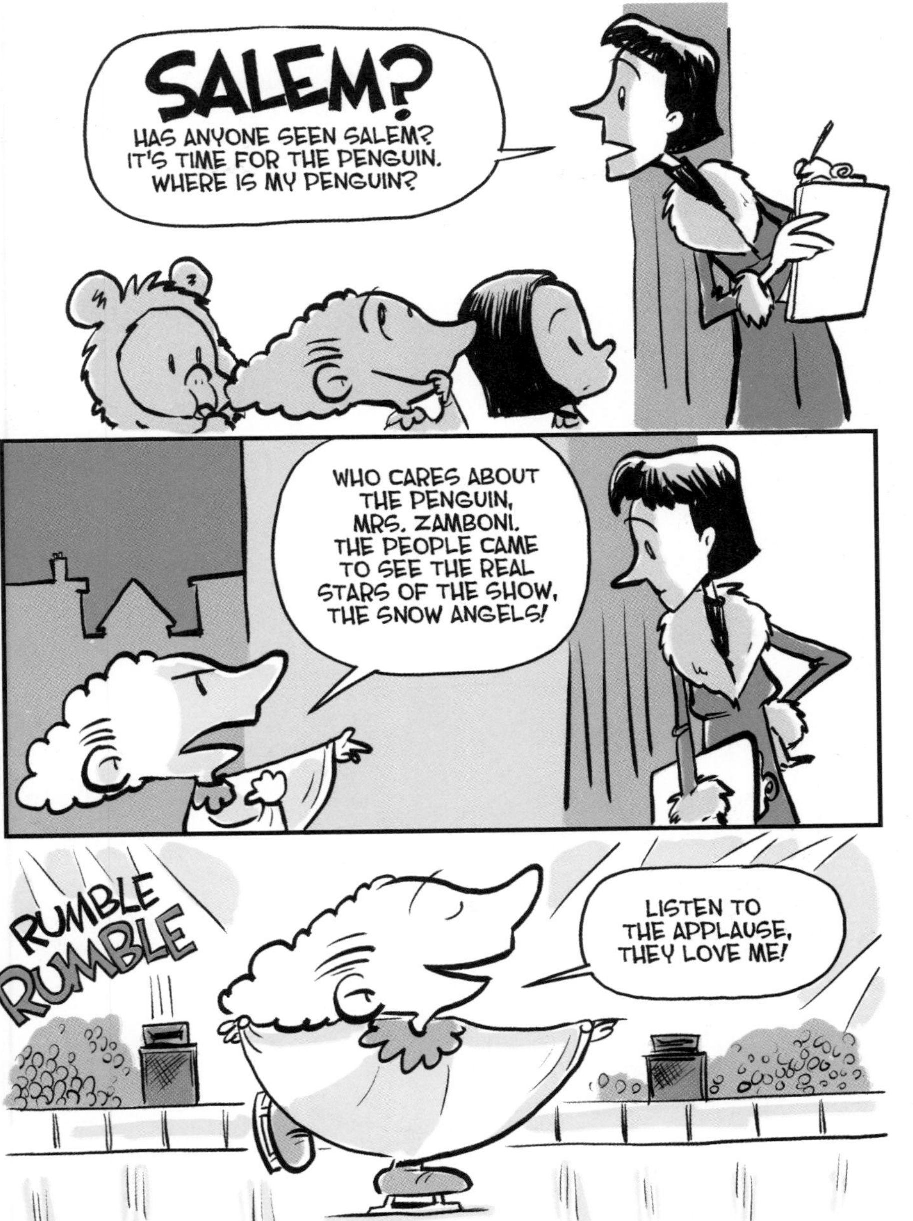
SALEM?
HAS ANYONE SEEN SALEM? IT'S TIME FOR THE PENGUIN. WHERE IS MY PENGUIN?
WHO CARES ABOUT THE PENGUIN, MRS. ZAMBONI. THE PEOPLE CAME TO SEE THE REAL STARS OF THE SHOW, THE SNOW ANGELS!
RUMBLE RUMBLE
LISTEN TO THE APPLAUSE, THEY LOVE ME!

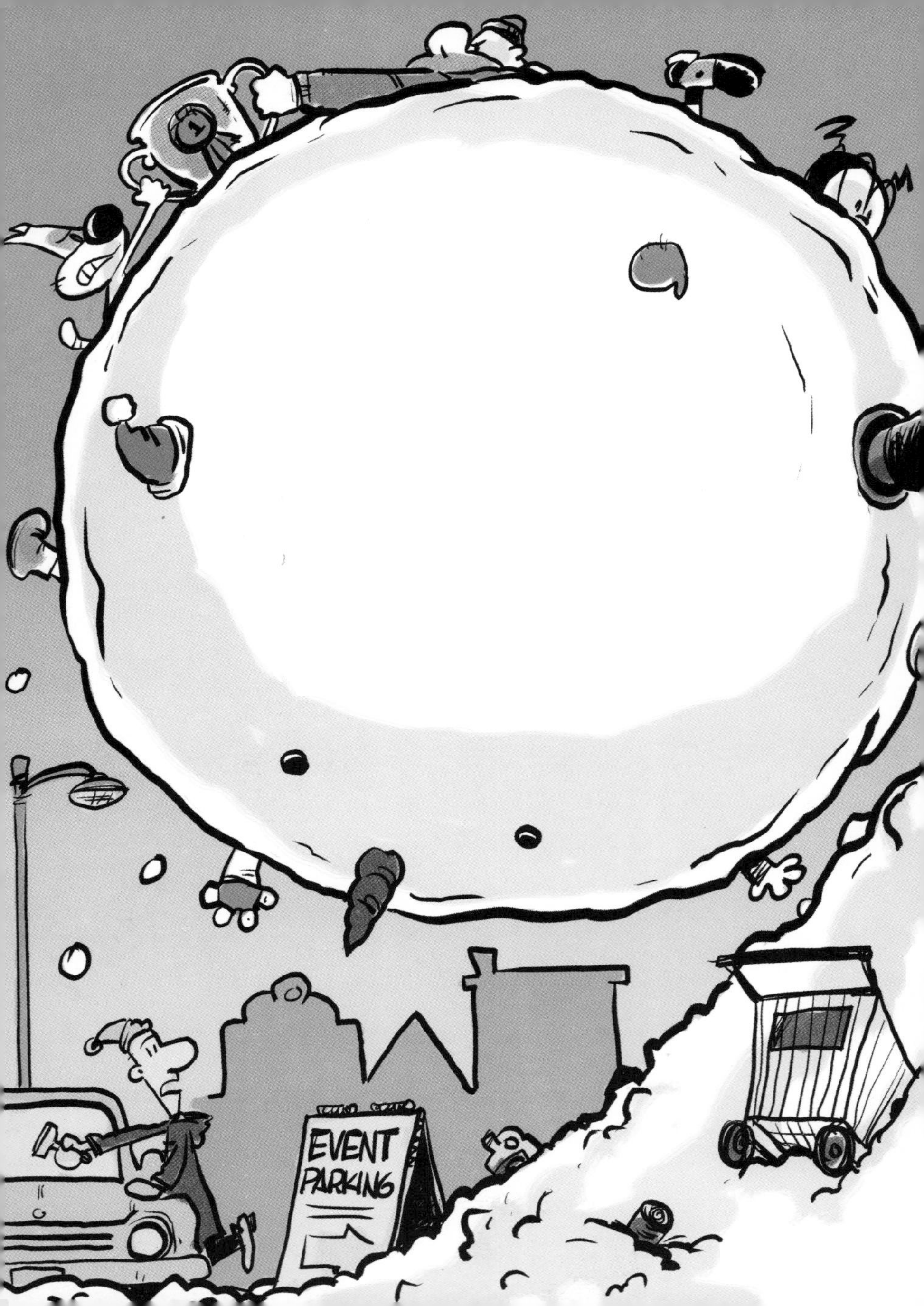
EVENT
PARKING

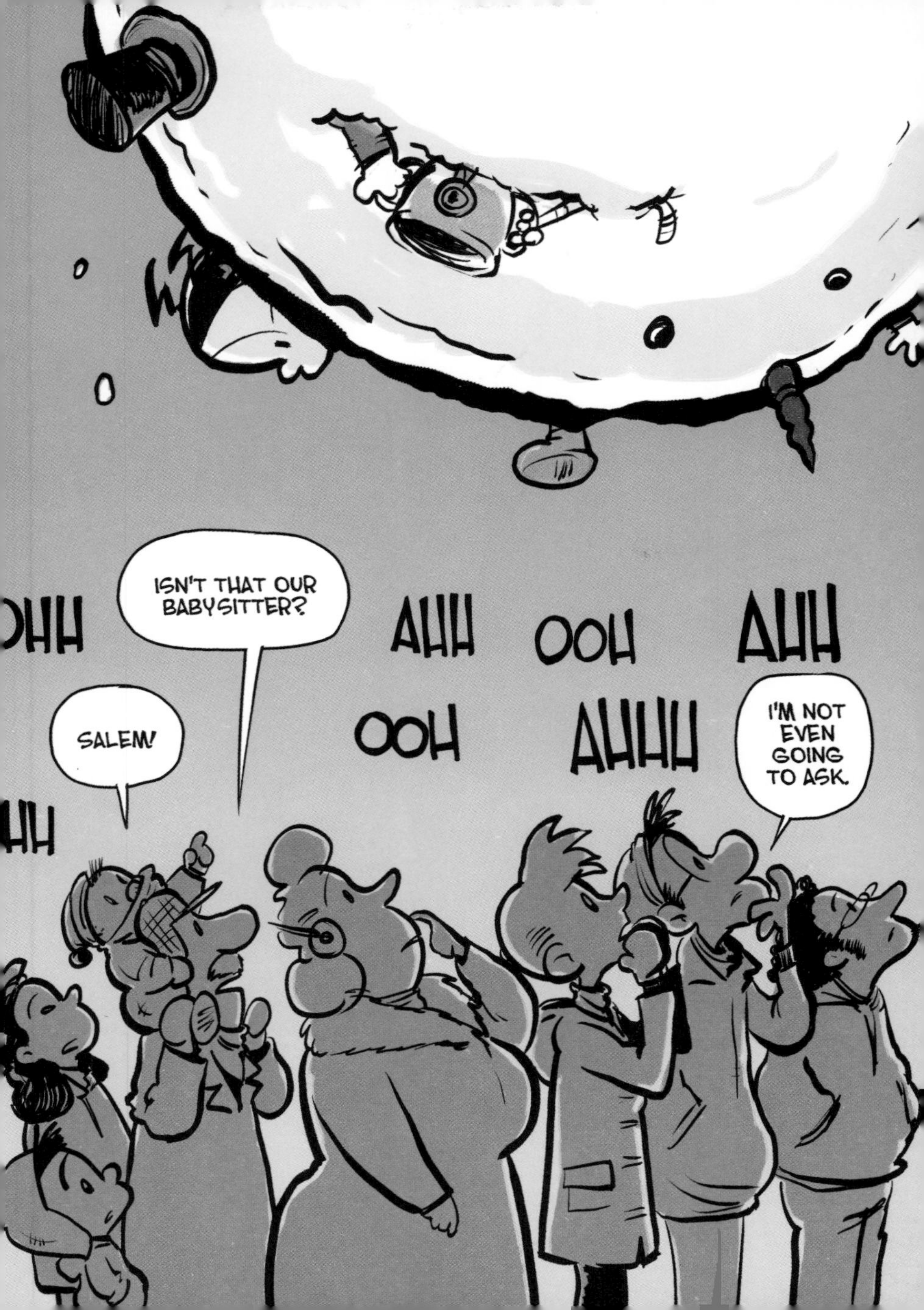
OHH
HH
ISN'T THAT OUR BABYSITTER?
SALEM!
AHH
OOH
OOH
AHH
AHHH
I'M NOT EVEN GOING TO ASK.

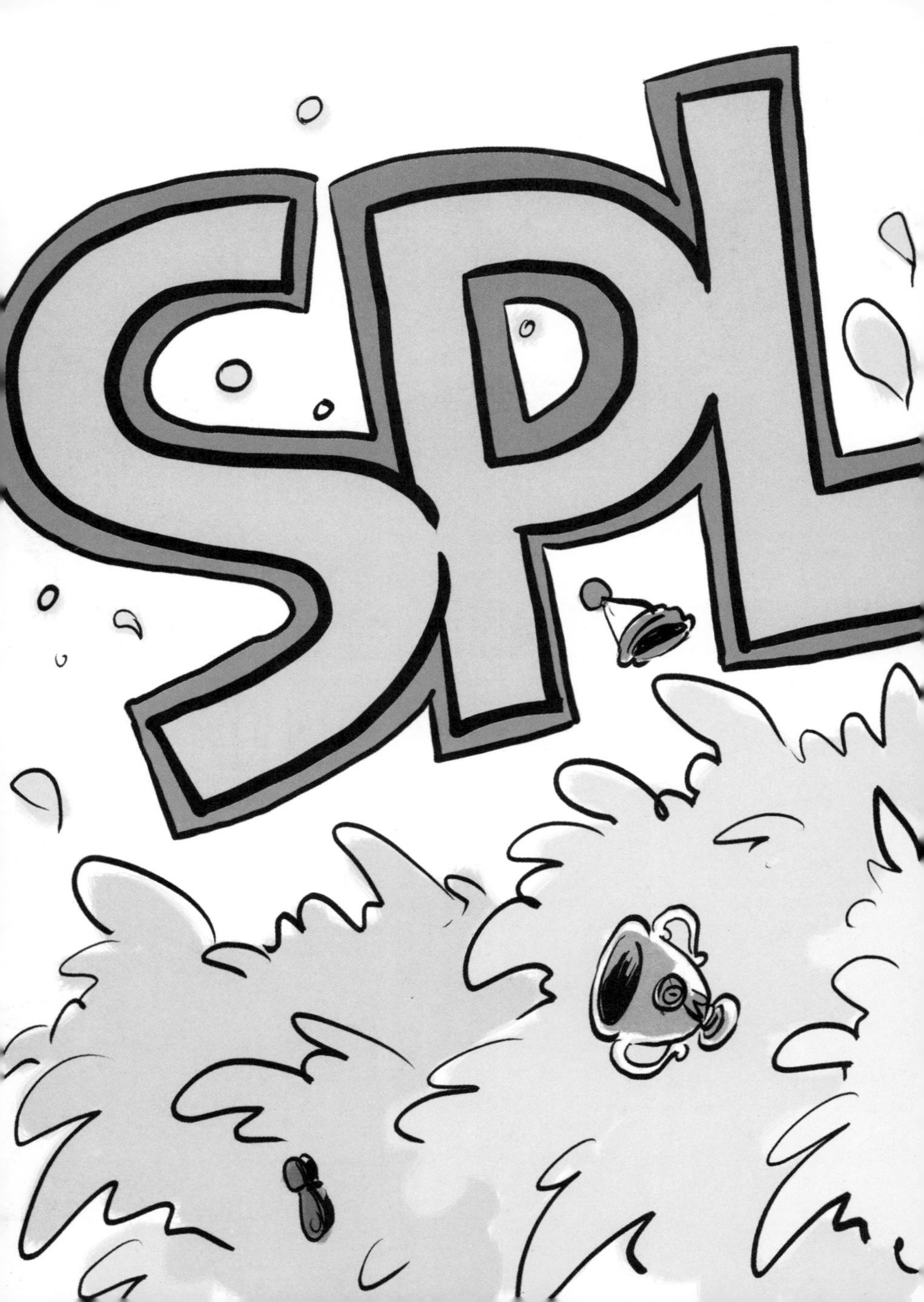
SPL

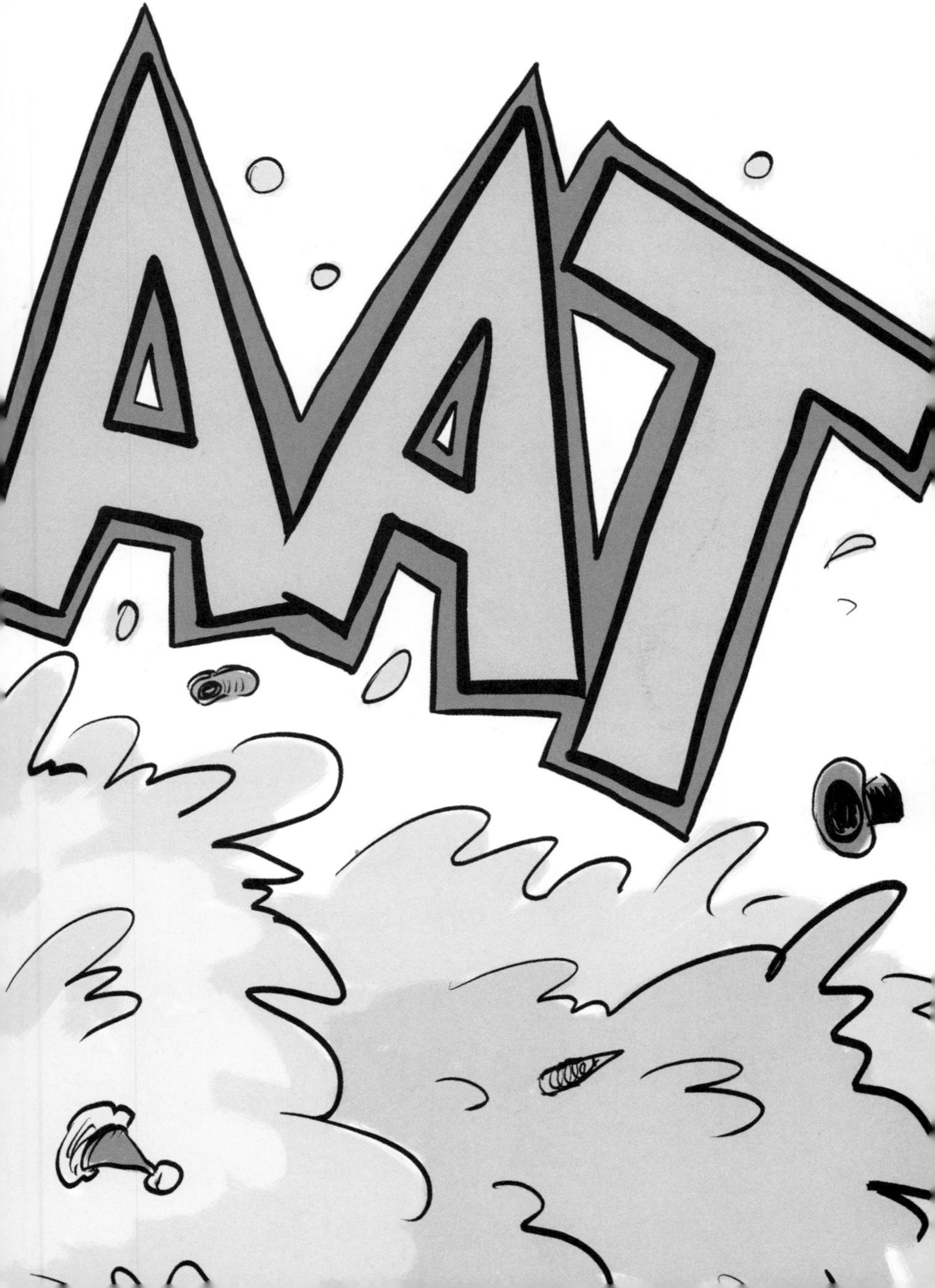
AAAT

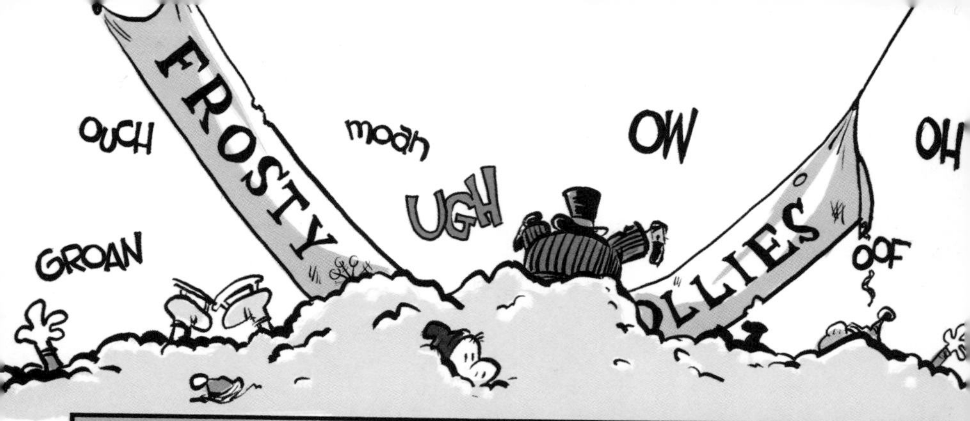
FROSTY
OUCH
moan
OW
OH
GROAN
UGH
OLLIES
OOF

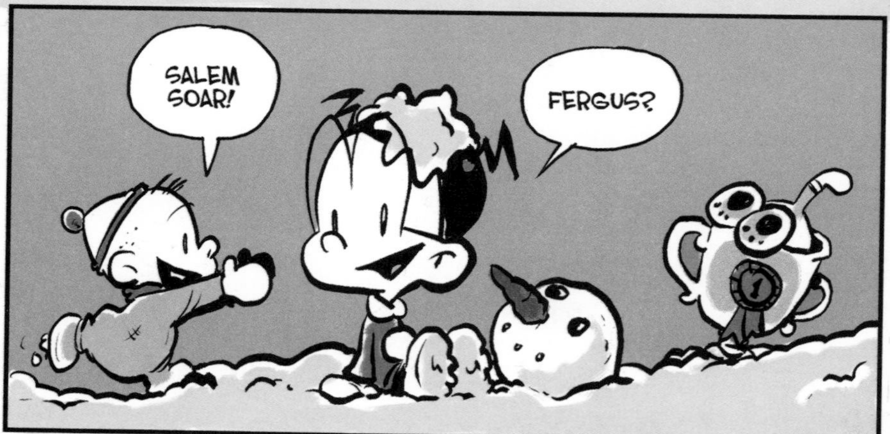
SALEM SOAR!
FERGUS?

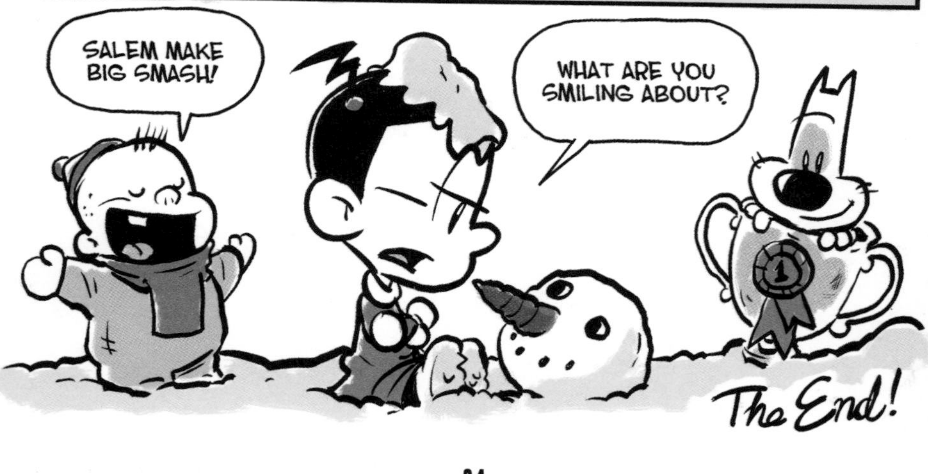
SALEM MAKE BIG SMASH!
WHAT ARE YOU SMILING ABOUT?
The End!

Getting to know FRANK CAMMUSO

FRANK LIKES
1. WINTER
2. CHILI (ALL KINDS)
3. DRAWING
4. RED PLAID FLANNEL SHIRTS

FRANK DISLIKES
1. ICY DRIVEWAYS
2. MAYONNAISE (ALL KINDS)
3. SHOVELING SNOW
4. ICE-SKATING

FUN FACT: DID YOU KNOW . . . FRANK CAMMUSO MAKES A PRETTY MEAN CHILI.

SPECIAL THANKS TO . . .

Ngoc and Khai, Kathy Leonardo, Nancy Iacovelli, Nicole Sclama, Alyssa Nassner, Jim Armstrong, Elizabeth Peskin, Charlie Kochman, Chad Beckerman, Morgan Dubin, and Judy Hansen.

FOR MORE FUN STUFF ABOUT
SALEM AND WHAMMY
CHECK OUT MY WEBSITE AT . . .

WWW.CAMMUSO.COM

ALSO AVAILABLE

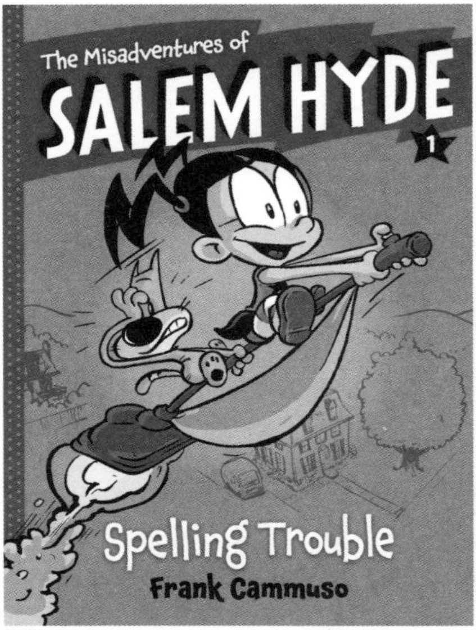

The Misadventures of
SALEM HYDE
1
Spelling Trouble
Frank Cammuso

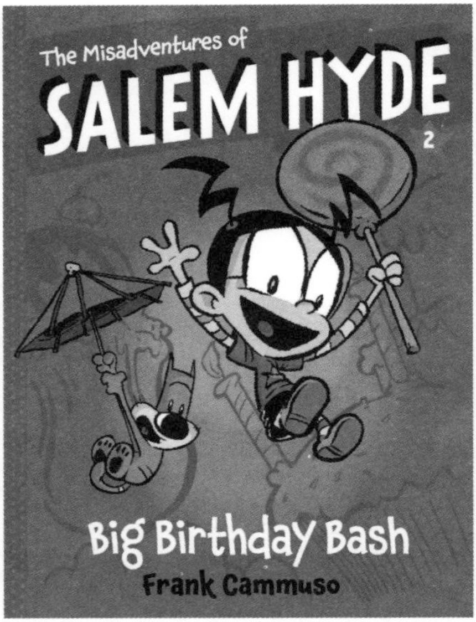

The Misadventures of
SALEM HYDE
2
Big Birthday Bash
Frank Cammuso

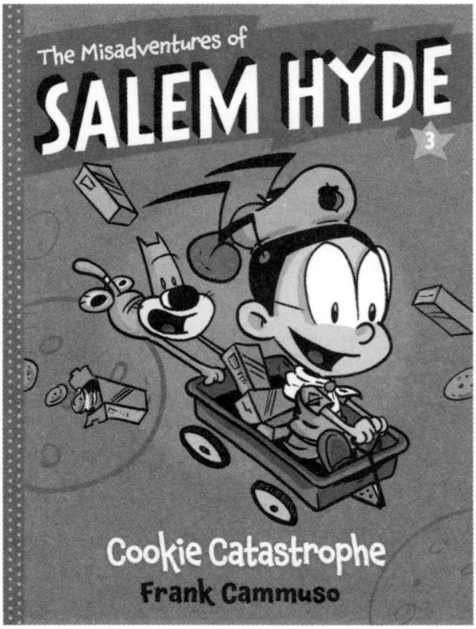

The Misadventures of
SALEM HYDE
3
Cookie Catastrophe
Frank Cammuso

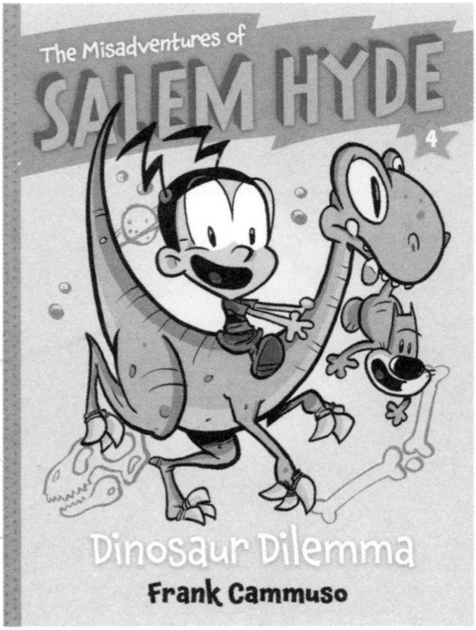

The Misadventures of
SALEM HYDE
4
Dinosaur Dilemma
Frank Cammuso

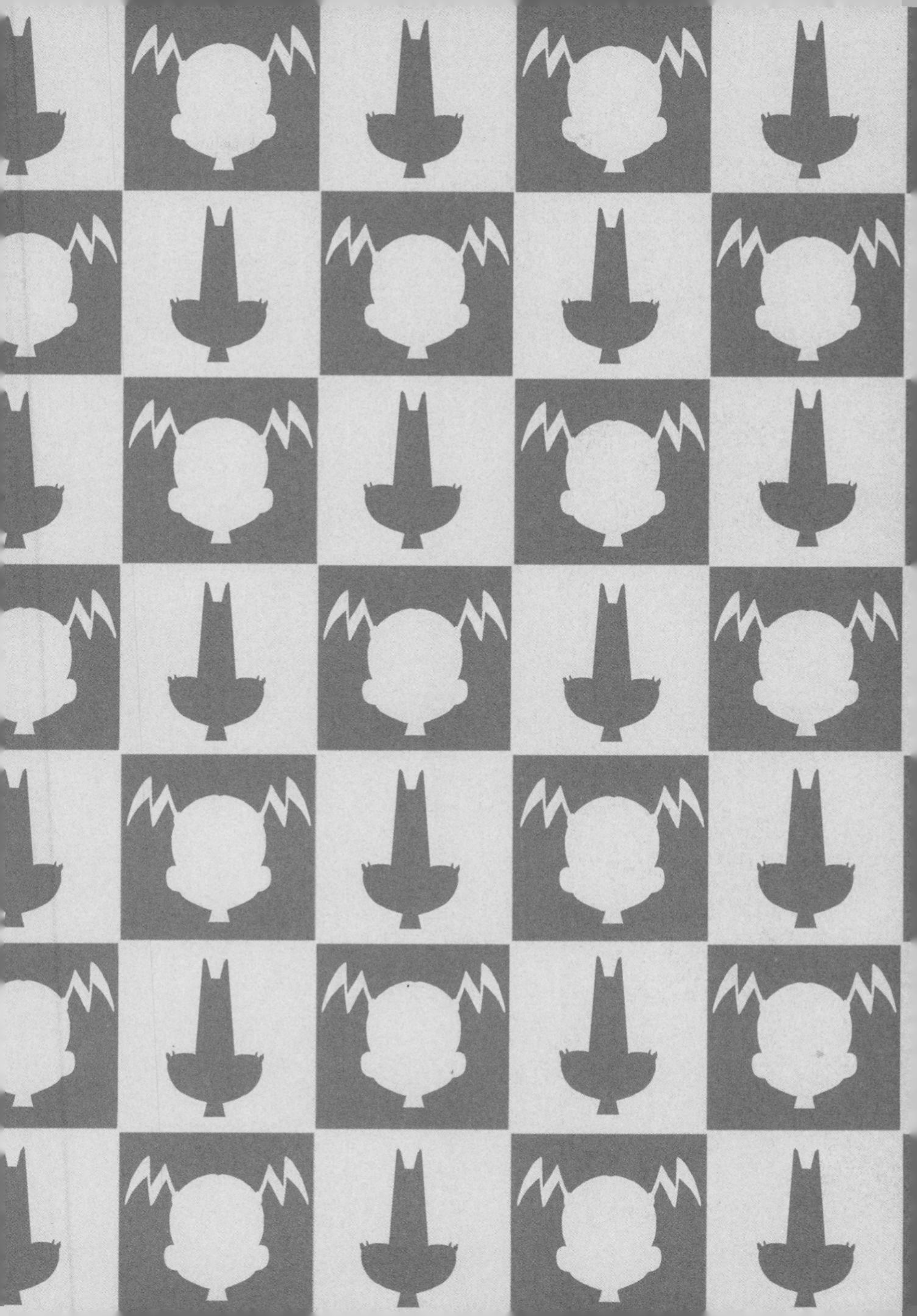

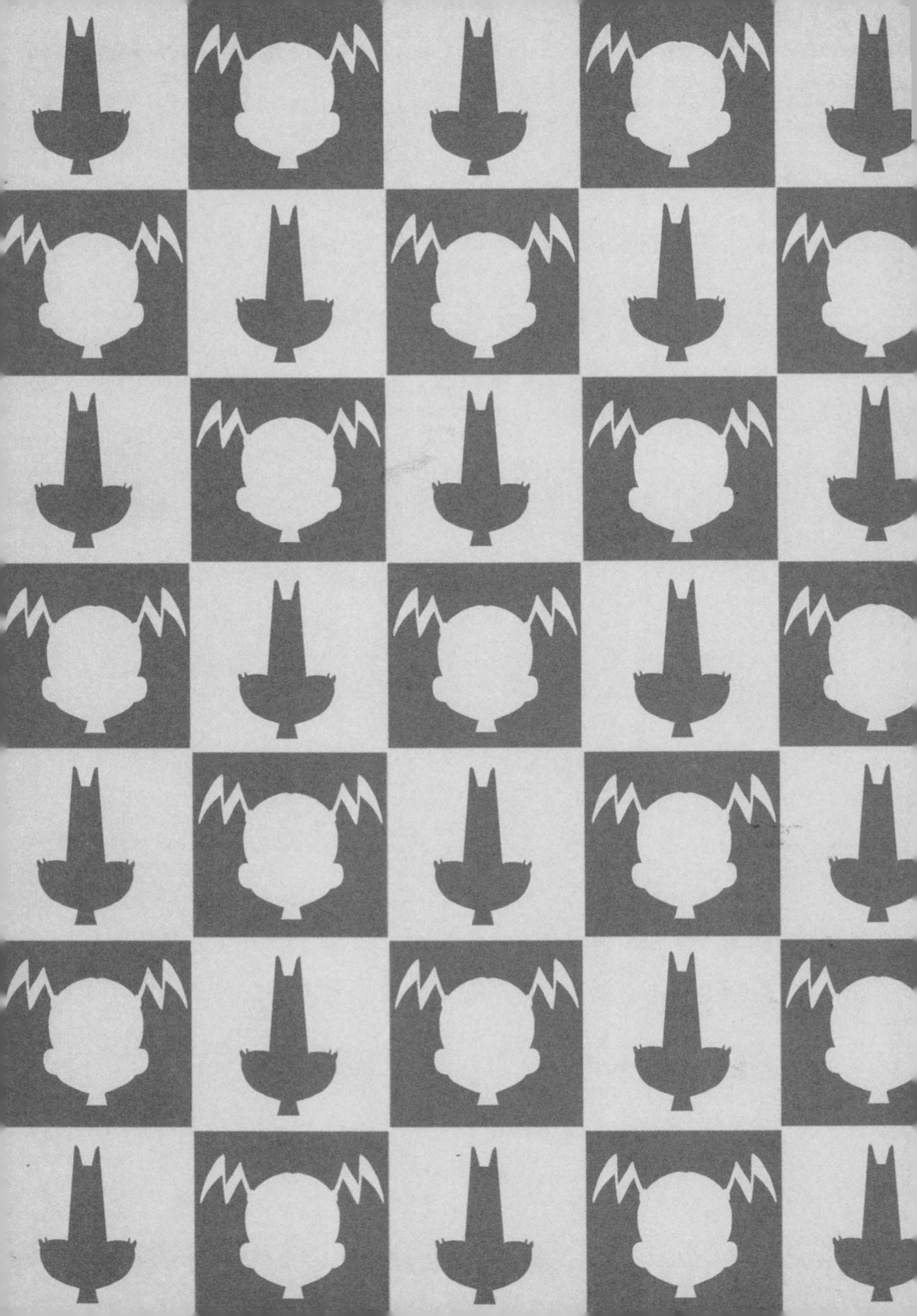